I0525930

Eric Wilder

Wild Magnolias

Gondwana Press

Edmond, Oklahoma

Other books by Eric Wilder

Gondwana Press
1802 Canyon Park Cir. Ste C
Edmond, OK 73013

Front Cover by Gondwana Graphics

ISBN: 978-1-946576-21-7

for Marilyn

What is there worth the effort and despair of writing about, except love and death?

— William Faulkner, Mosquitoes

Wild Magnolias

A novel by
Eric Wilder

Chapter 1

In the Big Easy, the party never ends. I realized this truism as I waded through the waves of jubilant tourists who had invaded the French Quarter, searching for beignets and the blues. Though New Orleans sprawls far and wide, the French Quarter is just one square mile.

Size doesn't matter here because thousands of tourists flock to this historic neighborhood yearly. The city planners like it that way and constantly seek ways to increase tourism. Ever resourceful, they envisioned a festival that would keep the visitors coming, even after Jazz Fest. One such idea has succeeded far beyond expectations.

With its world-renowned lineup, Jazz Fest brings together the best musical acts from around the globe. Yet, New Orleans has countless exceptional musicians and unique musical groups. It was natural that someone would create a festival to showcase our local talent and the unparalleled cuisine found nowhere else on earth. French Quarter Fest was born, quickly evolving from a mere idea into a phenomenal success story.

While an economic boon to the city and the state's many musicians and restaurants, the festival was a pain in the neck to me, the giant crowds jamming the streets and disturbing the ambiance. Next year, I vowed to take my cat, Miss Kisses, and leave town for the duration of the fest. Next year would have to wait. Today, someone awaited me at Bertram Picou's Bar on Rue Chartres, and I looked forward to seeing them.

With a smile and a bounce in my step, I navigated through the music coming from several directions, crowd noise, and the commingled aromas of fabulous French Quarter cuisine being sold from kiosks. I had another destination.

There are many iconic bars in the French Quarter, none quite like Bertram's. It was almost empty, most tourists outside watching the many free musical performances or eating fried alligator from one of the food concessions. Four customers at the bar were talking with the wild Cajun bartender. I recognized them and smiled as I joined them.

Bertram had dark hair, eyes, a mustache, and a Gallic nose. His Cajun accent always grew more pronounced when he talked to customers. Like most Cajuns, he'd be unable to speak if you tied his hands behind his back.

When he spotted me walking toward them, he said, "Where you been?"

The four people across the bar from Bertram turned and smiled when they saw me.

"You didn't see my request for a hall pass?" I asked.

"Okay, Mr. Smartass. There are people here waiting on you."

Two of the people were longtime friends, Lil and Tony Nicosia. Tony was a former N.O.P.D. homicide detective, and Lil was his long-suffering wife. Lil was an inch taller than Tony's five-eight. She was attractive, though not pretty in the truest sense.

Tony was my sometimes P.I. partner. During a recent out-of-town case, we'd met Maya Henstooth. Maya was a no-holds-barred homicide detective for the Rapides Parish Sheriff's Department, a prestigious position she held despite being female and black. She wore a blue dress, and her hem touched the floor. It was the first time I'd seen her in something other than her police uniform, and the transformation was stunning.

The fourth person in the group was someone I'd met only once, though I recognized him instantly. The little man with short-cropped gray hair topped with a fedora wore horn-rimmed glasses. The day I met him, he wore a priest's garment. Today, his pinstriped pants and subdued sports shirt indicated he'd retired from the clergy.

"Maya," I said, embracing her. "Forgive me for staring. Your uniform disadvantaged me, and I didn't realize how gorgeous you were. Father Piastri, you look so casual."

"Call me Adano," the former priest said. "I'm a civilian now."

"Maya was telling us about how Adano had caused her to return to singing," Bertram said.

4

"And Wyatt was there when he did," Maya said. "He and my sister-in-law tricked me into performing a pop song that night at my brother's barbecue restaurant. Now, I'm singing there every Wednesday."

"And I haven't missed a show," Adano said. "Maya has the voice of an angel, and her brother cooks the best barbecue in the world."

Someone walked in the door and said, "Help me out here. I haven't had any good barbecue since I left Tulsa."

Recognizing Jake Huntington's voice, Maya and Father Piastri both smiled. Jake wasn't alone; his significant other, Mama Mulate, and chopper pilot Colley Hornbeck were with him. They joined us at the bar.

Jake was tall and fifty-something with the athletic body of a dedicated runner. With a becoming smile, he extended his hand and introduced himself to Maya and Adano. They were starstruck upon meeting the host of Cryptid Hunter, the most popular reality show on television. Jake was used to the adoration and smiled as Adano pumped his hand.

Colley Hornbeck looked like an aging movie star. Bertram already knew he was drinking straight whiskey with an Abita chaser. He handed them to him. Jake and Mama were two of his best customers, and they were soon also drinking.

Colley grasped Maya's hand, kissed it, and said, "I love barbecue. I'll fly us to your brother's place, pretty lady, if you tell me where it is."

"No need," Maya said. "Leo is one of the French Quarter Fest's food vendors this year and has a kiosk not far from here."

"Then let's go," he said.

Maya laughed when she pulled away her hand. "I'm singing in a few hours and don't want to spoil my vibe."

"Bertram, make this beautiful young woman a drink and put it on my tab."

"Already tried," Bertram said. "She's Southern Baptist and doesn't drink."

"How narrow-minded of you," Colley said.

Maya was smiling and said, "And I'm still a virgin and will be until my wedding night."

"Whoa!" Colley said. "That exempts me. Marriage is the last thing on my mind."

"Good," Maya said. "My Baptist deacon daddy would kill me if I brought home a white man."

Maya shook her head when he said, "Your dad doesn't believe in mixed marriages? We could do what Bossman and Mama do."

Mama Mulate was a longtime friend, sometimes business partner, and Jake's significant other. She was tall, her skin the color of café au lait, and her curly hair draped to her svelte shoulders.

"Which is?" Maya asked.

"Hang out together and enjoy each other's company."

It was apparent that Maya was enjoying her exchange with Colley.

Adano was thinking about Mama and said, "Wyatt tells me you're a voodoo mambo."

Mama smiled and said, "Among other things. I also teach English lit at Tulane."

"I'm impressed," he said. "What religion do you practice?"

"Vodoun, though the way the original religion was practiced has changed immensely since arriving in this country."

"I'd love to discuss it with you sometime," he said.

"Good," Mama said. "Maybe I can convert you."

"It's probably a little late for that to happen," he said, though I'm all ears."

"Vodoun, as practiced in New Orleans, draws heavily on Catholicism. You might be surprised."

"This is my first visit to New Orleans," he said. "I'm looking for someone to show me St. Louis Cathedral."

"Wyatt and I will take you," Mama said. "He knows more about the old cathedral than most tour guides."

"Are you Catholic?" Adano asked.

"Me and most of the people in New Orleans," I said. "I'd be happy to give you a personal tour."

"Wonderful," he said.

Adano's eyes sparkled when Bertram handed him a fresh martini.

"You looked as if you were getting a little dry, Padre," Bertram said.

"Thank you, my son," Adano said. "Are you Catholic?"

"Born and raised," Bertram said. "My momma would spank my ass if she knew the last time I attended Mass."

"Do you need for me to hear your confession?" Adano asked.

"We ain't got enough hours in the day," Bertram said.

"Bertram's banking on his gift of gab to get him into heaven," I said.

"What about you?" he asked.

"I'm probably doomed," I said.

"There's always time to repent, my son," he said.

Maya squeezed the old man's hand and said, "You're retired. Remember? You promised we wouldn't talk religion."

"Sorry," he said. "I have a hard time passing up the chance to save lost souls."

"This is the Big Easy, Padre," Bertram said. "You know what they say?"

"What?" he asked.

"In the Quarter, everyone's soul is pretty much lost, so laissez les bon temps rouler.

"Let the good times roll," I said.

"Is this town beyond wicked?" he asked.

"Andy Jackson's wife called it the Great Babylon," Mama said.

Jake tapped Adano's martini glass and said, "This is New Orleans, Padre. Some things are unchangeable."

"Holy Mother of God!" Adano said.

"It's past time for lunch, and my stomach is growling," Jake said. "Let's get off the subject of religion and visit your brother's barbecue stand."

"Wyatt?" Maya said, glancing at me.

"You know how much I love your brother's cooking," I said. "Let's do it."

After Bertram had cleared everyone's tab, we started for the door as a stately older woman entered. Bertram spoke with her, signaling me to return to the bar before I managed to walk out the door.

"Go ahead," I said. "I'll catch up."

The woman waiting at the bar smiled when I reached her.

"I'm Evelyn DuPont," she said, extending her hand.

I recognized Ms. DuPont. The handsome fifty-something woman with gray hair and the cheekbones of a former model was part of the French Quarter elite. Though her family's wealth and influence ensured she would never have to work if she didn't want to, she'd spent years posing for many magazine covers.

8

Evelyn DuPont had devoted her life to the arts and charitable works, giving away much of her vast fortune. She held my hand a bit too long as if reaching out for a life preserver. Her slight tremble didn't go unnoticed.

"How can I help you, Ms. DuPont?" I asked.

"You know who I am?"

I smiled and said, "Me and every other resident of the Quarter."

"I'm looking for someone to recover something for me," she said.

"Please," I said. "Tell me more."

"People in the Quarter know who I am. Few of them know my greatest passion."

"Which is?" I asked.

"Rare books with a New Orleans' connection."

"I've heard you have an extensive library."

"Oh? How did you hear that?" she asked.

"Two of my closest friends, Madam Toulouse and Armand, are rare objects appraisers."

Evelyn DuPont smiled. "Armand and Madam Toulouse gave me your name to help with my problem."

"What exactly is your problem, Ms. DuPont?"

Evelyn DuPont didn't answer my question, glancing briefly at Bertram instead. The nosy Cajun bartender was hanging on to every word of our conversation. I noticed, and so had Ms. DuPont.

"I have a booth that's private," I said. "Can Bertram bring you a drink?"

"New Orleans milk punch," she said.

Duly chastised, Bertram ducked his head and began preparing Ms. DuPont's specialty drink with a New Orleans twist.

"I'll bring your drink to Wyatt's booth," he said.

I had no formal office and maintained a large booth in the back of Bertram's bar. It wasn't free. I rented an upstairs apartment from Bertram, who added an extra one hundred fifty dollars to my monthly rent. I was okay with the arrangement because the booth was all I needed. I let Evelyn Dupont slip into the booth before sliding in beside her.

Bertram arrived with Ms. Dupont's New Orleans milk punch and a glass of lemonade for me. He also brought a bowl of salty pretzels.

Ms. DuPont smiled and said, "Thank you, Bertram."

"My pleasure," Bertram said. "Wave if you need another."

When he was gone, Ms. DuPont said, "I hope I'm not causing you to miss French Quarter Fest with your friends."

"No problem," I said. "Work always comes before play."

I eyed her cocktail and said, "Not many know about the New Orleans milk punch."

"Whiskey is my drink of choice, preferably Wild Turkey, though I also like a good martini occasionally. Armand and Madam Toulouse said you were good at what you do."

"Please forgive me. I'm so used to seeing your face on the covers of magazines that you aren't quite real to me."

"You're forgiven. I've grown old, and most people no longer remember me."

"I remember," I said. "Now, please tell me how I can help you."

"I've lost something and need you to find it for me," she said.

"Happy to help," I said.

As a pre-teen, I'd had a picture of Evelyn DuPont ripped from one of my mother's fashion magazines. She was one of the first glamour models to do full-frontal nudity. I thought about the picture as she slid into the booth, her slitted dress hiking up over her thighs, giving me a momentary flash of her marvelous legs.

Ms. DuPont was still stunningly beautiful, and her glance told me she saw me looking. When I turned my attention toward the bar, her smile informed me she was probably enjoying the moment. I sipped my lemonade, hoping my face hadn't turned red.

Though my prurient interest in her long legs probably pleased her, she let me off the hook as she explained her reason for speaking with me.

"One of my most prized possessions has disappeared, and I want you to retrieve it."

"Happy to help," I said. "Tell me more."

"William Faulkner is often referred to as a New Orleans author. He was not, though he lived and wrote in New Orleans for part of 1925. He moved to Paris, where he wrote *Mosquitoes,* a novel with a New Orleans setting."

Ms. DuPont took a pretzel from the bowl, nibbled on it, and then sipped her New Orleans milk punch.

She grinned when I said, "Go on."

"These pretzels are tasty, and Bertram's New Orleans milk punch is a close second to the best I've ever drunk."

"Bertram is the best bartender in the Quarter," I said. "I doubt you'd find a better New Orleans milk punch elsewhere."

"That's a tall claim," she said. "Maybe now. It wasn't always the case."

"Only Bertram's predecessor, Gil LaPiere, was better, and Gil is dead."

"I knew Gil," she said. "I couldn't have been more than fourteen the first time I skipped school and spent the day in the French Quarter, finally ending up here. Gil knew my parents and recognized me. It was he who mixed my first New Orleans milk punch. It's been my favorite ever since."

"Gil's ghost haunts the bar," I said.

"No way!" she said.

"We have something in common," I said. "Gil mixed my first drink."

"You're shitting me!"

"I was in the bar one night long after it had closed. Gil's ghost appeared and apologized for launching me on the path to alcoholism."

"Did he?" Ms. DuPont asked.

I laughed. "I was primed, ready, and needed no assistance."

Ms. DuPont and I were sitting closely. She clutched my hand and pressed it into her warm breasts. I could feel her heartbeat; the picture from my adolescence was all I could think about.

"Please, Wyatt, call me Evelyn."

They say the mind is the body's largest sex organ. At that moment, mine was engorged, and Evelyn DuPont had me in the palm of her hand. I raised a finger to signal Bertram to bring us more drinks.

"Thanks, Bertram," I said when he arrived.

"Wimp," she said when he was gone.

"Ms. DuPont, are you trying to seduce me?"

"Not just trying; succeeding, I'd say. And Wyatt, my name is Evelyn."

"Okay, Evelyn. Do you want me to find your book or a roll in the hay?"

"What's wrong with doing both?" she said.

"Nothing I can think of," I said.

"Have you ever made love to an older woman?" she asked.

"Yes," I said.

Evelyn pulled me closer and said, "Tell me."

12

"Bertram will kick us out if I rip off your clothes, throw you on the table, and hump you in front of God and the world."

"How narrow-minded of him," she said. "Maybe you're right. Let me continue."

She grinned when I said, "I might need a cold shower first." Evelyn moved away from me in the booth and asked, "Better?"

"Depends," I said.

"There's always time for sex," she said. "Let's take care of business first. I'm missing something and need someone to recover it."

"A copy of Faulkner's *Mosquitoes*?"

"Not just any copy of *Mosquitoes*," she said. "The volume I'm missing is one of the most valuable books on the face of the earth."

"Please explain," I said.

"Mosquitoes was little more than a pastiche of characters Faulkner had met during his tenure in the Quarter. It was racy, highlighting both lesbian and gay sex. Three chapters were too racy for the publisher, so they were omitted from the book. The University of Virginia houses the original text and the deleted three chapters."

"And?"

"There's a copy of Mosquitoes containing the deleted chapters. Faulkner signed it."

"The original publisher?"

"A local publisher. Someone who knew Faulkner and the real identities of the characters portrayed in his book."

"Why did you have the book?" I asked.

"My grandparents were benefactors to Faulkner during his tenure in New Orleans. Faulkner had two copies of the original manuscript containing the omitted chapters printed using leather and gold leaf, one for himself and one for my grandparents. I believe Faulkner's copy is in Oxford, Mississippi. Someone recently stole mine."

Evelyn shook her head when I asked, "Have you contacted the police?"

"The book is private, and few people know about it. I don't want to involve the police. That's where you come in."

"I understand," I said. "Where did you keep the book, and when did you first notice that it was missing?" I asked.

"I maintain a rare book library in my home."

"Tell me about it," I said.

"As you might imagine, the temperature, humidity, mold count, etc. are meticulously regulated. There are tables and chairs for visiting scholars. Special lighting prevents light damage to the book's pages or covers."

"Such a room must have cost a small fortune to install," I said.

Evelyn nodded and said, "You don't want to know."

"Do you keep the room under lock and key?" I asked.

Evelyn nodded. The walls are steel, like a vault, and you must know the combination code to unlock the door."

"Who other than you has access to the room?" I asked.

"Libby Tanner, my social secretary. Why are you smiling?"

I wiped the smirk from my face and said, "Sorry for my reaction. You're the only person I know with a social secretary. Please continue."

"My best friend, Veronica LaSalle. She's a rare book dealer and owns Wild Magnolias on Magazine."

"Who else?" I asked.

"That's all," she said.

"Does anyone live at your house other than you?"

"Alicin, my daughter. My son, Rodney, has a room, though he's presently away."

"Anyone else?"

"I have a waitstaff that includes cooks and their helpers, several maids, and a butler. Jonathan Stallings, my butler, and Sara Sloan, my chief maid, maintain rooms on the premises. Everyone else goes to their own homes at night."

"I'll need to see your library and interview the others you named," I said.

"Whatever it takes," she said. "I want the book returned to me," She opened her purse and handed me a check for twenty-five grand. "This is a retainer. Please feel free to hire whatever help you may need. Present me with weekly invoices. I pay promptly."

Evelyn DuPont grinned when I said, "I'm on it, Boss."

"That's what I like to hear." She handed me a card with her address and a phone number." She slid past me, smiling as she grabbed my crotch. "Call me when you have an update. Here's hoping you know how to multitask."

I returned to the bar as the gorgeous older woman exited the door.

"What happened?" Bertram asked.

"Crazy shit!" I said.

"That woman is trouble," he said.

"Tell me about it," I said. "Doesn't matter because she's now my employer."

Bertram's eyes grew large when I handed him Evelyn DuPont's check and asked him to deposit it for me.

"What you got to do for her for this much money?"

I smiled and said, "Don't know. Right now, I need some barbecue."

Bertram shook his head as I left the bar to join Maya and her crew at her brother's French Quarter Fest barbecue kiosk.

Chapter 2

My meeting with Evelyn DuPont raised more than questions. The sidewalks were crowded when I left Bertram's, and I decided to detour before heading to Leo's barbecue kiosk. Two people held the answers to many questions. Armand and Madam Toulouse had given Ms. Dupont my name and probably knew more than they'd told her. I decided to pick their brains.

New Orleans, especially the French Quarter, is a mecca for eclectic bars. It mattered little that there was no sign out front. Everyone in the Quarter knew about Allemand's, a dive bar near Canal and Bourbon. Armand and Madam Toulouse could almost always be found there.

Needing to take them something for their trouble, I stopped at a food kiosk before leaving the Quarter. The line was long, though I finally departed the kiosk with a paper sack of tasty Fest Food. Allemands wasn't far, my stomach growling, causing me to regret that I hadn't bought something myself to eat.

No one glanced up when I entered the creaky front door. A dozen people sat around the circular bar. Recognizing me, the bartender waved. The place reeked of stale beer and cigarette smoke. The bar was dim, the clatter of pool balls coming from a back room. Armand and Madam Toulouse were at their usual table and smiled when I handed them an oily sack of Fest food.

"Brought you something," I said.

Looking like a quintessential beatnik, Armand tore it open, smiling as he popped one of the still-warm fried oysters into his mouth.

"You the one, Cowboy," he said. "Me and Madam Toulouse were thinking about braving the crowds and buying some fried oysters."

"There's more than just oysters," I said. "They threw in some stuffed jalapenos and a couple of freshly baked chocolate chip cookies."

Madam Toulouse hugged me when I slid into the booth beside her. "You always know the way to a girl's heart."

Madam Toulouse loved red down to her fingernails, toenails, and bright lipstick. Even her leather miniskirt was red. As usual, she was sucking a sugary drink through a long red straw.

Armand's dark hair had thinned since I'd last seen him, and his cookie-duster mustache was beginning to turn gray. Not so his clothes, which were all black.

Armand was grinning as he forked an oyster and doused it with hot sauce. Not to be outdone, Madam Toulouse stuffed a jalapeno pepper into her mouth. The bartender arrived with a pitcher of lemonade for me, his sleeveless shirt displaying many colorful tattoos.

"Me and the Madam were wondering how long it would take for you to come calling," Armand said.

I laughed and said, "Am I that transparent?"

"You're like family," Madam Toulouse said.

I nodded when Armand said, "You're here to find out about Evelyn DuPont's dark secret."

"The thought crossed my mind," I said. "Can you help me?"

"Tell you about Ms. DuPont's copy of *Mosquitoes*, yes. How to find it, no."

"She said she consulted you. If you had known where to find it, you'd have told her," I said. "I need a clue or two to get me started in the right direction."

"Like what?"

"I tried reading *Mosquitoes* when I took English lit as a freshman at L.S.U. All I can remember about it was the language was flowery and hard to read, and the entire book was about sex, any flavor you like."

Armand and Madam Toulouse laughed. "*Mosquitoes* is an overlooked masterpiece written during a different era," Armand said.

"Faulkner was still a young man when he lived in the French Quarter and became part of the small yet vibrant art and literary community," Madam Toulouse said.

"Twenty-eight," Armand said.

"He was from a small town in Mississippi. The people he met in New Orleans profoundly changed his worldly views," Madam Toulouse said.

"Faulkner moved to Paris after his short stay in the French Quarter, and that's where he began writing *Mosquitoes*," Armand said. "The opening is dense, though the book gets imminently readable when it becomes mainly dialogue.

"Maybe I gave up too soon," I said.

"If you didn't read the book from start to finish, then yes, you did," Armand said. "In *Mosquitoes*, Faulkner delves into sexuality and human desire, often using innuendo and explicit references to challenge the social norms of his time. More?"

"Please," I said.

"By openly discussing sexual matters, Faulkner critiques the prudishness and hypocrisy of early 20th-century American society. He exposes the gap between public morality and private behavior. He uses sexuality to explore and reveal his characters' inner lives and complexities."

"Maybe I was too hasty in my assessment of the novel."

"Very much so," Madam Toulouse said. "Faulkner was part of a broader modernist movement that sought to break free from Victorian constraints and explore the full range of human experience, including frank discussions of sexuality as a way to push artistic boundaries and innovate within the literary form."

"The characters were always swatting something," I said. "I can imagine mosquitoes were rampant in the French Quarter then. How do these little blood suckers tie to the theme of the book?"

"There are artists, and there are benefactors," Armand said.

"And?"

"Mosquitoes is a simile for benefactors."

Armand nodded when I said, "Then the benefactors, the patrons of the arts who support the creatives, are blood-suckers."

"Literary parasites demanding a symbolic drop of blood from creatives," he said. "Anything else?"

Armand blinked away a grin when I asked, "Is Evelyn DuPont a mosquito?"

"Ms. DuPont pays the madam and me very well," Armand said. "You'll never hear a bad word about her from our lips."

I had to suppress a grin. Armand and Madam Toulouse knew everything about everyone in New Orleans and loved to gossip. If they knew any of

Evelyn DuPont's dark secrets, I would hear them before leaving the booth.

Armand and Madam Toulouse shook their heads when I asked, "Have you ever visited her rare book room?"

"We don't rate that highly," Madam Toulouse said.

"Then how did you appraise the book?"

"Ms. DuPont allowed us to keep the volume at our apartment overnight," Armand said.

"She won't invite you to visit her library but trusts you enough to let you keep the most valuable book in New Orleans overnight."

"Trust isn't our problem with Ms. DuPont," Armand said.

"Then what is?"

"Our social status," Madam Toulouse said.

"Are you kidding me? You live in the Lower Pontalba, the most prestigious and expensive apartments in New Orleans, and if I had your money, I'd burn mine."

"At arm's length, Ms. DuPont loves us. Doesn't matter because her social peers would banish her if they knew we had something other than a business relationship."

"Because?"

Armand grinned. "Because Madam Toulouse is black."

"That's crazy," I said.

"You're colorblind, Cowboy. Not everyone in New Orleans' polite society is as liberal-minded."

"Did Ms. DuPont bring the book to you?"

"Heavens, no!"

"Then how did you get it?" I asked.

"Her son Rodney brought it to us," Madam Toulouse said.

"What's his story?"

21

"Evelyn has two children, Rodney and Alicin. They're fraternal twins. They've never worked, and Alicin's a stumbling drunk."

"They both have their mother's good looks," Madam Toulouse said.

"How is it Ms. Dupont trusted Rodney to take the book to you," I said.

"Go figure," Armand said.

"According to Ms. Dupont, only two other people know the combination to her rare book library," I said.

Madam Toulouse nodded. "Her social secretary, Libby Tanner, and best friend, Veronica LaSalle."

"What's their story?" I asked.

"Libby is Ms. DuPont's niece," she said.

"Why does Libby work if she's a DuPont heir?" I asked.

Armand snickered. "You'll find out soon enough."

I moved on because neither Armand nor Madam Toulouse would tell me more about Libby Tanner.

"And Veronica LaSalle?"

"I'm surprised you don't recognize the name, Cowboy," Armand said.

"Jog my memory."

"She's a rare book expert and owns Wild Magnolias," he said.

"Which is?"

"The most exclusive bookstore in the French Quarter. If Ronnie doesn't have the book you want, she'll find a way to get it for you," Madam Toulouse said.

"Sounds like a perfect motive for theft," I said. "Like the fox guarding the henhouse. Why does Ms. Dupont trust her?

"In case you haven't noticed, Ms. DuPont has powerful sexual urges. She and Ronnie are lovers," Armand said.

Madam Toulouse and Armand grinned when I said, "Lesbians?"

"Ms. DuPont is straight, lesbian, and everything in between," Madam Toulouse said. "Ronnie LaSalle uses her sexuality to get what she wants. Both women have powerful desires."

"I see," I said. "Ronnie and Libby Tanner are the only two with the combination to the rare book room. Who else could have done it?"

"The question you should be asking is who had a motive to steal the book," he said.

"That isn't much help."

"When in doubt, follow the money," Armand said.

"There's someone Armand and I suspect," Madam Toulouse said.

"Oh?" I asked. "Who?"

"A man named Samuel Penrose."

"What's his story?" I asked.

"Self-made millionaire. Fine Arts degree from L.S.U. He deals in rare books. Never married and as sexually kinky as anyone in the Quarter," Armand said.

"That's a powerful claim."

"But true," Madam Toulouse said. "He owns a million-dollar shotgun house on Bourbon. It's where he resides when in the Quarter."

"And when he's not?" I asked.

"A plantation on River Road in St. Charles Parish," Armand said. "He likes to host exotic parties if you get my drift."

"Sounds too wealthy and successful to steal," I said.

"How long have you lived in the Quarter, Cowboy?" he asked.

"Long enough. Why?"

"Then I don't have to tell you that the rich are the first to steal the pennies off a dead man's eyes."

"Penrose didn't steal the book," Madam Toulouse said. "If he's responsible, he paid someone else to take it."

"Libby Tanner or Veronica Lasalle?" I asked.

"Or any of the houseful of servants Ms. DuPont has," Madam Toulouse said. "I doubt there are many secrets they don't know."

"Damn!" I said again.

"Hope Ms. DuPont is paying you well," Armand said.

"You've given me a place to start," I said. "It would have been nice to see Ms. DuPont's book so I'd know what I was looking for."

Madam Toulouse smiled and pulled a Manila envelope from her massive purse.

"When we authenticated Ms. DuPont's *Mosquitoes*, we made a copy."

I thumbed through the pages of the reproduction of Evelyn DuPont's *Mosquitoes* Armand and Madam Toulouse had lovingly made.

"Ms. DuPont said a local publishing house published the two books," I said.

"Lower Pontalba Press," Armand said.

"Too bad they aren't still in business," I said.

"They are," he said.

I gave him a skeptical look and said, "You're kidding me."

"They have a printing plant on the edge of the Quarter, near the Mint," Madam Toulouse said. "It's still family-owned by the founders."

"Who is the present owner?"

"Toby Coleman-Labissiere III," Armand said. "He's hands-on, and you can almost always find him at the plant."

"Any connection to the DuPont family?" I asked.

"Toby is part of the good ol' boy network," Armand said. "No pie gets divided in New Orleans without Toby having a piece of it. He and Evelyn DuPont are distant cousins."

"Sounds as if I'm going to need help on this investigation," I said.

"Or grow another set of arms and legs," Armand said.

I glanced at the copy of *Mosquitoes* and said, "This is more than I expected. I'll copy it and return it to you."

"It's a copy of our copy," Armand said. "You don't think we'd entrust our personal copy with anyone, do you? It's yours to keep."

I slid out of the booth and said, "Thanks."

Armand's comment stopped me before I could start for the door.

"And Cowboy, I suggest you read it to the end, including the four missing chapters."

"Four?" I said. "Ms. DuPont said there were only three."

Madam Toulouse and Armand laughed, and Armand said, "Like you, Ms. DuPont never read the entire book. If she had, she'd have had a conniption."

Chapter 3

It was late when I left Allemand's, my growling stomach reminding me I'd missed lunch. The hours of the French Quarter Fest were from eleven a.m. to eight p.m. The music venues cranked, the food kiosks winding down as the tourists took their food to enjoy the free entertainment. When I reached Maya's brother's barbecue kiosk, I was surprised.

Neither Leo, Maya's brother, nor his wife, Pepper, were working at the food kiosk. Instead, Mama and Jake, both attired in white aprons, filled orders for many enthusiastic customers. I pushed through the crowd and entered through the back of the kiosk.

Mama and Jake were working feverishly, dishing out plates of ribs, chopped beef sandwiches, and hot links with sides of fried okra, curly-cues, and potato salad. After donning an apron hanging from a chair, I began helping.

"You two look like you're about to drop," I said. "Take a break. I got this."

"You can't handle it alone," Mama said.

"I help Bertram all the time. I'm used to demanding crowds."

Jake reached into the cooler and grabbed two cans of Abita, tossing one to Mama and holding the other frosty can to his forehead.

"Thanks," he said.

Two old recliners sat in the back of the kiosk, and Mama and Jake quickly occupied them. An hour passed before the lines subsided, which was good because Leo's larder was all but empty, replaced by lots and lots of cash. I filled a plastic cup with iced tea, drank it dry, and refilled it.

"Where's Leo and Pepper?" I asked.

"They wanted to hear Maya perform. Mama and I volunteered to man their food kiosk," Jake said.

"Looks like it almost got the best of you," I said.

Mama pulled herself out of the recliner and hugged me. "Wyatt, you saved our lives. I was about to cry uncle."

"Happy to help," I said. "I only wish I'd saved a plate for myself. I'm starving."

"Got you covered," Jake said, pulling out two paper plates from one of the coolers. "I don't know about Mama, but I'll share."

"You can have mine," Mama said. "I'm so exhausted. All I need is one of Bertram's martinis."

I was already nibbling on a tasty rib when I said, "Sure about that?"

Mama laughed and said, "I think I'd lose a hand if I tried to come between you and those ribs."

"Try some of Leo's barbecue sauce," Jake said. "Best I've ever tasted."

"Wonderful," I said, "Though I could eat shoe leather right about now."

Jake and I were licking the crumbs when Colley, Adano, Leo, Pepper, Tony, and Lil returned from Maya's performance.

"I was hoping we'd have a crowd when Maya's concert ended," Leo said.

"We sold out," I said. "Hope you have a place to put all that money you made."

"Good God Almighty!" Leo said when he glanced into the till.

"Where's Maya?" Mama asked.

"Changing clothes," Pepper said. "The audience loved her, and she's on cloud nine."

"Thanks for covering the kiosk for us," Leo said.

Jake gave him a thumbs-up. "No problem. You needed to see your sister perform on the main stage."

"How can I thank you?" he asked.

"Seeing your happy faces is all we needed," Jake said.

"We're going to Bertram's bar on Chartres," Mama said. "He mixes the best martinis in town, and right now, I need a double. Join us?"

"I better put some meat on the slow cooker, or I'll have some disappointed diners tomorrow. Pepper will go with you, and I'll join her when I can."

"No way, Macho Man," Pepper said. "I'm going no place without you. "I'll help you prepare the meat and sides, and then I'm retiring to our lovely little bed and bath. I'm beat!" Pepper embraced Mama. "You were wonderful. Thank you."

"Thank Wyatt," she said. "He saved our lives."

When we reached Bertram's, it was rocking with tourists who'd departed the Fest to enjoy cocktails in a comfortable drinking establishment. There was barely room at the bar, though we somehow managed to shoehorn our way in. I was clutching the Manila folder, and Tony noticed.

"What you got, Cowboy?" he asked.

I removed the copy of the manuscript and showed him.

"I have a new client. This is a copy of a missing book she wants me to find. I can use your help. Interested?"

"If Lil will let me out of the house," Tony said.

Lil was kibitzing with Bertram, drinking wine, and having a wonderful time.

"Have at it," she said. "We haven't been ten feet apart for the past two weeks, and I'm ready to spend some time alone."

"Put me to work," Tony said. "I'm ready."

"Our client is Evelyn DuPont," I said.

"So that's who it was," Lil said. "I told Tony she looked familiar."

"She has a collection of expensive first editions with a New Orleans twist. Her most valuable book has gone missing."

"May I take a look?" Adano said.

"Of course, Padre," I said, sliding the copy of *Mosquitoes* down the counter toward him.

Mama was sitting beside Adano, and they were soon pouring over the book.

"This must be some sort of a joke," she said.

"Why is that?" I asked.

"The frontispiece says this copy of *Mosquitoes* was published in 1926 by Lower Pontalba Press in New Orleans. The actual first edition was published in 1927 by Liveright, a New York publisher."

"You're correct," I said. "Liveright removed three chapters they felt were overly salacious during editing. Faulkner was pissed and had a local publisher do a limited-edition printing of the entire book; one for him and one for Ms. DuPont's grandparents, who were his benefactors during the time he lived in New Orleans."

Adano pulled a jeweler's loupe from his pocket to examine the frontispiece.

"Three," he said.

"Pardon me?" I said.

"Three copies of the novel were produced in the limited edition. This is copy three of three."

"How do you know that?" I asked.

Adano pointed to the frontispiece directly below the words, Limited Edition.

"Faulkner signed the frontispiece. If you look closely beneath his signature, you'll see the numbers 3/3," he said. "This was the third copy of three produced in this edition."

"Impossible," I said. "Armand wouldn't have missed something as important as that."

Mama borrowed Adano's magnifier for a better look at the frontispiece.

"Faulkner's signature obscured the edition marking. It's hard to see without Adano's loupe," she said.

"Do you always carry a jeweler's loupe?" I asked.

"Old habits die hard," Adano said. "I apprenticed in Italy studying rare and ancient documents. I'm not mistaken."

"He's right," Mama said. "What difference does it make how many were produced?"

"Faulkner paid for two copies, one for him and a second for the DuPont's. It means this copy was produced without his permission."

"The copy Ms. DuPont lost is valuable, though not as much as the first two," Mama said. "Let me have another look."

Mama began thumbing through the volume. Holding it at a distance, she shook her head.

"What?" I asked.

"You said this edition of Mosquitoes contains an extra three chapters. This version has four," she said.

"How do you know?" I asked.

"The title of my dissertation was *The Life and Times of Influential Southern Author William Faulkner.* I've read everything he ever wrote. The New York version of *Mosquitoes* isn't divided into chapters."

"Then how do you know there's extra text?" I asked.

"*Mosquitoes* chronicles a four-day yacht excursion in Lake Pontchartrain. The novel begins with a lengthy prologue and an equally lengthy epilogue, and each day is subdivided into hours of the day."

"And?" I said.

"The chapters deleted from the New York version are present in this one," Mama said.

Tony's hand covered his grimace. "Give me a good old murder case any day," he said.

"The devil's in the details," Mama said. "Such is the life of a bibliophile."

"What about the fourth added chapter?" I asked.

"It's extra, though not exactly a chapter," Mama said.

"Then what is it?" I asked.

"An extra dedication," she said.

"Extra?" I said.

"He dedicated Mosquitoes to Helen Baird, a young woman from a southern aristocratic family. Though he loved her or thought he did, she married someone else. There's an extra dedication at the end of the book."

"Is that normal?" I asked.

"Someone other than Faulkner put it there," she said.

Mama nodded when I said, "Sure about that? Who is it dedicated to?"

"Anthony and Julia DuPont."

"Evelyn DuPont's grandparents," I said.

Mama continued, "The dedication is in the form of a poem titled *In Shadows Veiled.*"

"Is that important?" I asked.

"None of the other poems in the book are titled," she said.

"Read it to us," I said.

In Southern halls where secrets lie,
Beneath the moon's unblinking eye,
A tale of whispers, dark and deep,
Where restless spirits fail to sleep.

In madness born from fevered dreams,
Where river's song and silence scream,
The mind unravels, thread by thread,
In tangled webs, the heart is led.

A garden's bloom of perfumed sin,
Where passion's flame consumes within,
In twilight's grasp, two souls entwine,
Beneath the veil of jasmine vine.

Betrayed by blood, by ties unspoken,
The vows once sworn now cruelly broken,
In shadows' grip, the truth is bared,
A lover's gaze, a conscience snared.

The specter of forbidden kin,
A legacy of hidden sin,
In gilded rooms where echoes sigh,
Their bond profane, a silent cry.

A tale to stain a name revered,
To strip away what time endeared,
By rival's hand, the verses penned,
To shatter trust, and friendships end.

Yet, in these lines, the truth remains,

A haunting song of loss and gains,
In whispered tones, the past returns,
As candles flicker, shadows burn.

"What's it supposed to mean?" Tony asked.

"I'm unsure. I need to analyze it," she said. "One thing I'm sure of. Faulkner didn't write it."

"How do you know?" I asked.

"The meter is simple, unlike the complex and layered poems he penned," Mama said.

"You think someone other than Faulkner wrote it?" I asked.

"I'm positive that's the case. Can I keep it overnight? I may be able to provide more insights."

"You bet," I said. "Your thoughts are valuable to me."

Tony slugged his scotch and motioned Bertram to bring him another. Bertram had already anticipated Tony's thirst and immediately handed him one.

"This is all a bunch of gobbledygook to me," he said. "I ask again, what does it all mean?"

Maybe the most important clue we have," I said. "Someone at the Lower Pontalba Press created three copies of a limited-edition Mosquitoes instead of two."

"And added a dedication that Faulkner didn't write," Mama said.

"Lower Pontalba Press is still in business," I said. "I need to get over there and check it out."

"Let me," Tony said. "I'll go first thing tomorrow."

Everyone's attention turned to Maya when she entered Bertram's carrying a large suitcase. A short green skirt and simple white blouse replaced her floor-length dress, making her seem younger than she was. Seeing us at the bar, she smiled and joined us.

"What's the deal with your suitcase?" Tony asked.

"Every room in the Quarter is taken," she said. "I bunked last night with Leo and Pepper."

Maya laughed when Bertram said, "They kick you out?"

"No way! It's their first trip out of Rapides Parish since they were married. They need time alone. I thought Wyatt might let me sleep on his floor."

"Ain't going to happen," Bertram said. "I got a guest suite just begging for a pretty lady to occupy." Bertram took Maya's suitcase, ducked under the counter, and said, "Follow me."

When they returned, Maya smiled and said, "Thank you, Bertram. It's nicer than the bed and bath where Leo and Pepper are staying."

"You were fantastic tonight," Colley said.

"Maya has the voice of an angel," Adano said. "Too bad you only had one performance."

"No kidding," Mama said. "Jake and I wanted to hear you."

When Bertram handed her a colorful mixed drink, she pushed it away.

"You know I don't drink," she said.

"It's a mocktail. Ain't no alcohol in it. Just the other good stuff."

"You sure?"

"If I'm lying, I'm dying," he said.

Everyone soon forgot the copy of *Mosquitoes* as they enjoyed Bertram's cocktails—everyone except Maya.

She looked at Tony and said, "You two are working a case, aren't you?"

"Guilty as charged," Tony said.

"I'm off until the end of French Quarter Fest; my stage performance is over. Can I help?"

"I thought you were here to enjoy your time in the French Quarter," I said.

"I'm bored. Please let me help."

Lil had Tony's arm and was pulling him toward the front door.

"Meet me here tomorrow morning," he said. "I'll tell you what Wyatt and I are doing, and you can go with me."

Chapter 4

Someone knocked on my apartment door later that night. It was Maya dressed in a light blue nightgown.

"I couldn't sleep," she said. "Am I disturbing anything?"

"Your daddy, if he knew his baby daughter was visiting a man's apartment after midnight dressed in a little bit of nothing nightgown," I said.

"I've seen you naked," she said. "It doesn't feel like a stretch being here in my nightgown."

I grabbed her arm and directed her into my apartment.

"You're lucky I have my boxer shorts on. If I were naked, I might pull you to the bed and ravish you."

Maya laughed. "I have a brown belt in karate."

"Yeah, well, I have a black belt in seduction," I said.

Maya didn't wait for me to pull her to the bed. My cat, Kisses, was lying beside a pillow. Maya picked her up and flopped on the bed without my help.

"Your cat is beautiful. What's her name?"

"Kisses," I said. "She likes you."

"I hope you aren't getting the wrong idea," she said. "I'm here strictly as a friend."

"Glad you informed me," I said. "Wild thoughts were flying through my head."

I lay on my small bed beside her.

"Maybe I should go back downstairs," she said.

The room's lighting was muted, and dim illumination from a nightlight in my kitchenette was the only concession to total darkness. My patio door leading to the balcony overlooking Chartres was open, its curtain flapping in a gentle breeze blowing through the French Quarter, distant music from Bourbon Street echoing against the walls.

"Don't go," I said. "I'll try to keep my hands to myself."

"Maybe I don't want you to keep your hands to yourself," she said.

She laughed when I said, "Then why do I get the idea you'd break my hand if I tried to cop a feel?"

"You're the first man to see me in my nightgown."

"How about totally naked?"

Maya slapped my hand and sprang off the bed.

"Stop it right now!" she said. "I'm not here for sex."

I went into the bathroom. When I returned, I was carrying a bathrobe.

"Put this on," I said.

"For what reason?" she asked.

"You're hot, and your body is giving me too many ideas. Put on the robe, or else go back to your room."

Maya still had Kisses in her arms when she sprawled back on the bed. I lay beside her, putting a sleep mask on my face.

"You don't like looking at me?" she asked.

37

"I don't have to look. Your perfume is intoxicating, and we're lying so close I can almost taste you," I said.

"You want me to go?"

"I want you to put on the robe I gave you or strip off your nightgown and have wild sex with me. You're driving me insane."

Maya got out of bed, put on the robe, and sat in my old recliner.

"Better?" she asked.

She laughed when I said, "I'll know in a minute or two. It's late. Why aren't you asleep?"

"I'm used to my job keeping me up at all hours. I couldn't sleep, so I knocked on your door to see if you were awake."

"You're on vacation."

"I've never been on vacation," she said. "I need to be doing something."

Maya laughed again when I said, "Take off the robe, and I'll give you something to do."

Maya ignored me and said, "I love your apartment. Have any coffee?"

"You need something to help you sleep, not keep you awake," I said. "I have just the thing."

I had a whiskey jigger in my little kitchen that was once my mainstay when I was drunk and needed sleep. The whiskey was gone, replaced by a bottle of tart cherry juice. I filled the jigger for Maya and then added two drops of onion juice from a dropper bottle I kept in the refrigerator.

The concoction worked, and I'd used it every night until it had replaced my craving for whiskey. Though I no longer needed it, I kept it as a crutch in case I ever did.

"What is it?" Maya asked when I handed her the jigger.

"Tart cherry juice with no added sugar and two drops of my secret guaranteed sleep inducer."

Maya drank the concoction and said, "Not bad. What's the secret ingredient?"

"Onion juice. Maternity ward nurses give it to babies to help them sleep. It works."

Maya was soon yawning. "Guess I better go before I fall asleep on your bed."

"Good idea," I said, kissing her forehead and pushing her out the door. "See you tomorrow."

When Maya exited Bertram's apartment the following morning, she found Tony and Father Piastri sitting at the bar. She wore shorts, a white blouse, and comfortable walking shoes.

"Morning, sleepy head," Bertram said.

"The bed in your guest suite is the most comfortable I've ever slept in. I don't believe I've ever had a better night's sleep."

"Good," Tony said. "We've got work to do."

"Not before you have some of ol' Bertram's Cajun breakfast, you don't."

"I already ate," Tony said.

"Well, this pretty girl hasn't, and neither has the padre. They ain't going nowhere until they do," Bertram said.

"Then you better bring me another scotch."

Bertram smiled and said, "Yes, sir, Mr. Tony." Adano nodded when he said, "You, Padre?"

"Martini, please."

Tony was soon drinking another scotch while Maya and Adano dined on Bertram's version of grillades and grits.

"This is wonderful," she said.

"It beats my usual oatmeal," Adano said. "Your wonderful martini makes it even better."

Tony was carrying something, and Maya asked, "What's in your hands?"

Bertram held up a souvenir t-shirt emblazoned with the words Bertram's Bar, Rue Chartres, and French Quarter America.

"I had a bunch of these printed up last fall, intending to sell them for twenty-five bucks a pop. I'd be honored if you'd wear it today," Bertram said.

Maya had finished her last bite of Bertram's succulent breakfast. After dabbing her lips with a napkin, she took the colorful shirt.

"Thank you, Bertram. I'll put it on now."

Maya returned dressed in shorts and Bertram's t-shirt decorated in green, gold, and purple, the colors of Mardi Gras.

"I love it," she said.

Bertram frowned when Tony said, "You ought to make him pay you for advertising this place."

Maya finished the last sip of her strong Cajun coffee and said, "No way!"

"Then let's go to work," Tony said. "I got bills to pay. My car's not far from here."

"Mind if I tag along?" Adano asked.

"My car has plenty of room, Padre," Tony said. "You're welcome to come."

"How far is it from here to where we need to go?" Maya asked.

"Less than a mile," he said.

"It's a beautiful morning. Let's walk. I haven't had time to explore the Quarter."

"This is business, not an excursion," Tony said.

"Can't we do both?" Maya asked.

"I second the motion," Adano said.

Tony's surgically repaired knee had long since healed. He was no longer in pain when he walked, and his leg muscles were much stronger. It didn't matter because he never liked to walk when he could drive.

"We don't have all day," he said.

"I do," Maya said. "Let's walk.

Tony grumbled but followed her and Adano out the door. "Why not," he said. "It's not that far."

"And you can point out some sights on the way," she said.

"Do I have a choice?" he said.

"Stop grumbling," Maya said.

The day was beautiful, and the sidewalks were crowded with tourists and locals enjoying the succulent aromas and diverse sounds of French Quarter Fest.

"I was so worried about my performance that I've had no time to see much of the Quarter What's the building up ahead with the big steeple?"

"Bertram's is on Chartres, and so is Jackson Square. The building up ahead is the St. Louis Cathedral, possibly the most famous building in New Orleans."

"Wyatt and Mama are going to give me a tour," Adano said.

"Why wait?" Tony said.

A brass band belted a symphonic melody before hundreds of admiring music lovers gathered around the open-air stage.

"This is a dream come true," Adano said.

"You won't be disappointed," Tony said.

When they entered the doors, Adano was overcome with emotion. Dropping to his knees, he buried his face in his hands and began to weep. Feeling his passion, a tall woman hurried up the aisle, knelt before him, and wrapped her long arms around his shoulders.

Tony thought he recognized the handsome woman, though she wore a nun's habit the last time he'd seen her. Her short-cropped hair was uncovered, and her clothes were a modest yet stylish skirt and blouse.

"Is that you, Sister Lydia?"

"Tony?" she said.

"It's me, Sister," he said. "Father Piastri just retired from the clergy. He's never visited St. Louis Cathedral. This is Maya."

"It's Lydia now," she said. "I've retired, and yesterday was my final day."

"Retired?" Tony said. "You aren't a nun anymore?"

"I'll always be a nun," she said. "God has directed me to explore my secular side."

Adano beamed. "Then we are star-crossed because that's exactly what he has directed me to do."

"You've been a nun forever," Tony said. "What will you do with yourself?"

Lydia smiled. "Almost forever. Now, I intend to do what I've wanted for years. Travel and see the world." She took Adano's hand and said, "This wonderful old building has the same effect on me. Come. I'll give you a tour."

Maya and Tony watched as the former-nun Lydia led the former priest Adano to the front of the magnificent cathedral.

"Who is she?" Maya asked."

"A retired nun. She worked for the Greater Archdiocese of New Orleans a few years ago when she hired Wyatt."

"To do what?" Maya asked.

"Investigate a satanic altar in a closet in the Old Ursuline Convent."

"Are you making this up?" Maya asked.

"If you don't believe that, then you aren't going to believe the rest of the story," Tony said.

"Tell it to me before you piss me off," Maya said.

Tony laughed. "Sister Lydia was married to the first vampire to come to New Orleans. He was the grandson of the 'Sun King, Louis XIV. They had a son together."

Maya found it hard to suppress a grin. "Where is her husband now?"

"Sister Lydia drove a wooden stake through his heart."

"I'm not laughing," Maya said.

"Neither am I," Tony said. "You're going to have to trust me on this. I'll tell you the story later."

"Let's follow Adano and Sister Lydia. Sounds as if she's the best tour guide in New Orleans."

They listened as Lydia recounted the building's history and architecture and showed them the Stations of the Cross. Adano had many questions, and Lydia had all the answers. An hour passed before she concluded her tour.

"When I left Italy, I dreamed of serving God at St. Louis Cathedral. My tiny church in Rapides Parish is modeled after this wonderful building. Fifty years have passed, and this is my first visit to New Orleans."

"Now that you're here," Lydia said. "I hope you stay awhile."

Like Adano, Lydia was seventy-something and had devoted her life to the Church. Taken by her stately beauty, he held her hand and stared into her clear eyes.

"That was lovely," he said. "I've waited all my life to visit this cathedral, and you made the event memorable."

"I sensed you were a man of God when I saw you on your knees," Lydia said. "Are you going to Bertram's? I could use a stiff drink right about now."

"We're working a case and, on our way, to interview someone of interest," Tony said.

"All three of you?" Lydia asked.

"I'm just along for the ride," Adano said. "Join us, and I'll buy the drinks at Bertram's when we finish."

Lydia looked at Tony for confirmation and said, "May I? I promise I won't get in the way."

"Why the hell not?" he said.

Chapter 5

It was the weekend, tourists and locals flooding the French Quarter for the Fest. Music and the wonderful aroma of Cajun and Creole cooking wafted in a gentle breeze. Maya was all eyes as they strolled past Café Du Monde. When they entered the French Market, she stopped at a vendor's cubicle and squeezed a foam rubber alligator.

"Ohh!" she said. "I need some souvenirs to take home."

"You'll have lots of time to return later," Tony said. "The French Market isn't far from Bertram's. The Lower Pontalba Press closes at noon on Saturday, and we have to hurry."

Maya gazed around, taking in the sights and smells. "I think I love this place. There's so much to see."

"And it changes daily," Lydia said.

Adano was also pawing through a box of New Orleans souvenirs at one of the open-air vendors.

"I could spend all day here," Maya said.

"But not now," Tony said. "We have work to do."

"Spoilsport," Maya said. "At least give me some detail on the case on the way there."

"Our wealthy client owns a valuable book. It's gone missing, and she wants us to find it," Tony said.

"How valuable?" Lydia asked.

"A million bucks," Tony said.

"No book is worth a million bucks," Maya said.

"This one is."

"I love a good mystery," Adano said.

"Me too," Lydia said.

Adano smiled and said, "One more thing we have in common."

The sky above the French Quarter was robin egg blue. Overhead, a snowy egret buoyed by a thermal updraft was winging toward Lake Pontchartrain. The crowd noise was beginning to disappear as they approached Esplanade Avenue and the edge of the French Quarter.

"What makes the book so valuable?" Maya asked.

"It's one of three," Tony said. "That's not our only problem."

"What is?" Maya asked.

"There were only supposed to be two made. Our client's edition was number three. Evelyn DuPont's grandparents were supposed to receive number one. Instead, they ended up with a book that wasn't authorized to be printed. The Lower Pontalba Press printed all three books."

Tony nodded when Maya said, "The place we're headed?"

"Why is the third copy of the book so important?" Lydia asked.

"It had extra text added to the end of the book," Tony said.

"Extra text?" Lydia said.

"In the form of a long poem," Tony said.

"About what?"

"I'm not exactly sure," Tony said. "I don't understand much about poetry; this poem was cryptic."

"You mean it contained a hidden message?" Lydia asked.

"That's what Mama Mulate thinks," Tony said. "She has Wyatt's copy of the missing book and is analyzing the poem."

"I've loved poetry and have studied its structure and content for years. I'd like to see the poem," Lydia said."

"Why not?" Tony said. "Mama will be at Bertram's later."

"You think the person we're interviewing knows about the book?" Maya asked.

"Don't know. The three books were published in 1926. The current owner wasn't even alive at the time."

"Then why waste our time?" Maya asked.

"The press is a family-owned business, and Toby Coleman-Labissiere is the owner. Maybe he knows why there were three books published instead of two."

"If he happens to be a student of history," Lydia said.

"Or perhaps his predecessors maintained exquisite records," Adano said.

"Why not?" Lydia said. "Business owners were more responsible back then."

"That's why we're checking it out," Tony said.

They realized something was wrong when they reached the building housing the Lower Pontalba Press. Cop cars with blue flashing lights circled the building.

"What the hell!" Tony said.

The cop at the doorway smiled when he recognized Tony. Tony shook his hand.

"Lieutenant Nicosia," he said.

47

"What you got, Charles?" Tony asked.

"A dead man," the cop said.

"Murder?" Tony asked.

"Don't know yet," Charles said.

Officer Charles didn't stop them as they pushed through forensic technicians who were combing the place for clues. In the owner's office, two people Tony recognized stood beside a body in a chair behind an executive desk.

The two men turned when Tony said, "Tommy, Marlon, what happened here?"

"Homicide investigation. You back on the clock, Tony?"

"Lil would divorce me if I was. These galoots, Maya, Lydia, and Adano, are the two best homicide detectives in New Orleans. Tommy O'Rear and Marlon Bando. I know because I trained them."

"Happy to meet you," Tommy said. "We're kind of busy."

Tommy and Marlon stopped what they were doing when Tony said, "Maya is a homicide detective in Rapides Parish."

"Are you now?" Tommy said. "Are there many murders in Rapides Parish?"

"You'd be surprised," Maya said. "It's near an Army base, and we have more murders per capita than New Orleans."

Tommy smiled and said, "Damn!"

"I have time on my hands and will help with the investigation if you'd like," Maya said.

"I doubt the Chief would go along with that," Tommy said. "What do you have time off from?"

"Maya's a lead singer with a band from Pinebridge," Tony said. "She performed last night on the main stage."

"Thought you looked familiar," Tommy said. "Marlon and I caught your show last night."

"And?" Maya said.

"You got a set of pipes," Tommy said. "You blew us away."

"Thanks," Maya said. "It was my first time performing outside Rapides Parish, and I was worried."

"You were wonderful and have nothing to worry about," Marlon said. "I checked online to see if you had any recordings."

"Not yet," Maya said. "I'm working on it."

Tommy glanced at Lydia and Adano and said, "You working a crew now, Tony?"

"Adano and Lydia recently retired from the clergy. They're friends of mine. We weren't expecting a murder scene."

"Don't know yet if that's what we got," Tommy said. "We don't even know how he died."

Tommy was a large man with an Irish complexion and unruly red hair. When he shook Maya's hand, his own felt like a bearpaw. Marlon was also tall, though not as stocky as his partner.

"Marlon's shy," Tony said.

"Are you really a homicide detective?" Tommy asked.

"For the past five years," Maya said. "Who's dead?"

"The owner, Toby Coleman-Labissiere," Tommy said.

"You don't know how he died?" Tony asked.

"Nope," Marlon said. "Want to take a look at the body?"

Tony gave his ex-partner a perplexed glance. "Then how do you know it's murder?"

"Like I said. "We don't."

"Someone called 9-1-1 and said Coleman-Labissiere had had a heart attack. When EMTs arrived, they found the body and a trail of blood leading out the front door," Marlon said.

"Mind if I take a look?" Maya asked.

"Knock yourself out," Tommy said.

Maya had a pair of latex gloves in her pocket and began rotating the head of the victim.

"Do you always have gloves with you?" Tommy asked.

"Old habits die hard," she said. "Look at his neck."

Tony, Tommy, and Marlon stared at the red mark on the victim's neck.

"What is it?" Tony asked.

"Snakebite," Maya said. "A snake killed him."

"Whoa!" Tommy said. "Never seen that before. Sure about that?"

"I grew up in Rapides Parish. I'm sure," Maya said. "Better tell your techs to look for a snake. It's probably in here somewhere."

"The victim must have died shortly after the snake bit him. The venom of Louisiana vipers doesn't act that fast," Adano said.

"How do you know?" Tony asked.

"My family wasn't exactly Catholic," he said.

Lydia gave him an appraising glance and said, "What were they?"

"In this country, we would have been called evangelicals. My family handled snakes as part of our religious practice. I began handling snakes before I ever attended school."

"I wasn't aware that there are evangelicals in Italy," Lydia said.

"Less than one percent of the population. I learned the error of my ways when I began attending school. Though a hundred percent Catholic now, I still love snakes and other reptiles."

"Interesting," Lydia said.

"Whatever bit the victim immobilized him immediately," Marlon said. "Someone went to the bar, broke a glass, and sustained a wound."

"They must have cleaned up the glass after cutting themselves but failed to staunch the bleeding," Tommy said.

"The person who broke the glass is your murderer," Tony said.

"And he or she was friends with the victim," Maya said.

"How do you know?" Tommy asked.

"There's an unfinished drink on the desk. Coleman-Labissiere was sharing a drink with someone he knew," Maya said. "The murderer produced the snake and plopped it into his lap. He panicked, and the snake bit him."

A crime tech hurried into the office. "We found the snake," he said. "Someone's on their way from Audubon to capture it."

"You fellows scared of a snake?" Tommy asked.

"It's spitting at us," the tech said.

"Spitting at you? What the hell are you talking about?"

"It's a cobra, Lieutenant Blackburn. A king cobra. Someone braver than me is going to have to capture it."

"I'll do it," Adano said. "Show me where it is."

The forensic team had gathered around and opened the door of a credenza. Adano knelt and began speaking Italian in a soothing voice. Soon, he reached into the credenza and emerged with the snake. The entire forensic team took backward steps.

"He's as frightened of you as you are of him," Adano said. "No problem because he has submitted and will not harm anyone."

"Remarkable," Lydia said. "Aren't you frightened?

Adano touched the reptile's mouth with his lips. "God protects me because I'm a true believer.

My parents handled snakes for years and were never bitten."

"We have snake handlers in Rapides Parish," Maya said. "Not all evangelicals handle snakes."

Tony shook his head and said, "Padre, I think you missed your calling."

"What the hell are you doing here, Tony?" Tommy asked.

"To interview the victim," Tony said.

"For what purpose," Tommy asked.

"Wyatt and I are investigating the theft of a book printed here nearly a hundred years ago. I was hoping Toby Coleman-Labissiere could shed some light on our search."

"You probably came to the right place," Tommy said. "From the looks of things, this office hasn't changed much in the last hundred years."

"Is there anyone else I can talk to?" Tony asked.

"It's Saturday, and the victim was the only person working," Marlon said.

"Who usually works in the office?" Maya asked.

"Toby's niece, Bambi Coleman-Labissiere," Tommy said.

Tommy smiled when Tony said, "Bambi?"

"Hell, Lieutenant, I couldn't make this shit up."

"What now?" Tony asked.

"Let forensics do their work. When Audubon Zoo gets here, Marlon and I will be off duty. You buying?"

"Don't I always?" Tony said. "Join us at Bertram's."

Handlers from the Audubon Zoo's herpetology department arrived and took custody of the king cobra. The forensic techs continued scouring the office for clues. Tommy and Marlon gave Tony and the others a ride to Bertram's in their squad car.

Bertram smiled as he began dispensing drinks and putting them on Tony's tab. Tony didn't mind because he was on retainer. However, he intended to glean as much information as possible from Marlon and Tommy.

"Why didn't the murderer collect the snake before leaving the premises?" Marlon asked.

"Something disturbed them and caused them to drop their drink," Tommy said. "He or she sustained a cut and vacated the premises quickly."

Tommy and Marlon smiled when Maya said, "I like you two."

"Then come with us to Carlucci's," Tommy said.

"Where is that?" Maya asked.

"A bar in the Central Business District," Tommy said. "It's where all the New Orleans cops hang out. It'll be rocking right about now."

"I don't have a car," Maya said.

"You can ride with us," Marlon said. "We'll bring you back here when you're ready."

"Tony?" Maya said.

"Go," Tony said. "These guys are honorable, and you'll love Carlucci's and all the gang."

Tony watched as Maya, Tommy, and Marlon disappeared out the door. Adano and Lydia were drinking martinis, and both had silly grins.

"Why are you so amused?" he asked.

"Bertram's martinis are wonderful," Lydia said.

"That's not why you and Adano are grinning,"

"While with the Greater Archdiocese of New Orleans, I worked in administration and knew where all the bodies were buried," Lydia said.

Tony knew she was about to tell him something and said, "And?"

"While you and your buddies played cops and robbers at the crime scene, I cased the joint for information."

Tony gave her a look. "You found something important to the case?"

Lydia nodded. "The name of the person who ordered the creation of the third copy of Mosquitoes."

Chapter 6

My yearly physical exam had rolled around, and I'd left my apartment early to attend it. My doctor was an attractive middle-aged woman who'd been a pharmacist before becoming a doctor.

"Your cholesterol is a little high," she said. "I want to put you on a statin."

"I don't like drugs," I said. "I'm healthy and don't need to take statins."

The doctor frowned. "That's what you said last time you were here. Your cholesterol is still high. You could be setting yourself up for a heart attack or a stroke. I'm writing you a prescription. I'll call it in. What's the name of your pharmacy."

"I don't have a pharmacy," I said.

"There's one in this building. I'll call, and you can pick it up on your way out," she said.

The previous day, I'd run five miles in under forty minutes and felt as strong as I ever had. Still feeling the pressure, I filled the prescription before leaving the building and left the pharmacy with mixed emotions about the medical profession.

The French Quarter Fest continued with hundreds of people enjoying the music and succulent aromas wafting in the breeze above the sidewalks and streets. Bertram's was less crowded, with only some regulars drinking at the bar. I thought I recognized the woman talking with Adano, Bertram, Mama, and Jake, though I wasn't sure.

"Is that you, Sister Lydia?"

The handsome older woman smiled and said, "Just Lydia now. I'm retired."

"You're looking fantastic. Retirement must agree with you."

"Don't know yet since this is my first full day. Ask me again next week," she said.

"You met Jake and Mama?" I asked.

"We've had a lovely conversation," Lydia said. "I'm one of the Cryptid Hunter's biggest fans."

"What's in your hand?" Mama asked.

"Nothing," I said.

"Looks like medicine to me," she said. "Are you sick?"

"My doctor thinks my cholesterol is too high and wants to put me on a statin."

Mama snatched the small sack from my hand and tossed it into Bertram's trash.

"Don't you dare," she said. "I have something natural to lower your cholesterol. I'll have it next time I see you."

"What about my doctor?"

"They'll never know the difference," Mama said.

"Good," I said, taking the lemonade Bertram handed me. "What's everyone doing here?"

"Lydia and Adano accompanied Maya and me to interview Toby Coleman-Labissiere," Tony said.

"You need a crew to do an interview now?"

"I wasn't given a choice. Turns out, they came in handy."

"What did Coleman-Labissiere tell you?"

"Not a damn thing," Tony said.

"He wasn't there?"

"He was dead," Tony said. "Tommy, Marlon, and their forensic crew were on the scene when we arrived."

"Murder?"

"I think so."

"Tommy and Marlon must have been surprised seeing you."

Tony smiled. "Just like old times."

"How did he die?" I asked.

"Snakebite," Tony said.

"Excuse me?"

"I didn't stutter," Tony said.

"Snakebites don't kill you instantly. What stopped him from driving himself to the emergency room?"

"The bite of a king cobra can kill an elephant in an hour and a man in fifteen minutes," Adano said.

"What the hell was a king cobra doing in his office?" I asked.

"Someone brought it in with them," Tony said. "Someone Coleman-Labissiere knew. As I see it, he was having drinks with them when they handed him the snake. Something caused the killer to drop their tumbler. It was broken on the floor, and a trail of blood led out the door."

"Something or someone must have spooked the killer," I said.

"They cleared out pronto without retrieving the snake or cleaning up the blood," Tony said. "With DNA and fingerprints, they'll be easy to find. We'll know more about the motive when we find out who the killer is. Lydia found something interesting."

"What?" I asked.

"Maybe the most important clue yet," Mama said. "The name of the person who paid Lower Pontalba Press for the third copy of *Mosquitoes*."

"Wonderful," I said. "How did you do that?"

"While everyone was looking for the snake, I took the liberty to examine the file cabinets. Records of the creation of the business were superbly kept. While scanning the files, I hit the jackpot."

Lydia nodded when I said, "The name of the person who commissioned the extra book?"

"Bingo," Tony said.

"Who was it?" I asked.

"A man named Laceigh Rutherford, a contemporary of Anthony DuPont," Lydia said.

"What's the connection?" I asked.

"Both were bank owners about the same age and social status. Rutherford was murdered, his killer never found," Lydia said. "That's all I know so far. I'm still looking."

"Where did you find the connection?" I asked.

"I did a quick check of the Internet. I'm sure there's much more to the story, but that's all I found doing a cursory search."

Bertram and Mama shook their heads when I asked, "Do either of you know anything about Laceigh Rutherford?"

"Before my time," Bertram said.

"How do you know the snake was a king cobra?" I asked.

"A forensic tech found it. Adano captured it and held it for us until Audubon Zoo people arrived."

"I'm good with snakes," Adano said.

"Glad someone is." I glanced at Mama and said, "Did you have any luck deciphering the meaning of the poem?"

"Lydia, Adano, and I were discussing it when you arrived," Mama said.

"Any ideas?"

"We think it's an accusation and a threat," she said.

"Against who?"

"The dedicatees, Anthony and Julia DuPont," Mama said.

Could you reread the poem?" I asked.

Mama opened the copy of *Mosquitoes* and said, "Of course."

> In Southern halls where secrets lie,
> Beneath the moon's unblinking eye,
> A tale of whispers, dark and deep,
> Where restless spirits fail to sleep.

> In madness born from fevered dreams,
> Where river's song and silence scream,
> The mind unravels, thread by thread,
> In tangled webs, the heart is led.

> A garden's bloom of perfumed sin,
> Where passion's flame consumes within,
> In twilight's grasp, two souls entwine,
> Beneath the veil of jasmine vine.

> Betrayed by blood, by ties unspoken,
> The vows once sworn now cruelly broken,
> In shadows' grip, the truth is bared,
> A lover's gaze, a conscience snared.

> The specter of forbidden kin,
> A legacy of hidden sin,
> In gilded rooms where echoes sigh,
> Their bond profane, a silent cry.

> A tale to stain a name revered,
> To strip away what time endeared,
> By rival's hand, the verses penned,
> To shatter trust, and friendships end.

Yet, in these lines, the truth remains,
A haunting song of loss and gains,
In whispered tones, the past returns,
As candles flicker, shadows burn.

"Sounds like a bunch of malarkey!" Tony said.

"And you don't believe that Faulkner penned the dedication?" I asked.

Mama laughed. "Faulkner was a poet laureate. The person who wrote this poem was a hack. It doesn't come close to a poem Faulkner would have written."

"Then who wrote it?" I asked.

"Laceigh Rutherford," Lydia said.

"How do you know?" I asked.

"From the stanza, 'By rival's hand, the verses penned. To shatter trust, and friendships end.' Rutherford and DuPont were both bankers. That means they were rivals. He penned it to spill the goods on Evelyn DuPont's grandparents."

"For what reason?" I asked.

"Revenge, maybe," Mama said. "Rutherford apparently had a gripe with Anthony and Julia DuPont."

"We think he knew something horrible about Anthony and Julia and wanted them to know it," Lydia said.

"How horrible? I said. "Spell it out to me."

"Incest," Mama said.

"One of the stanzas tells you that?" I asked.

Mama nodded and said, "The one that goes, 'The specter of forbidden kin, A legacy of hidden sin, In gilded rooms where echoes sigh, Their bond profane, a silent cry."

"It has to be an accusation of incest," Lydia said.

"Whoa!" Tony said. "In this town, that kind of talk could get someone murdered."

"And did," Lydia said.

"If Rutherford had a beef with the DuPonts and had status-ending dirt on them, then why did he tell them about it instead of spreading the accusation around town?"

"I'm sure there's a reason," Mama said. "We just don't know what it is."

"Maybe he was trying to blackmail them," Jake said.

"Maybe," I said.

"Rutherford had a relationship with Toby Coleman-Labissiere's grandfather, or he wouldn't have published an illicit copy of *Mosquitoes*," Adano said. "Perhaps he was in on the extortion."

"Makes sense," I said.

"Maybe the disappearance of Ms. DuPont's book and the murder of Toby Coleman-Labissiere are linked," Tony said.

"Could be," I said. "Fast forward to the present. Someone murdered an heir of the original owner of the Lower Pontalba Press. Maybe the past is the key to the future."

"Crazy but plausible," Mama said. "And anything but simple."

"Murder never is," Tony said.

"Where's Maya?" I asked.

"Carlucci's with Tommy and Marlon," Tony said.

"Oh my! You think that's a good idea?" I asked.

"Maya is attractive, and Tommy and Marlon are bachelors. They'll watch out for her," Tony said. "Besides, she's a cop and probably knows what to expect."

I smiled and said, "Heaven help her."

"Maya can take care of herself. She'll be fine," Tony said. "Where do we go from here?"

"We have three generations to decode," I said. "I have an appointment with the owner of Wild Magnolias, a bookstore here in the Quarter."

"What do you hope to learn?" Mama asked.

"Veronica LaSalle, Evelyn DuPont's best friend, owns the bookstore. It's where collectors go for book advice and to purchase valuable first editions. By all accounts, there's little she doesn't know about *Mosquitoes* and Evelyn DuPont. Afterward, I'll drop in on Ms. DuPont. Now that I see where this investigation is heading, I better understand what questions to ask.

"The Greater Archdiocese of New Orleans has always maintained meticulous records," Lydia said. "I'll see what more I can find about Rutherford and Ms. DuPont's grandparents." Adano beamed when she added, "Adano can help me."

"Maybe we can have dinner and discuss it," he said.

"If it's at Leo's barbecue kiosk," Lydia said. "You're bragging about the ribs has me craving them."

"Love it," Adano said. "We'd better hurry before they run out."

"Wait," Bertram said. "Take a couple of go cups. Nobody mixes martinis like ol' Bertram does."

Lydia and Adano had mile-wide grins as they waited for Bertram to mix their martinis and transfer them into colorful go cups. Music and crowd noise flooded through the front door as they exited the bar and attacked the crowd, still holding sway outside Chartres Street.

"I think they like each other," Mama said.

Jake squeezed her hand and said, "I'm hungry. Maybe we should join them."

"Hang on, big boy," Mama said. "I have one more thing to tell Wyatt."

"Hit me," I said.

"The Tulane Library also has a wealth of old newspapers and historical records," Mama said. "Jake and I will access them and concentrate on generation two."

"Sounds like a plan," I said.

Tony slammed his drink and said, "Put these drinks on my tab."

"Where are you going?" I asked.

"Carlucci's. By now, the N.O.P.D. will have the coroner's report on the victim, as well as blood tests, fingerprints, DNA, and more. Tommy and Marlon need a little bird-dogging to get the job done, and there's no one better to do it than me and Maya."

"You aren't going to join everyone at Leo's kiosk?" I asked.

Tony smiled and nodded. "Good idea. Wouldn't hurt to take some barbecue to the gang at Carlucci's."

Tony followed Mama and Jake as they exited the bar. Bertram's smile had disappeared. There was no one else at his establishment except him and me.

"This festival is wrecking my business," he said.

"No one's here," I said. "Shut down the bar and try some of Leo's barbecue. You'll love it."

"What if a crowd shows up while I'm gone?"

"You'll have no more customers than now until the fest shuts down. By then, you'll be back behind the bar, filling your stomach with Leo's barbecue. It would be best if you rewarded yourself with something you didn't cook for a change," I said.

"Does sound pretty good," he said.

"Sure it does. Take Lady and knock yourself out. She'll love it, and so will you."

"You're right," he said. "Let's get out of here and lock the door before someone shows up."

Chapter 7

I followed Bertram out the door and watched him lock it. I thought about joining the rest of the crew at Leo's. I had something else on my mind as I hurried toward Royal Street. The short walk took me to a shop called Wild Magnolias, which alluded to the all-black marching club that dressed in flashy costumes during Mardi Gras.

Wild Magnolias sold books, though it wasn't a Barnes & Noble Superstore. The woman behind the sales counter dropped her celebrity magazine when the bell on the door rang, her relieved smile indicating she was glad to see me.

"I'm Wyatt Thomas. Thanks for agreeing to talk with me."

"Veronica LaSalle. Evelyn would kill me if I hadn't. And you can call me Ronnie."

I shook her hand and said, "Now I know why your name is so familiar. You're Ronnie LaSalle, one of the original supermodels. I've seen your face in dozens of magazines. Is that how you met Evelyn DuPont?"

"We had the same agent," Ronnie said. "Evelyn's the most beautiful woman on earth."

As I stared into Ronnie's vivid hazel eyes, I had yet to release her hand.

"Evelyn is drop-dead gorgeous, though she doesn't hold a candle to you."

"You're a liar, Mr. Thomas, but I love it."

Ronnie's flowing violet designer dress was cut so low that it almost made me blush. Almost. Her surgically enhanced breasts were challenging to take my eyes off of. When I did, I looked up into her smile and understood my reaction had had the desired effect. Her face was a little too perfect, and I saw she was a Botox fan. It didn't matter. Older women were my kryptonite, and Ronnie LaSalle was still a knockout.

"I hope I'm not disturbing your business," I said.

"You kidding? I haven't sold a book since the Fest began. As usual, I'll be glad when it's over."

"So sorry to hear that," I said.

"I shouldn't complain. The French Quarter Fest is good for everyone in New Orleans." Ronnie locked the front door and put the closed sign in the window. "Please come with me."

I followed her down the hall to a room in the back that was not only bolted but also triple-locked. She opened the door using keys on a large brass ring and then re-locked all the bolts once we were inside. Sitting behind an antique desk, she directed me to an empty chair.

"You're familiar with my little shop, Mr. Thomas?"

"I presume you're a bookseller."

"Outside's a façade, a few magazines, and slick best sellers for the average Beaumont or Little Rock tourist. It's not where I make my real money."

"I see," I said, even though I didn't.

Veronica LaSalle pointed to her racks of old books and said, "I generate my real money in this room. Wild Magnolias specializes in rare first editions, especially books with a New Orleans connection."

"Then you must be familiar with Armand and Madam Toulouse."

"You know Armand and the Madam?" she asked.

"They're friends of mine," I said.

"Lucky you. They charge me an arm and a leg for their services."

"And worth every penny," I said.

"You don't have to tell me. They are irreplaceable, indispensable, and any adjective you want to apply."

I glanced around the room as Veronica LaSalle spoke. It was different from the shop in front. Instead of movie posters and linoleum, expensive wallpaper and a Persian rug dominated the decor. Real art, not cheap lithographs, hung from the walls. I began to appreciate the three locks on the door.

"These volumes are valuable," she said.

"How valuable?" I asked.

"Would you like an example?"

"Please," I said.

"Faulkner's book of poetry, *The Marble Faun*, is the type of book I sell. In perfect condition and with dust jacket intact, it might go for ten to twenty thousand dollars."

"A lot of dough for an old book," I said.

"It is, and I have such a volume. It bears a special inscription, signed in New Orleans, in the author's own handwriting. One of my collectors is ready and willing to pay fifty thousand for the book. Are you a collector, Wyatt."

"I love to read. I usually buy my books at the thrift store or check them out at the library."

"If everyone were like you, I'd be out of business," Ronnie said. "Thank God they're not."

"Evelyn DuPont calls you her best friend. I had assumed your friendship began as book lovers," I said. "I see now you met much earlier."

"As I said, Evelyn and I had the same agent and worked for the same modeling agency. We both made tons of money over the years. Evelyn is from a socially elite New Orleans family, has old money, and doesn't need any more than she already has. I was nouveau riche, naïve, and spent most of my newly found wealth purchasing disposable luxuries."

"I've never had that problem," I said.

"It's more of a curse than a problem. My money went out the door as fast as it came in. Evelyn helped me change that."

"Oh? Please explain."

"Evelyn and I are both avid readers. Modeling can be extremely boring, and we spent our time between photo shoots reading. It was she who turned me on to rare book collecting."

"Collecting and not selling?"

"I'm a better seller than I am a collector. I also have a God-given talent," she said.

"Which is?"

"The innate ability to spot the proverbial diamond in a pig's ass. I began buying and selling and was soon making more dealing in old books than modeling."

"Did Evelyn help you acquire Wild Magnolias from the previous owner?" I asked.

"Not Evelyn; someone else," she said.

"Mind sharing that information with me?"

"Why not?" she said. "It's common knowledge. Samuel Penrose purchased Wild Magnolias. Believe me when I tell you it wasn't cheap."

"I can only imagine," I said. "Who is Samuel Penrose?"

"A powerful man who knows the dirt on every important person in New Orleans."

"So, Penrose owns Wild Magnolias?"

"Sam recognized my talent as a seller. He deeded Wild Magnolias to me in exchange for a cut of the profits."

Ronnie nodded when I said, "An ongoing relationship?"

"The commissions he has made have repaid his investment many times over," she said.

"You sound bitter."

"Samuel is like a leech attached to my jugular."

"I was a lawyer in another lifetime," I said. "There's no agreement that can't be terminated."

Ronnie snickered. "There is no agreement, at least on paper."

"Verbal agreements are worthless," I said. "Just quit paying him."

"Not so simple," she said. "Sam would ruin me both socially and financially if I discontinued giving him his blood money. I can't afford to lose all of my clients."

"You're one of the most attractive women in the world. Can't you use your feminine guile on him?"

My comment made Ronnie laugh. "Sam is gay and would like you better than me."

"Sorry I asked," I said.

"Don't be. I've tried everything short of murdering him."

Her remark caught me by surprise. "Don't do that," I said.

"Just joking," she said. "I would never even consider killing someone, much less actually doing it."

"Did you know Toby Coleman-Labissiere?" I asked.

"Everyone in the Quarter knows Toby."

Ronnie's hand went to her mouth when I said, "He was murdered."

"You have to be kidding," she said.

"I'm not."

"How was he killed?" she asked.

"Snakebite. You know anyone who collects snakes?"

"Rodney DuPont, Evelyn's son."

I let the subject drop and said, "Coleman-Labissiere was a person of interest in my investigation because his publishing company printed the three extra copies of *Mosquitoes* with the additional chapters."

"Three copies? I was only aware of two that were printed," she said.

"Laceigh Rutherford, a contemporary of Evelyn's grandfather, had Lower Pontalba Press print a third copy. He added a dedication at the end of the book, a poem implying Evelyn's grandparents were incestual." When Ronnie didn't immediately reply, I said, "Something wrong?"

"Sorry," she said. "I need to consider what I tell you before blurting something out about my best friend's son."

"I understand," I said. "Can we talk about the disappearance of Evelyn's copy of *Mosquitoes*?"

"Of course," she said.

"Only two people other than Ms. DuPont have the combination to her private library. You and her social secretary."

"You aren't suggesting I took the book, are you?"

"Of course not," I said. "You aren't a suspect."

"You're a liar, Wyatt," she said. "Why are you smiling?"

"That's the second time you've called me that."

"Then maybe I'm correct," she said.

"You are Evelyn's best friend. She would have given you the book if you'd have asked," I said.

"You'd be wrong about that," Ronnie said.

"Please tell me what you know."

"Evelyn's my best friend. I shouldn't talk behind her back."

"But?"

"Perhaps there's something you don't know about Evelyn. It may be pertinent to Toby's murder, and I think I should tell you about it."

"Such as?"

Ronnie hesitated before saying, "Evelyn has congenital mental problems."

"She didn't appear that way to me."

"She's fine as long as she's taking her meds. When she's not, there's hell to pay," Ronnie said.

"Congenital?"

"Her father was certifiably loony tunes," Ronnie said.

Ronnie laughed when I said, "David DuPont was a well-respected man. I've never heard anyone accuse him of mental illness."

"And you never will. His craziness was covered up for decades. Anyone who tried to leak the information was dealt with most severely."

"And he passed his mental illness on to Evelyn?"

Ronnie nodded. "And Evelyn passed the mental illness on to her daughter Alicin and Alicin's twin brother Rodney."

"Evelyn mentioned Alicin but not Rodney. He collects snakes?"

"Among other weird things," she said.

"Tell me about him."

"The family had him committed to a private institute in Alabama," Ronnie said.

"Is he still there?"

"He escaped," she said.

"When did that happen?"

"Recently," she said.

"Is he back in custody?"

Ronnie shook her head. "No one knows where he is. He disappeared like a will-o-the-wisp."

"Who tends Rodney's snakes when he's away?"

"Jonathan Stallings, Evelyn's butler."

"How long has Stallings worked for Evelyn?" I asked.

"For as long as I've known her," she said. "He lives on the premises."

"Is it possible that he murdered Coleman-Labissiere?"

"Jonathan is one of the creepiest persons I know. I don't believe I've ever seen him smile."

"Is that a yes?"

Ronnie shook her head. "I don't know."

"What about Alicin?" I asked.

"She's more beautiful than her mother and crazy as a bed bug."

"She's not on medication?"

Ronnie laughed. "Self-medication. Whiskey and illegal drugs."

Ronnie laughed again when I said, "Does she work?"

"Not a day in her life. She's an addict, and that includes sex. When she's not lying naked by the pool, she's screwing some vagrant she picked up in the park."

"Sounds as if she needs help," I said.

Ronnie was becoming agitated with the discussion of Alicin. She poured herself a vodka from the wet bar and threw it down in a single swallow.

"Alicin is a whore, pure and simple. The sad thing is that she has no clue. She converses with imaginary friends and believes in aliens and the craziest conspiracy theories."

"Could Alicin have stolen the missing copy of *Mosquitoes*?"

Ronnie poured herself another shot and said, "There's nothing she isn't capable of."

"Even murder?"

Ronnie glared at me, her scowl slowly disappearing as the flush faded from her neck and face.

"How rude of me not to offer you a drink," she said.

"I don't drink," I said. "I'm also an addict."

Ronnie's smile slowly returned. "Evelyn said you were a handsome man. She's going to put the moves on you, you know?"

"Should I be worried?"

"Only if you dislike beautiful women," Ronnie said.

"Seems I have a possible conflict of interest," I said.

"How much did Evelyn pay you?"

"A lot."

"How much?"

"Twenty-five grand," I said.

"Evelyn likes younger men," she said. "Trust me when I tell you she expects certain things for the money she paid you."

"Like what?"

"Your body," she said.

"I'm not a prostitute," I said.

Ronnie laughed again and said, "You're Alice, and you just fell down the rabbit hole. You don't really know crazy until you spend the night with Evelyn and her daughter."

Chapter 8

Ronnie's cell phone rang before I had a chance to conclude my interview. A glowing smile lit her face as she talked.

When she hung up, she said, "That was Evelyn. She wants us to join her at Galatoire's."

"I'll have to pass," I said. "Galatoire's is outside of my budget."

"Nonsense," Ronnie said. "Evelyn is buying. You're along for the ride,"

"I don't want to spoil the party."

"Evelyn explicitly asked for you to be there. She doesn't like taking no for an answer."

Galatoire's wasn't far away on Bourbon Street. It was dark as I stood on the sidewalk outside Wild Magnolias, watching Ronnie lock the door. It was a glorious spring night, and the weather was cool as we headed toward the crowd sounds emanating from Bourbon Street.

Since the Fest was over for the day, many older tourists headed for their hotels or a French Quarter bar for an adult cocktail. The younger, more adventuresome crowd wasn't finished for the night and headed for the cacophony and craziness of Bourbon Street.

Though Galatoire's was on Bourbon Street, it wasn't part of the craziness. The elegant old restaurant featured tuxedoed waiters and white tablecloths. The maître d' recognized Ronnie and led us through the main dining area to a secluded booth in a side room. Evelyn smiled as we approached the booth.

Ronnie slid in beside Evelyn, and I sat across from them. A waiter in a tux brought drinks, including a Wild Turkey and water for me.

"I can't drink this," I said. "I'm an alcoholic."

"Nonsense," Evelyn said. "One drink won't kill you."

I pushed the drink aside and motioned to the waiter. "No more for me," I said. "I'll have iced tea, please."

Evelyn prevented our waiter from whisking away the drink.

"Leave it, Rudy," she said. "Can't let good whiskey go to waste."

Rudy nodded, quickly returning with a glass of iced tea.

"Spoil sport," Evelyn said.

"You don't need to get me drunk," I said. "I'm happy being sober with the two most beautiful women in New Orleans."

Evelyn let the matter drop and said, "Did Ronnie tell you all of my secrets?"

"Your secrets are safe with Ronnie, though she helped me immensely with the case."

Our waiter returned and said, "Would you like to begin with an appetizer?"

"Bring us an order of oysters Rockefeller and one shrimp cocktail. We'll share," Evelyn said.

We soon shared appetizers while Evelyn and Ronnie worked on their second drink. After working through an avocado and crab salad, I ordered eggplant stuffed with lump crab and boiled shrimp with a special sauce.

Ronnie and Evelyn had equally ravenous appetites and were still ordering cocktails when they finished eating. The bandage on Evelyn's palm was noticeable when she and Ronnie touched their cocktail glasses.

"What happened to your hand?" I asked.

"Cut my hand by accident," she said. "Nothing serious. Have you learned anything about the case you'd like to share?"

"One thing," I said. "Faulker commissioned Lower Pontalba Press to print two special copies of *Mosquitoes*, one for you and one for himself. There were three copies printed. The copy you had was the third copy."

Evelyn slurred her words when she said, "Why would they have printed three copies?"

"Your copy had a special dedication: a poem accusing your grandparents of being in an incestual relationship."

Evelyn's smile disappeared, and her demeanor changed. She slugged her drink and motioned our waiter to bring her another.

"I hired you to find my missing book, not to dig up dirt on my grandparents."

"I'm sorry," I said. "There's more to the missing book than meets the eye. Your grandparents are integral to this case. If you want me to withdraw, I will."

"I paid you well to solve this mystery," Evelyn said. "I want you to find my book?"

"And all the trauma that comes with it?" I asked.

"What trauma?" Evelyn asked.

"Toby was murdered yesterday," Ronnie said.

Evelyn looked at Ronnie and then at me. "Toby Coleman-Labissiere is dead?" I nodded. "How did he die?"

"From the snakebite of a king cobra," I said.

Evelyn cast an accusing glance at Ronnie. "You don't suspect my son, do you?"

"I'm not the police," I said. "You're my only boss, and I have no ulterior motives."

My words seemed to calm her. "Who got the copy my family was supposed to have?" she asked.

"I'm guessing some private collector has it in their collection," I said.

"How did that happen?" Evelyn said.

"Coleman-Labissiere's relatives cut a fat hog when they printed the third copy of *Mosquitoes*," I said.

"The Coleman-Labissiere's are friends of the family. I grew up with Toby and knew his parents well. They wouldn't have done such a thing," Evelyn said.

"Did you know his grandparents or a man named Laceigh Rutherford?"

Evelyn averted her gaze. The front door opened, and we briefly heard the noise emanating from Bourbon Street.

"I was close to my grandfather," she said. "I heard him mention Laceigh Rutherford on several occasions."

"And?"

"There was bad blood between the two," she said.

"Enough so that Rutherford might have reason to cast aspersions on your family?"

"Perhaps worse," she said.

"Do you know what relationship Rutherford had with the Coleman-Labissieres?" Evelyn shook her head. "Know anyone that does?" I asked.

"Sam," she said.

Evelyn glanced at Ronnie and nodded when I said, "Samuel Penrose? I want to speak to him."

"Sam lives in an old plantation home on River Road and is wealthy and very reclusive," Ronnie said. "He only comes to town infrequently for business and other things."

"Other things?"

"To visit the gay bars," Evelyn said. "He calls on Ronnie every time he comes to town."

I looked at Ronnie and said, "Can you alert me when and where I can talk to him?"

Ronnie glanced first at Evelyn and then said, "He'll be in town tomorrow. I'll call you."

Our waiter appeared with fresh drinks and asked, "Will we have dessert tonight?"

Evelyn's smile returned. "The black bottom pecan pie for me, Rudy."

"Raspberry sorbet," Ronnie said.

"And you, sir?"

"What are my other choices?"

"Banana pudding with the chef's banana praline sauce is our specialty."

"No need to go any further," I said. "That's what I'll have."

"Coffee?"

"Please," I said.

Satiated by an excellent meal and topped off with a tasty dessert and numerous cocktails, Evelyn's smile returned.

"How did you learn so much so fast?" she asked.

"I've only scratched the surface," I said. "You want me to continue?"

"I want you to come home with Ronnie and me," she said.

"Can I take a raincheck on your invitation?" I asked.

"What's wrong with tonight," she said.

"I have an appointment I must keep and didn't know I would be dining with two gorgeous women when I made it. Can I beg off?"

"Whatever," she said.

Evelyn motioned for our waiter to bring our tab. Her limousine was waiting at the front, and her chauffeur ushered us into the back of the large vehicle.

"Home, madam?" the chauffeur asked.

"We'd like to do a little sightseeing first, so take your time," Evelyn said. "We don't need a bedroom to have some fun. The back of my limo is a perfect location for lust."

I soon found myself the object of Evelyn and Ronnie's ardor. Anesthetized by their exotic perfume, I had little will to resist. My shirt was unbuttoned, my fly down, as the chauffeur weaved a circuitous path through the French Quarter.

Ronnie and Evelyn's hands were all over me, and my hands were all over them. Their designer clothes were in disarray, and I was soon panting like the lead dog in a pack of huskies pulling a sled bound for the Iditarod.

I finally pulled away and said, "Uncle. This goes far beyond any client and attorney privilege. Please have your driver drop me off at Bertram's on Chartres."

"Even if the concept applied in this particular situation, which it doesn't, you're no longer an attorney."

"Doesn't matter," I said. "You know what I mean."

"Spoilsport," Evelyn said as the limousine stopped at Bertram's and let me out.

Bertram had a packed house, and I waved to him as I started upstairs. When I opened the door to my room, I noticed something was amiss. Maya was lying on my bed, my cat Kisses in her arms. Again, she was wearing her blue nightgown.

She smiled when I said, "Am I disturbing something?"

"Where have you been?" she asked.

"Business," I said.

"Funny business," she said.

"I had dinner with Evelyn DuPont and Veronica LaSalle."

"I can smell their perfume from here, and I see the hickey on your neck," she said. "Seems as if you were doing more than eating."

"Are you jealous?"

"Should I be?"

"Only if you want to doff that little bit of nothing blue nightgown of yours and engage in a roll on the bed."

"You wish," she said.

I stripped to my tee shirt and boxer shorts and lay beside her.

"How did you like Carlucci's?" I asked.

"You're changing the subject," she said.

"It's a legitimate question."

"Love the place," she said. "Tommy and Marlon were perfect gentlemen."

"And Tony?"

"Lil called. I could tell by the look on his face that she was angry and he was in trouble. He cleared everyone's tab and hurried out the door. What's the deal?"

"Tony had an affair with a much younger woman a while back," I said. "Lil forgave him, though from the sound of things, the wound hasn't quite healed yet."

"Sounds as if he needs Father Piastri to hear his confession," Maya said.

I laughed and said, "Tony's Catholicism is like mine: mostly gone, though not quite forgotten. Tell me about Carlucci's."

"A dive bar owned by a former cop and frequented by off-duty cops. They have a dartboard and a pool table. Tony is a dart shark who beat everyone in the place."

"Did Tommy or Marlon say anything about the murder?"

"Tommy had a call from one of his forensic techs. They told him the blood type of the person was B. They lifted a single print from the broken glass that wasn't the victim's and are running it through their system."

"They'll have a match before long," I said.

"Doesn't matter because the person who cut themselves wasn't the murderer."

"How do you know?"

"The blood was still wet and didn't match the victim's time of death," Maya said.

"So, they visited the victim's office unannounced and discovered the body. The person knew the victim well enough that they were drinking his half-finished whiskey when something caused them to drop it. They sustained a cut when it broke on the floor."

"My guess is the snake spooked them. Seeing it was unmistakably a cobra, they ran like hell," Maya said.

"Then the person who sustained the cut was a whiskey-drinking friend of the victim," I said. "Did they find any clues possibly left by the actual killer?"

Maya shook her head, "It has the techs baffled. Whoever murdered Coleman-Labissiere didn't leave a single clue. Tommy said it's like he or she is an apparition."

"What else?" I asked.

"The king cobra Adano captured wasn't from the Audubon Zoo. The Audubon herpetologist said it probably came from a private collection."

"Evelyn's son Rodney collects snakes," I said.

"What's his story?" Maya asked.

"An escapee from a private institution in Alabama. No one knows where he is. Jonathan Stallings, Evelyn's butler, is caring for the snakes."

Maya laughed and said, "I've never known anyone with a butler."

"He's a person of interest and on my list of people I need to speak with. Want something to drink?"

"I thought you might have another shot of your cherry juice concoction. I slept like a baby last night. First, I want to hear what you learned today."

"I met with Ronnie LaSalle, the owner of Wild Magnolias, a rare bookstore in the Quarter. She is one of two other than Evelyn DuPont, who has a key to her rare book collection."

"Evelyn must trust her," Maya said.

"They are best friends," I said. "More than best friends, actually. They are lovers."

"Lesbians?" Maya asked.

"They both like men as well," I said.

"Is that where you got the hickey?"

"I plead the fifth," I said.

"What else did they give you?" she asked.

"Let's move on," I said. "Ronnie and Evelyn are former supermodels. Evelyn turned Ronnie on to collecting rare books. Ronnie soon learned she had a knack for locating the rarest of books. A collector named Samuel Penrose noticed her talent. He bought Wild Magnolias and deeded it to her in exchange for an ongoing cut of the profits."

"Father Piastri told me French Quarter property is through the roof. How did he justify buying an expensive property and then giving it away?"

"Ronnie said he's returned his investment many times."

"How is he connected to the murder?" Maya asked.

"He was friends with Coleman-Labissiere. I'm going to interview him tomorrow."

"I want to go with you," she said.

"You may want to rethink that," I said. "Penrose is gay, and I'm probably meeting him at a gay nightclub."

"I'm an adult," she said.

The door to my balcony was ajar. A cool breeze was blowing in from the Quarter, and only the dim light of a distant streetlamp illuminated my apartment. Maya was lying so close to me that I could feel the warmth of her body. Her nightgown was all but transparent in the flickering glow from the patio. I rested my hand on the gentle curve of her stomach, and she didn't move away. When my hand wandered beneath the nightgown and touched her breast, she sprang from the bed.

"I'm going now," she said.

"Want a shot of my sleep elixir first?" I asked.

"If you can keep your hands to yourself," she said.

"Sorry," I said. "Your body is intoxicating,"

I filled my shot glass with the tart cherry juice and onion drops and handed it to her. She threw it back, kissed me on the cheek, and backed toward the door.

"Don't forget about the interview tomorrow. I'm going with you."

Chapter 9

Maya descended the stairs from Wyatt's room, her eyelids drooping as she felt the effect of his sleep-inducing concoction. Bertram's drinking establishment was closed for the night, and she wondered if she was already asleep and dreaming when she heard the sound of trumpet music. Someone was behind the bar polishing a glass. It wasn't Bertram.

The tall man had thin gray hair, a close-cropped beard and mustache, deep-set dark eyes, and skin that radiated a ghostly light. Maya should have been frightened, but the man didn't look scary or real.

"Who are you?" she asked.

"Gil LaPiere," he said. "I own this bar."

"Bertram owns the bar," Maya said.

"He does now. I sold it to him," Gil said. "He owns it most of the time, though when the bar closes and everyone goes home, it becomes mine again."

"Are you a . . .?"

"Ghost? Yes, baby, that's what I am."

Gil smiled when she said, "I don't believe in ghosts."

"You believe your own eyes, don't you?"

"I'm dreaming," she said.

"Dreams are nothing but reality seen through a different prism," Gil said.

"Why am I in this dream? I don't know you."

"You know Bertram. I taught him everything I knew. He's now the best drink mixer in New Orleans."

"I love Bertram," Maya said. "He's a wonderful person."

"And a great bartender," Gil said. "He's also a good cook. I didn't teach him that. He learned it on his own."

"You know Wyatt?" Maya asked.

"Since he was a boy," Gil said. "I mixed him his first drink."

"What do you think of him?"

"Wyatt's hard not to like," Gil said. "He's moody and insecure and one of the most intelligent persons I know. He has his shortcomings."

"Such as?" Maya asked.

"He's an addict. That will never change. He tries his best though never quite succeeds."

"I feel responsible for him," Maya said.

"Don't," Gil said. "Wyatt can take care of himself."

Gil smiled when she asked, "Where are all your customers?"

"Customers come and go in this part of the universe. Other than yourself, I'm mixing drinks for an extraordinary person. Someone who wants to meet you."

"Who?"

"You hear the music, don't you?" he asked. "Know who's playing it?"

"Louis Armstrong," she said. "Is it music from one of his records?"

"From Louis Armstrong himself."

"He's dead," she said.

"So am I," Gil said.

"Dead is dead," Maya said.

"Life is energy," Gil said. "Energy can neither be created nor destroyed. It simply takes a different form. In another dimension, I still exist, and so does Louis."

With his unmistakable trademark smile, Louis Armstrong appeared in a damp mist beside her. After resting his trumpet on the bar, he pumped her hand, his gravelly voice inimitable.

"Glad to meet you, Miss Maya," he said. "I caught your show the other night."

"You did?"

"I was playing along with the band. Did you hear me?"

"I felt something," she said. "I didn't know it was you."

"It was me," he said. "How do you like being the best vocalist in New Orleans?"

"I wish I was and didn't have so much insecurity."

"You're a star," Louis said. "No need for insecurities."

"I know, though I can't seem to rid myself of them."

"Tell me how you feel," he said.

"You really want to know?"

"Wouldn't have asked if I didn't," he said. "Something's troubling you, baby. What is it?"

"I'm not sure I can explain it. I'm torn."

"About what?" he asked.

"I have two passions: singing and law enforcement. I realized as much today when I was at Carlucci's, listening to the stories of the cops who go there. Feeling their pain and their joy. I haven't been off work for even a week and already miss it."

"So, what's your problem?" Louis asked.

"It says in the Bible that no man can serve two masters: for either he will hate the one, and love the other, or else he will hold to one, and despise the other."

"You're confused, baby," he said.

"How so?"

"That passage is talking about good and evil. It's true; you can't serve both good and evil. Music and the law are both good. If you want, you can do both."

Gil put a drink on the counter and said, "Here's something I mixed especially for you. Try it."

"What is it?" she asked.

"One of my famous Ramos fizzes," he said.

Maya pushed it away and said, "I don't drink."

"You're dreaming," Gil said. "Drink it. It isn't real."

Maya took a sip and said, "This is wonderful. Am I going to become an alcoholic like Wyatt?"

"Wyatt has his demons. Doesn't mean you will."

Louis touched her wrist and said, "Sometimes it's easy to get caught up in fame. When you realize it's happening, you must step back and see who you're leaving behind."

"Did that happen to you?" she asked.

Louis Armstrong nodded. "It's a universal reaction."

"I'm leaving no one behind," Maya said.

"Oh, but you are. You haven't visited your brother's food kiosk since your performance. He and Pepper supported you when you needed them most. You should return the favor."

"I'm trying to give them space. This is their first time alone together outside of Pinebridge. They didn't need me sharing their room."

Louis's gravelly laugh returned. "You got that part right. That isn't where they miss you."

"Good," Maya said. "Except for college, this is my first time away from home. I'll check on Leo and Pepper tomorrow,"

"Now you're on the right track. One more thing. You should also invite them to spend time here with Bertram's gang."

"I have. They've been too tired."

"Keep asking. They'll change their minds."

"I'll ask them tomorrow after I spend the day helping them," Maya said.

"You're a good sister," Louis said.

"Do you come here often?"

Louis grinned. "This has always been the best bar in the French Quarter. Gil makes the best drinks, and there's always people here to talk to."

"You knew William Faulkner?" Maya asked.

"We've met on more than one occasion. There's someone here who also knew Faulk. He wants to talk to you."

The person sitting at the bar beside her emanated an otherworldly glow like Louis and Gil. He smiled when Maya acknowledged his presence.

"Who are you?" she asked.

"Laceigh Rutherford," the ghost said.

"What's your claim to fame?"

Maya's interest was piqued when he said, "I'm the person who commissioned the third copy of *Mosquitoes* and penned the dedication and poem at the back."

The little man wore clothes from a different era. His long coat draped over the back of the adjacent stool. His hair was long and dark black. Though he had no beard, he did have a pencil-thin mustache.

"Mama Mulate and Sister Lydia said the poem implied Evelyn's grandparents were in an incestuous relationship," Maya said. "Is that true?"

The little man nodded. "Anthony and Julia DuPont were brother and sister, and they were definitely in an incestuous relationship."

"You have to be kidding. Isn't that illegal?"

"People like the DuPonts make the law," he said. "If they don't like it, they have it changed."

"How did you know about them."

"Growing up, Anthony and I were neighbors and best friends. I liked Julia and thought I loved her. I had hoped to marry her someday. I didn't know then that she and her brother harbored a dark secret."

Rutherford nodded when Maya said, "Their incestuous relationship?"

"I couldn't believe it when Julia cried and told me. She loved me, though her marriage to her brother was preordained."

"How is that possible? What church would condone such a relationship, much less allow it to happen."

"One church would," Rutherford said.

"None that I've ever heard of."

"In the Church of Lucifer, incest is not only condoned, it is encouraged."

"Is there such a church?"

"Yes, its followers are members of a cult called Ordre du Sang, French for Order of the Blood. The cult started here in New Orleans."

"Does the Church of Lucifer still exist?" Maya asked.

"Not to the extent it was, though many powerful people from New Orleans are still part of the cult."

Rutherford shook his head when Maya said, "You weren't a Satanist, were you?"

"Never," he said.

"How did you learn about it?"

"Faulk told me."

Rutherford nodded when Maya said, "William Faulkner? He knew his benefactors were Satanists?"

Rutherford nodded. "I was friends with young Faulkner and a benefactor of his, though not to the extent Julia and Anthony were. We had dinner when he returned to the city to commission the copies of *Mosquitoes*. I gave him the name of the Lower Pontalba Press."

"And that's when you decided to have a third book printed?"

"It was meant only for Anthony and Julia's eyes. I didn't expect it to cause such trouble."

Maya finished her Ramos fizz, and Gil began mixing another. When he handed it to her, she didn't turn it away.

So, Faulkner told you his plans. How did you convince Lower Pontalba Press to print the extra copy with an additional chapter?"

"Coleman-Labissiere took my money, though he had no intention of giving the unique version to me. When Faulk went to pick up his two copies of *Mosquitoes*, he was mistakenly given copies one and three instead of one and two. He kept copy one and gave copy three to the DuPont's."

"What did Coleman-Labissiere plan to do with the special edition of *Mosquitoes*?"

"Sell it at auction in London for a small fortune."

"Why would it be worth a small fortune?" Maya asked.

"Because he intended to claim the additional chapter was penned by Faulkner himself."

"But you knew he didn't write it."

"Coleman-Labissiere blackmailed me. He said he would ruin me if I divulged the truth. It didn't matter. When Anthony DuPont received the book, he went directly to Faulk. I was the only person the author had informed about his plans. Coleman-Labissiere told him that I had penned the dedication, and DuPont proceeded to ruin me."

"What happened to copy two?" Maya asked.

"I don't know. I salvaged what I could and fled to Paris to escape further persecution."

"Why are you telling me?" Maya asked.

"In hopes you will provide retribution for my soul," Rutherford said.

"Anthony and Julia are as dead as you are. What retribution do you expect, and from who?"

The image of Laceigh Rutherford began to fade. "I've told you too much. I must go now."

Rutherford disappeared in a blue wisp of water vapor.

"He's gone," Louis said.

"I had more questions."

"What you heard is what you have," Louis said.

Maya drank more Ramos fizz and said, "This is good. My daddy would kill me if he knew I was drinking alcohol."

Louis chuckled. "Your daddy has had more than a nip of the strong stuff in his life."

"Impossible," Maya said. "He's a Baptist deacon."

"And he's human," Louis said. "Do you forgive him?"

"I don't pass judgment. My brother and Pepper drink."

"Yes, they do."

Can I ask you a favor?"

"Of course," Louis said. "Name it."

"Will you sing with me?"

"You bet I will," he said.

Louis put the trumpet's mouthpiece to his lips and began playing *Summertime*. When he finished the lead-in, Maya began to sing. As the song reached its crescendo, Maya heard clapping. She turned to see Bertram dressed in a nightshirt and sleeping hat.

"Beautiful," he said.

"Did you see him?" she asked.

"See who?"

"Louis Armstrong."

There's no one here except you and me," Bertram said. "Who made you that drink?"

"Gil," Maya said.

"Gil's dead, baby."

"Then who made the Ramos fizz for me?"

"Wasn't me," Bertram said.

"It was Gil's ghost. Louis Armstrong was drinking at the bar and sang *Summertime* with me."

"If you say so," Bertram said.

"You didn't hear his horn?"

"Lady's barking woke me. All I heard was your beautiful voice. I got out of bed, and me and Lady came to see."

Lady's tail wagged, and she barked once when Maya rubbed her head.

"I'm not making this up," she said.

Bertram squeezed her hand. "You aren't the first person to see ghosts in this old place. Me, I ain't seen them. Wyatt has. It's three in the morning. You'd better get some sleep."

Chapter 10

Though early, there were already tourists and locals in the bar when I went downstairs. Maya sat at the old zinc countertop, enjoying grits and eggs and drinking Bertram's strong1Cajun coffee. When I sat beside her, he slid a steaming plate in front of me.

"Thought you were going to sleep all morning," he said.

"It's barely seven," I said. "Did you two stay up all night."

"Maya, Gil, and Louis Armstrong," he said.

Maya didn't glance up from her grits and eggs when I said, "Something you want to tell me?"

"Maybe later," she said. "After breakfast, I'm going to help Leo and Pepper."

"Feeling guilty?" I asked.

"Maybe. I have some things to tell you about the missing book. Come with me to Leo's, and I'll explain."

"I don't mind helping. Tell me now," I said.

Bertram was waiting on a couple near the back of the bar, far enough away that he couldn't hear what Maya had to say.

"Louis Armstrong and Gil weren't the only ghosts I saw last night."

93

"Who else?"

"I don't want to tell you in front of Bertram. He thinks I'm crazy. He told me that you've also seen Gil's ghost."

"I've seen Gil and other ghosts in the bar late at night. I believe you. Who did you see, and how are they relevant to Evelyn DuPont's missing copy of *Mosquitoes*?"

"First, let me tell you about Gil's Ramos fizz."

She nodded when I said, "You drank one of Gil's Ramos fizzes? You're Baptist. You're going to hell, you know."

"Shut up," she said with a silly grin.

"How'd you like it?"

"Wonderful. I told Bertram. He didn't believe Gil mixed it for me."

"Where did he think it came from?"

"I don't know. I didn't mix it for myself."

"What I can't believe is you actually drank an adult beverage," I said.

"Now, I'm an alcoholic just like you.".

Her statement made me laugh. "I don't think so. Your sobriety is safe."

"No, it isn't. I love the taste. I'm craving one right now."

When Bertram returned, I said, "Mix this young lady a Ramos fizz and put it on my tab."

When Bertram glanced at her, she nodded and said, "I'm helpless to resist."

Bertram smiled and said, "Good ol' Gil. He always knew how to sweet-talk pretty girls."

"Don't push it," Maya said.

Bertram smiled and rubbed his hands as he moved away from the bar to mix the Ramos fizz.

"Tell me who you saw before he returns with your drink," I said.

"The ghost of Laceigh Rutherford."

"Who the hell is that?"

"He grew up with Anthony and Julia DuPont. He loved Julia and wanted to marry her. It wasn't to be because the DuPonts belonged to a cult called Ordre du Sang."

"Order of the Blood," I said.

I nodded when Maya asked, "You're familiar with it?"

"Lydia and I had to deal with the cult a while back. They are Satanists."

"That's what Rutherford said. "Julia spurned his ardor because she was promised to her brother."

"Then Mama and Lydia correctly analyzed the dedication. How did Rutherford learn that Faulkner intended to print two books to include the edited chapters?"

"Rutherford was one of his benefactors and had dinner with Faulkner when he arrived in town. He was the person who recommended using Lower Pontalba Press."

"How did he convince Coleman-Labissiere's grandfather to print a third copy of *Mosquitoes*? Especially considering he added an extra chapter."

"According to Rutherford, Coleman-Labissiere intended to keep the book and auction it for big bucks in London. The problem is that Faulkner wound up with copies one and three instead of one and two. He signed both copies and gave three to the DuPonts."

Maya quit speaking when Bertram presented her with the Ramos fizz.

"Hope you like it as good as the one Gil mixed you," he said.

"I didn't think you believed me about Gil," Maya said.

"I believe you," he said. "Taste this one."

Maya took a sip of the Ramos fizz. When she nodded and gave him a thumbs up, he hurried away with a smile to wait on another customer.

Maya shook her head when I asked, "Is it as good as Gil's?"

"No, but I'm not telling Bertram."

"I don't blame you," I said. "What happened to copy two?"

"No idea. DuPont was incensed by the version he received and knew who penned it. He proceeded to ruin Rutherford both socially and financially. Rutherford salvaged what he could and moved to Paris."

"Coleman-Labissiere must have informed DuPont. Evelyn told me she knows Toby Coleman-Labissiere III, so it's logical that the families were friends even back in the day. Good work."

"It's the first time I ever interviewed a ghost."

"Don't tell your Rapides Parish boss. Trust me when I tell you it won't go over well."

"Bet that's right," she said. "I won't even share the story with Tommy and Marlon next time I'm at Carlucci's."

"Good idea," I said. "Few people are going to believe you saw a ghost."

"My daddy told me he saw a ghost," Maya said. "I thought he was pulling my leg."

"Well, there you go. You didn't believe him, and few people will believe you."

Bertram's customers were leaving the bar as the French Quarter Fest opened for the day. He wasn't happy when we started for the door.

"Are you abandoning me too?" he asked.

"Relax," I said. "We'll be back, and so will your customers. "Take a break and enjoy yourself. We're going to help Leo and Pepper."

"Me and Lady are coming with you," he said.

"You're shutting the bar in the middle of the day?" I asked.

"Why not? I ain't doing any business."

Maya embraced him and said, "I finally have you figured out. You have to be busy, or you aren't happy. You can help Wyatt and me run Leo and Pepper's kiosk."

It was spring in New Orleans, and a morning nip was in the air as we joined the crowd filling the French Quarter. Though the Fest had just begun for the day, a line of hungry tourists and locals waited for service from Leo and Pepper. Bertram, Maya, and I entered the kiosk through the back.

"What are you doing here, little sister?"

"You and Pepper need a break. Wyatt, Bertram, and I have this. Take the rest of the day off."

"No way," Leo said. "We can handle it."

Pepper wasn't so sure and tugged at Leo's hand. "We have some unfinished business. Wouldn't hurt to take a few hours off."

"That's your better half talking," Maya said. "Listen to her."

"You sure you can handle it?" Leo asked,

"Meet Bertram Picou, the best bartender in the Quarter," Maya said. "He'll be helping Wyatt and me."

"Take a break and have some fun," Bertram said. "Like your pretty sister told you, we'll run the show."

The French Quarter was alive with the fest's pulsing energy, and the smoky aromas of sizzling meats mingled with the tangy scent of barbecue sauce in the air. From every corner of the streets, the sounds of brass bands and blues guitarists created a rich tapestry of music, blending with the lively chatter of locals and tourists alike. Leo's kiosk was in the thick of it all, the perfect spot for people-watching and joining the celebration.

Bertram, with his easygoing charm, was in his element. The line at the kiosk stretched long, but no one seemed to mind the wait. His Cajun-inflected drawl rolled out like honey, greeting each customer with a wide grin and a playful quip.

"Well, chère, if that ain't the biggest appetite I ever seen!" he'd say, handing over a hefty plate of ribs to a woman whose eyes lit up at the sight of the food. "Better save some room, though—dessert's just around the corner."

Laughter rippled through the line as Bertram kept a running dialogue, commenting on everything from the weather to the jazz echoing from a nearby stage. "Y'all hear that? Now that's real music; makes the food taste even better!" he'd call out, drawing nods of agreement.

Meanwhile, Lady, Bertram's beautiful collie, was having the time of her life. She weaved in and out of the customers' legs, her tail wagging furiously as she sniffed the tantalizing smells drifting from the grill. Occasionally, someone would reach down to give her a friendly pat, and Lady responded with a happy bark, her eyes sparkling with excitement.

While working alongside Bertram, Maya and I shared amused glances as the Cajun bartender entertained the crowd. I took in the sights and sounds. Maya smiled at Bertram's antics, enjoying the moment as she helped with the food orders. Bertram handed over another plate of brisket and winked at the customer.

"Now don't y'all go spillin' that sauce. It's liquid gold! And Lady here's liable to steal a bite if you're not careful!"

The customer chuckled, dodging Lady's playful nudge as they moved away with their prize.

The rhythmic thump of a bass drum from a nearby stage shook the ground, and a cheer rose from the crowd. The French Quarter Fest was in full swing, and with Bertram at the helm of the barbecue kiosk, it felt like New Orleans' heart was beating in the music-filled air.

After lunch hour, the crowds thinned, and only one of us needed to fill the orders. Bertram manned the kiosk while Maya and I loaded paper plates with smoked ribs coated with Leo's tangy sauce. The wooden picnic table near the kiosk was finally empty, and we took it. We were almost done eating when we heard Adano's Italian-inflected voice.

"Look, Lydia, we don't have to eat alone."

Lydia and Adano grinned as they joined us at the table. The line had disappeared, and Bertram left the kiosk, his arms filled with more ribs, brisket, and fixings. Adano followed him, returning with sodas for Maya and me and cold beer for everyone else. Lady was happy to lay at our feet, chewing on a rib bone.

Another line had begun forming as we finished eating. "I got this," Bertram said.

Adano followed him to the kiosk. "I'll help," he said.

"You and Adano are getting along," I said.

"He's a jewel," Lydia said. "We spent the day at the Greater Archdiocese of New Orleans. The man is a wonderful researcher."

"Learn anything you'd like to share?" I asked.

"A lot," she said. "We learned about a man named Laceigh Rutherford. His business failed, and his reputation was tarnished."

Lydia nodded when I asked, "Was it Anthony DuPont who caused it to happen?"

"DuPont doomed Rutherford's life in New Orleans. He moved to Paris, where he lived for about a year before being murdered."

"Was the murderer caught?" I asked.

Lydia shook her head. "The official police report said he was the victim of cult violence."

"The official report?"

"A newspaper account stated he was a victim of Ordre du Sang and that he died a heinous death and was perhaps a victim of human sacrifice."

Maya and I exchanged glances. "Damn!" I said.

"What else?" Lydia asked.

"Maya and I are meeting with a person of interest tonight. A rare book collector and someone familiar with the people here in New Orleans who might be involved in selling or trading rare books, both legally and illegally."

"What's the name of this person?" Lydia asked.

"Samuel Penrose. He financed Veronica LaSalle's purchase of Wild Magnolias, the rare bookstore in the Quarter."

"Where are you meeting him?" Lydia asked.

"The Office," I said.

"The Office is a gay and lesbian nightclub, you know," Lydia said.

"I was born," I said, "Though not yesterday."

Lydia smiled. "Good hunting," she said. "Adano and I will dig up what we can on Samuel Penrose.

Leo and Pepper returned to the kiosk at closing time, their smiles indicating how much they appreciated our assistance.

When Leo counted his money, his smile grew larger. "As soon as I get more meat in the smoker, Pepper and I will buy drinks for the rest of the night. Where can we meet you?"

"Right down the street at my place," Bertram said. "I'll bet I have a crowd gathering."

"Pepper and I will help you serve and mix drinks," Leo said. "I've never been to an honest-to-God French Quarter bar, and I look forward to it."

Sounds like a plan," Bertram said. "Maybe later, we can exchange some recipes. I love your barbecue sauce."

Leo smiled and said, "Everything except that. My sauce is secret and will go to the grave with me."

Pepper was smiling and hugging his big tattooed arm. "Maybe after today, you'll have an heir to pass your secret sauce to."

Chapter 11

Spring rain had swept through the French Quarter as Maya and I hurried back to Bertram's to change clothes. When we met at the bar, she was dressed in a short skirt and low-cut blouse, which looked fetching. Bertram and Lady were back behind the counter, and tourists and locals had begun to trickle in from outside.

"Where you two going all dressed up?" he asked.

"The Office," I said.

"Hell, Cowboy, you ain't got no office unless you count the booth in back."

"The nightclub," I said.

"Something you want to tell me?"

I smiled. "Maya and I are questioning someone who may know something about Evelyn DuPont's missing book."

"I went there once," he said.

"Something you want to tell me?" I asked.

"Just checking the competition," he said. "It's quite a place."

"We're about to find out," I said. "Umbrellas or call a taxi?"

"It's barely raining," Maya said. "Let's walk."

"French Quarter weather can change in a heartbeat," I said.

"We can call a cab when it does," Maya said.

Bertram reached under the bar and handed me an umbrella. "This will keep you dry."

Maya's short skirt highlighted her athletic legs, and I glanced at them as we opened the umbrella.

"Nice legs," I said.

Maya did something unexpected, pinching my rear. "Nice ass," she said.

"Okay," I said. "I'm done with sexist remarks for a while."

"Good," she said. "This is business. How far is it to the Office?"

"On Bourbon, not far from here," I said.

The rain was light as Maya and I huddled beneath Bertram's colorful umbrella. A loud clap of thunder shook the old French Quarter walls, informing us it might not stay that way for long.

After taking a cross street, we stood outside the Office, the neon sign casting a rainbow-hued glow over the cobblestones of the French Quarter.

The nightclub appeared unassuming from the outside, tucked between a row of historic buildings, its entrance guarded by a discreet velvet rope. The rhythmic pulse of disco music could be felt even here, Donna Summer's voice beckoning us inside like a siren call.

As we entered the door, a curious clash of the mundane and the vibrant greeted us. The downstairs shop was cluttered with cheap souvenirs—rows of garish tee shirts emblazoned with slogans, plastic Mardi Gras beads, and stuffed animals that seemed out of place in the Quarter's sophisticated charm.

The faint smell of incense and a hint of something industrial lingered in the air. Maya also noticed and glanced at me. She shrugged, her eyes scanning the surroundings, taking in every detail.

Upstairs, the atmosphere changed dramatically. The music's driving beat grew louder, vibrating through the polished wooden floor. Disco balls spun overhead, casting glittering reflections that danced across the room while the rich scent of expensive cologne mingled with the faint aroma of bourbon.

The oak bar stretched along one wall, gleaming under the dim lights, tended by bartenders in crisp uniforms who moved with the precision of seasoned professionals. The clientele was a mix of sharp-dressed men in tailored suits and women in chic cocktail dresses, their laughter and conversation a harmonious counterpoint to the music.

For the patrons, this was a sanctuary—a place where New Orleans' gay and lesbian elite could relax, free from the masks they wore during the day. Our arrival drew a few curious glances but most quickly returned to their worlds, content to let strangers remain strangers.

I looked for the person we were there to meet, my gaze sweeping the room, finally landing on a corner booth shrouded in shadow. There, Samuel Penrose sat, a figure of quiet authority amidst the revelry.

Penrose was impeccably dressed in a black silk suit that clung to his lean frame with tailored perfection. A deep burgundy tie contrasted against the crisp white of his shirt, and a single diamond stud glinted in his ear—a subtle but striking piece of jewelry. His eyes, sharp and calculating, were the color of dark amber, and his neatly trimmed beard added to his air of sophistication. He wasn't alone.

Beside him was a mysterious companion who exuded an unsettling presence. Dressed in all black, his clothing was more casual yet carefully chosen to convey a sense of purpose. His slicked-back hair shone under the lights, and his angular features gave him a predatory look. He sat silently, one arm draped casually over the back of the booth, his gaze fixed on the dance floor as if waiting for something—or someone.

Penrose noticed our approach and offered a thin smile. His voice was smooth and cultured when he spoke, though it had an undercurrent of something darker.

"Mr. Thomas, Ms. Henstooth," he said, "Please, join us. We have much to discuss."

As we slid into the booth, Penrose's companion finally turned his gaze toward us, his eyes cold and unreadable. I couldn't shake the feeling that this man was more than just an acquaintance of Penrose—he was a protector, a shadow ready to strike if things took a wrong turn. The tension was palpable, even as the music played on and the revelers continued their night of carefree abandon.

"Thanks for agreeing to meet with us," I said. "Ronnie Lasalle said you know as much about the rare book trade as anyone in New Orleans."

"Did she now?" he said. "Let me introduce my friend, Victor Malveaux."

Malveaux's name struck me as dark and enigmatic, fitting his unsettling presence. He nodded, though he didn't bother smiling or reaching across the booth to shake our hands.

A waiter appeared at the booth with fresh drinks for Penrose and Malveaux. Through my years as an alcoholic, I'd noticed that a person's favorite adult beverage spoke volumes about their personality. Neither man's drink was typical.

"What can I get you to drink," the waiter asked.

"Ramos fizz for me," Maya said.

"Iced tea," I said.

"Ronnie told me you don't drink, Mr. Thomas. I didn't think such a person existed in New Orleans," Penrose said.

"Please call me Wyatt," I said. "There aren't very many of us. What are you drinking?"

"You can call me Sam; my drink is a negroni," he said.

"What a beautiful drink," Maya said. "What's in it?"

"It's a classic Italian cocktail with a balance of bitterness from the Campari, sweetness from the vermouth, and strength from the gin."

"Interesting," Maya said. "The deep red color and complex flavors you describe suggest you have a taste for the finer things in life."

"Very observant," Penrose said. "What line of work are you in?"

"Maya's a singer," I said. "She performed at the French Quarter Fest and is in town until it's over."

"Nice to meet you, Maya," Penrose said. "Victor's Sazerac is a perfect example. Its potency and history as one of the world's oldest cocktails resonate with someone deeply rooted in tradition yet dangerous and unpredictable."

Malveaux didn't answer when Maya leaned across the table and asked, "Are you dangerous and unpredictable, Victor?"

"Victor is a doer and not a talker," Penrose said.

When my eyes had sufficiently dilated to compensate for the bar's dimness, I realized how large it was. Same-sex customers were dancing on a large dance floor to the explosive strains of some disco anthem I didn't recognize. The place was crowded, though everyone was minding their own business.

"Evelyn DuPont hired me to find her lost copy of *Mosquitoes*," I said. "I was told Toby Coleman-Labissiere, Sr. intended to keep the book and sell it at auction in London."

"Who told you that?" Penrose asked.

"A French Quarter ghost," I said.

Penrose didn't seem to mind the seemingly evasive answer I gave him.

"I understand your reluctance to share your sources."

I glanced at Maya to see if she was keeping a straight face.

"Sorry," I said.

"No problem. Toby Coleman-Labissiere's grandfather was more interested in something other than Evelyn's interesting although pedestrian anomaly."

"You're suggesting her version of *Mosquitoes* isn't valuable," I said.

"To her, perhaps," Penrose said.

"It's one-of-a-kind. Why, exactly, isn't it valuable?"

"Anyone can create a knockoff of a valuable book. Faulkner didn't authorize the book's printing or even know about it," Penrose said. "He did authorize the printing of the other two copies and the value of one of them is through the proverbial roof."

"How much?" I asked.

"Millions," Penrose said. "It's quite possibly the most valuable book in the world."

"Which book?" I asked.

"The signed first copy of *Mosquitoes* Coleman-Labissiere printed for William Faulkner."

"Faulkner kept it," I said.

"Did he? Perhaps he took the wrong copy. Even so, where is it now?"

"Oxford, Mississippi, I presume."

107

"Faulkner left most, if not all, his literary works to the University of Virginia. That includes the original material for *Mosquitoes*. The copy of *Mosquitoes* printed by the Lower Pontalba Press isn't included in that collection."

"What happened to it?"

"No one knows."

"Someone does," I said. "What about Ms. DuPont's version? Any idea where I might look?"

"My best guess is some private collector now possesses it. If so, your chances of locating it and returning it to Evelyn are low."

"Why would a collector want it if it has no value?" I asked.

"Collectors come in all varieties," Penrose said. "Sometimes, only they know the reason."

Steam wafted up through the dance floor as the dancers began performing synchronously. Sparkling colors from the rotating disco ball painted the nightclub walls as Donna Summer's moans strengthened. The music made concentrating on anything other than the resounding beat complicated.

"Other than Ms. DuPont, only two people have the combination to her private collection: Ronnie and Ms. DuPont's social secretary, Libby Tanner. I haven't talked with Ms. Tanner yet. Do you know her?"

"I know Libby very well," Penrose said. "She's Victor's sister. It was I who got her the job with Evelyn, and I can vouch for the fact that she had nothing to do with the theft."

"That leaves Ronnie," I said.

Penrose smirked. "Ronnie didn't take Evelyn's book."

"That doesn't leave many options," I said.

"Evelyn's a scatterbrain sometimes. She probably ran an errand and left the door ajar."

"I have no reason to suspect either Ronnie or your sister," I said. "I'm sure you're right."

"I am," Penrose said.

"Is the murder of Toby Coleman-Labissiere somehow tied to the disappearance of the book?"

"Your guess is as good as mine," Penrose said. "I have an idea who killed him, though."

"Mind sharing it with me?" I asked.

"Evelyn's crazy son, Rodney."

"Because?"

"Who else in New Orleans do you know who has an exotic snake collection?"

Penrose focused on Maya when she asked, "What was his motive?"

"Crazy people don't need motives," he said. "Victor and I need to go. Any more questions before we do?"

"You've been accommodating," I said. "It was nice meeting you. We'll take care of your tab."

Penrose and Malveaux nodded and left the table; Maya and I were soon alone amid the din of the noisy bar.

"Well?" I said.

"Malveaux's the strangest person I've ever met, and Penrose was lying."

"What was your first clue?" I asked.

"Who is he trying to convince? Ms. DuPont's copy of *Mosquitoes* is valuable because it has intrinsic historical significance and was signed by William Faulkner."

"Seems obvious to me that Penrose is covering something up," I said.

"Big time," Maya said.

"How was the Ramos fizz?"

"Sucked," she said. "Even Bertram's version is ten times better."

"Not all bartenders are created equally," I said.

That's a fact," Maya said. "This bar is spectacular. Not so much for the bartender."

"Though I'm not sure what we learned, I feel meeting Penrose and Malveaux wasn't a waste of time," I said.

"It wasn't," Maya said. "Those two are somehow involved."

"No kidding. Malveaux's sister is one of two people with access to Evelyn's private library," I said.

"We need to talk to her."

"The sooner, the better," I said.

"We should get Tommy and Marlon to run Malveaux's record. He's scary."

"The way he glared at us, I wondered if he was going to come across the booth and attack us," I said.

Maya nodded and said, "Want to dance?"

Grabbing her hand, I pulled her toward the dance floor and said, "Why not?"

Maya and I spent the next hour dancing at the Office and having a wonderful time.

"What now?" I finally said.

"Clear our tab and return to Bertram's," she said. "I need a Ramos fizz, and the one I got here isn't cutting it."

Chapter 12

When we exited the Office, the rain was no longer light. A spring storm had engulfed the French Quarter, with thunder booming and rain falling in sheets. We stood beneath the overhang, not bothering to raise the umbrella.

"What now?" Maya asked.

"Call Bradley," I said.

"Who is Bradley?"

"Jake's chauffeur," I said. "He's probably in the neighborhood. He'll rescue us."

Maya waited as I spoke with Bradley on the phone.

"Well?" she said when I returned the phone to my pocket.

"He's on his way."

The storm's intensity continued as we waited for Jake's big black limo to arrive. If pulled around the corner, parking on the street beside us. A young man dressed in a black suit, tie, and chauffeur's cap carried a colorful umbrella and hurried through the downpour to the overhang protecting us.

Bradley, Jake's chauffeur, stood six feet six inches tall. He was a former pro football player and even a part-time stunt driver. The bulge beneath his coat was a pistol because he doubled as Jake's bodyguard.

"Where to?" he asked.

"Bertram's. Bradley, this lovely young woman is Maya."

"Pleased to meet you, ma'am," he said as he opened the backdoor of the limo.

Mama and Jake greeted us in the passenger compartment when we slid beside them.

"Love your limo," Maya said. "This is a first for me, and I'm impressed."

"Bradley, give Maya a tour through the French Quarter before we hit Bertram's."

"Yes sir, Bossman," Bradley's voice sounded through a speaker.

As Bradley navigated the sleek limo through the rain-soaked streets of the French Quarter, the world outside the tinted windows shimmered with a liquid glow. Rain tapped rhythmically on the roof, and neon signs blurred into streaks of color against the wet pavement. Maya gazed wide-eyed out the window, taking in the iconic sights of New Orleans.

Some streets in the Quarter are restricted to foot traffic only. Jake's limo had no such restrictions. Bradley drove down Bourbon Street, where the storm hadn't entirely dampened the spirits of the revelers. Beneath balconies dripping with wrought iron lace, clusters of tourists huddled under umbrellas, some daring to dance naked in the rain, their laughter mingling with the muffled strains of jazz and blues.

The flickering gas lamps cast a ghostly light over the scene, illuminating the cobblestone streets slick with rainwater as a street performer, drenched but undeterred, belted out a soulful tune on his saxophone, the notes haunting and beautiful in the rain-drenched night.

Bradley turned onto Royal Street, where the elegant galleries and antique shops stood like silent sentinels, their windows reflecting the storm. We glided past opulent mansions with ivy-clad walls and hidden courtyards, their secrets masked by the swirling rain. Here, the streets were quieter. The gentle lapping of rainwater against the curbs and the occasional clap of thunder echoing in the distance were the only sounds.

"It isn't a stretch imagining the ghosts of old New Orleans wandering these narrow streets, and their whispers lost in the downpour," Maya said.

Mama hugged her shoulder and said, "New Orleans is heaven on earth."

She nudged Jake with her elbow when he said, "At least most of the time."

As we approached Jackson Square, the towering spires of St. Louis Cathedral loomed through the mist, shrouded in a veil of rain. The square was nearly deserted, save for a few brave souls seeking refuge under the eaves of nearby buildings.

The statue of Andrew Jackson on his rearing horse seemed even more imposing in the storm, a dark silhouette against the backdrop of the cathedral's illuminated façade. Bradley slowed the limo so Maya could take in the scene—the heart of the French Quarter, timeless and resilient, standing defiant in the face of the storm.

When we reached Bertram's bar, the rain had grown stronger, turning the streets into shallow rivers. Bradley pulled up to the curb, the limo's headlights cutting through the sheets of rain.

"Quite a tour, huh?" I said.

"I'm awestruck," she said. "Thank you."

"Thank Bradley, not me," Jake said. "The big guy possesses the heart of a tour guide."

The electricity went out the moment we entered Bertram's front door. Intimately aware of the vagaries of the local electrical company, he'd had a generator installed. Because he was cheap, he hadn't purchased one big enough to restore the bar to full power. There was enough electricity to power the air conditioning and refrigeration, though it was only sufficient to provide dim overhead lighting.

"I like it," Jake said. "The dimness enhances the bar's ambiance."

The rain continued to fall in bucketloads as thunder rocked the old wooden structure and lightning flashed through the big window in front. As Jake had said, the atmosphere was conducive to drinking, though most tourists and Bertram's regulars had already gone home for the night. What was left were Leo, Pepper, Lydia, and Adano. We joined them at the bar.

Leo and Pepper were drinking Abita, and Leo did a double-take when he saw Maya's short skirt and low-cut dress.

He whistled and said, "Oh my, you look good, little girl. You got a boyfriend you haven't told us about? I may have to tell Daddy on you."

"You do, and I'll break your fingers," Maya said.

When Bertram handed her a Ramos fizz, Leo said, "You drinking now?"

"You and Pepper drink," Maya said.

"Leave her alone, Leo, or I'm going to smack you," Pepper said.

"I'm just pulling your leg, baby. You're a grown woman and free to do anything you please," he said.

"Thank you," she said.

"No, thank you, and Wyatt, Bertram, Lydia, and Adano," he said. "We were worn out and talking seriously about taking the day off."

"We were happy to help," Maya said. "We'll be there tomorrow if you need us."

Leo glanced at the lightning flashing through the open window.

"The weather may take care of things for us," he said. "Looks as if we're going to get rained out."

"It's just as liable to be sunny tomorrow," Bertram said.

Pepper blushed when Leo said, "Damn! I was hoping Pepper and I could spend another lazy day in our room."

Pepper was grinning but said, "Leo, shut your mouth."

"Yes, ma'am," he said.

"We're approaching the end of French Quarter Fest," Pepper said. "Neither of us can believe how much money we've made. We have reservations at Antoine's and plan to celebrate and spend a chunk of our bounty."

"Good for you," Maya said.

"Will you join us?"

"You bet I will," Maya said.

"When you're ready, I'll call Bradley and have him take you," Jake said.

Before Maya, Leo, and Pepper could leave, Tommy O'Rear and Marlon Bando walked in the door.

"Wait," she said.

"Friends of yours?" Leo asked.

"N.O.P.D. homicide detectives. I joined them earlier at a bar for cops and haven't had so much fun in ages."

It was apparent from their smiles that Marlon and Tommy felt the same.

"Look at you! Maya, you are hot," Tommy said.

Maya didn't seem to mind the compliment. "Tommy and Marlon, this is my brother Leo and his wife Pepper."

Tommy slapped Leo's shoulder and said, "Marlon and I ate at your kiosk twice this week. You should open a place in New Orleans. We'd help keep you in business."

"Thanks, Tommy," Leo said.

"How's the murder investigation going?" I asked.

"Confusing," he said.

"How so?"

"The person who cut themselves isn't our killer. The blood was still wet and didn't match the victim's time of death," Marlon said.

"They discovered the body when they showed up at Coleman-Labissiere's office unannounced," Tommy said.

"They knew the victim well enough that they were drinking his half-finished whiskey when something spooked them and caused them to drop it. They sustained a cut when it broke on the floor," Marlon said.

"How did they not know that Coleman-Labissiere was dead?" I asked.

"Hell, Cowboy, this is the Big Easy. They were probably drunk," Tommy said. "The cobra scared the hell out of them, and they fled the scene."

"Lots of whiskey drinkers in New Orleans," Marlon said.

Marlon and Tommy's smiles disappeared when I said, "Evelyn DuPont, for one."

"You know something you ain't telling us, Cowboy?" Tommy asked.

"Just saying."

"What else do you know?" he asked.

"Maya and I had drinks with Samuel Penrose and his pal Victor Malveaux earlier, and they seemed to think Evelyn's son is the killer."

"How the hell would they even have a clue?"

Tommy said.

"They were aware Evelyn DuPont's son collects exotic snakes," I said.

"Did they, now? How did they know the victim died of a snakebite?" Marlon asked.

"They said it was in the police report," I said.

"We haven't issued a police report," Tommy said.

Marlon had his notebook out and said, "Who did you say told you the victim died of a snakebite?"

"Samuel Penrose. His partner is Victor Malveaux," I said.

"What do you know about them?" Tommy asked.

"Penrose is a rare book dealer. I know nothing about Malveaux except he never smiled and looked dangerous."

Maya took Tommy's hand and said, "Leo, Pepper, and I are having dinner at Antoine's. Please join us."

"Sorry, Little Sis. Our reservation is for three, and the maitre d' insistent about it," Leo said.

"I can get us in if you let Mama, me, and everyone else tag along," Jake said. "And the treat's on the Cryptid Hunter."

"Us too?" Lydia said.

"I'd love your company," Jake said.

Before Leo could reply, Jake dialed his assistant Angie. "Can you call Antoine's and get me a reservation for twelve?"

Jake's phone rang five minutes later. He was smiling when he returned the phone to his pocket.

"You got it?" Leo asked in disbelief.

"No one ever turns down the Cryptid Hunter," Mama said.

"Angie and Bradley are a number," Jake said. "Angie's on vacation, so Bradley's dining with us, if that's okay."

Mama put her hand to Pepper's ear and said, "Angie's black and Bradley white."

"Please join us, Adano and Lydia," Jake said. "I'm not Catholic, but I enjoy an occasional religious conversation."

Adano and Lydia held hands as they drank their martinis. "Right now, we're thinking secular thoughts," Adano said.

"What's with you two?" I asked. "Priests and nuns are supposed to be celibate. You two don't look celibate to me."

"We served the Mother Church for decades," Lydia said. "We are both retired, and I believe I've found the love of my life."

"I know that I have," Adano said.

"Wonderful," I said. "What's your plans?"

"Adano's taking me to Italy," Lydia said.

"Are you going to marry?" I asked.

Lydia grinned. "Heavens no. We intend to enjoy each other's company until we die."

"Why not?" I said.

Mama and Jake looked as relaxed as I could remember seeing them. They'd recently returned from visiting Mama's sister in South Carolina, and it was the first time since meeting Jake that he wasn't working on a project.

He smiled when I said, "Did Cryptid Hunter get canceled?"

"The new season begins in September. We have all new episodes in the can and don't need to film again until next February. All my people, except Colley and Bradley, are on vacation."

"Jake's bored," Mama said.

"I'm coping," Jake said. "Mama and I plan to spend a few weeks in Tulsa, relax, and do lots of jogging."

"You've earned it," I said.

"Jake and I spent the day at the Tulane library. We have an interesting take on Ms. DuPont's father."

"I'm all ears," I said.

"I had to employ all my research skills to get you this information," Mama said.

"Don't keep me in suspense," I said.

"David DuPont, Evelyn's father, was certifiably insane," Mama said. "It's probable, even likely, that he had sex with his daughter."

Mama nodded when I said, "Evelyn?"

"I'll tell you more when we get to Antoine's," she said.

Jake cleared everyone's tab, Bertram looking dejected as we started for the door. I didn't make it as Evelyn DuPont came in as we were exiting.

"Am I interrupting anything?"

"Nothing I can't change." I waved to the others and said, "Have fun, and I'll catch everyone later."

Chapter 13

Even though she was obviously drunk, Evelyn DuPont looked stunning in her designer dress with shoes to match that must have cost thousands. The rain outside continued, though her hair wasn't damp.

Bertram was happy to see a paying customer and said, "New Orleans milk punch, Ms. DuPont?"

"Excellent memory, Bertram," she said. "Your New Orleans milk punch was terrific, but tonight I'm drinking Wild Turkey, neat."

"You got it," Bertram said.

"So sorry to pop in on you unannounced," she said. "I thought you might have something to tell me about my book."

"I spoke with Samuel Penrose earlier today, and he seemed to think a private collector has it."

"Samuel knows every private collector in town. If it's in a collection, you can be sure he knows who has it and where it is."

"Which brings me to Ronnie LaSalle. Only she and your social secretary have the combination to your library. Ronnie and Penrose are partners."

Evelyn bristled and said, "Ronnie has nothing to do with the disappearance of the book."

"Sure about that?"

"Ronnie's like a sister to me."

"Sisters can quarrel and have disagreements. There's always sibling jealousy."

"If Ronnie had asked me for the book, I'd have given it to her."

"Maybe Penrose pressured her to snatch it for him."

Evelyn sipped her shot and said, "Sam isn't above something like that, though I believe Ronnie would have told me."

"Penrose bought Wild Magnolias and gave it to Ronnie. Even though they have no written contract, Ronnie continues giving him a hefty cut of every book she sells."

"What are you getting at?" Evelyn said.

"Maybe Penrose saw a chance to cut a fat hog, and Ronnie saw an opportunity to get out from under his thumb."

Evelyn killed her shot and motioned Bertram to bring her another.

"What else?" she said.

"What do you know about Victor Malveaux?"

"He's Sam's lover, if that's what you mean."

"I met him today, and he seemed more than that."

"Victor is part of the Baton Rouge Malveauxs, an old-money family that owned plantations on River Road and were one of the wealthiest families in Louisiana."

"What happened to them?"

"The Malveaux family was the largest slave owner in Louisiana. Following the Civil War, they had no workers to tend the crops."

"Other plantation owners found ways to cope," I said.

"A family scandal precluded that," Evelyn said. "An older brother had been embezzling money for years, maybe decades. When the family needed to dip into the till, they found it was nowhere near full."

"What did he do with the money?"

"A gambling addict who lost millions. The family began selling land, and their fire-auction tactics led to a sharp devaluation of property along the river," Evelyn said.

"Still, they must have made lots of money even at depressed prices."

"They tried to diversify their income through investments in railroads and shipping, but bad luck or poor management led to catastrophic losses and wiped out much of their fortune," Evelyn said.

"And Victor Malveaux was left with no inheritance and nowhere to turn," I said.

"His father was the bad actor and was avoided by the family. His father's brush tarred Victor. The angst caused by his father's fall from grace shaped his personality for the worse."

"I can relate," I said. "My parents were far from perfect."

"Nor were mine, God rest their souls," Evelyn said.

"Victor was dressed in expensive clothes when I met him today and didn't appear to have suffered financially."

"He latched on to Sam like a buoy in a storm, and they've been a couple ever since."

Thunder shook the roof, and the bar went dark momentarily before the lights and air conditioning returned. Heavy rain pounded the front window, and I knew there would be standing water in the streets.

"What's your blood type," I asked.

"Why do you need to know?"

"Someone at the murder scene got cut when they broke Coleman-Labissiere's whiskey glass. The blood type was B. Is that your blood type?"

"Yes," she said.

"Did you visit Toby on the day of his murder?"

Evelyn's tone was defensive when she said, "What makes you think that?"

"The bandage on your hand and, like your cousin Toby, your fondness for Wild Turkey whiskey."

"Many people like Wild Turkey."

"I'm not the police, Evelyn, and I'm not sharing my information with them. Were you the person who found Toby and then cut your hand when you dropped his unfinished glass of Wild Turkey?"

Evelyn turned away from me, took a sip of whiskey, and then turned back.

"I thought he was asleep. I was going to prank him and drink his whiskey."

"Until the snake frightened you?"

"It wrapped around my leg, and I almost peed my pants."

I smiled and said, "I would have. Thankfully, it didn't bite you."

"Jonathan handles snakes all the time," she said. "They're more likely to run than to bite you."

"Tell that to your cousin, Toby," I said. "Was it one of your son's snakes?"

"No," Evelyn said.

"I don't know anyone in New Orleans who owns a king cobra."

"There are lots of snake collectors. You'd be surprised. Doesn't matter because I'd just as soon you didn't tell the police."

"They already know the cause of death and captured the cobra. One thing bothers me."

"What?" she said.

"Samuel Penrose knew Toby was killed by a snake even though the police haven't released that information. Any idea how he might know?"

"Ronnie could have informed him," Evelyn said. "I told her my story about the snake and Toby."

"Another reason to believe she's complicit in the disappearance of your copy of *Mosquitoes*."

"I refuse to believe it," Evelyn said.

"Something else Penrose told me," I said.

"Tell me."

"He said the only value your copy of *Mosquitoes* is as a curiosity."

"If it has no value, why did someone steal it?"

"My thoughts exactly," I said.

"You don't believe him, do you?" she asked.

"Penrose has ulterior motives, though I don't know what they are yet."

"How is it my grandparents wound up with the copy of *Mosquitoes* that they did?"

Bertram came out of the back and poured Evelyn another shot of whiskey before I could answer.

"Sorry," he said. "The storm has caused my generator to act up, and I was working on it."

"At least we have electricity," I said. "The rest of the Quarter has gone dark."

"And I have a paying customer," he said.

"Two," I said. "You never fail to charge me for my lemonade."

Bertram grinned and rubbed his hands together when Evelyn said, "Put Wyatt's lemonade on my tab."

"Thanks," I said.

When the generator sputtered again, Bertram hurried away to tend to it. Evelyn reached across the bar, grabbed the bottle of Wild Turkey, and poured herself another shot.

"When you're a runway model, you quickly learn to be self-sufficient. Now, why did my grandparents end up with the third copy of *Mosquitoes*?"

"Laceigh Rutherford paid Toby's grandfather to deliver that particular copy."

"Faulkner kept the original copy. What happened to the second copy?"

"Good question," I said.

"What's the answer?"

"Penrose cast doubt that Faulkner had the original. He said Faulkner willed all his notes and manuscripts to the University of Virginia and that the Lower Pontalba Press version of *Mosquitoes* wasn't part of the donation."

"He took it to Oxford, Mississippi, when he returned there," Evelyn said.

"Then where is it?"

"If he took it, it's there someplace," she said. "Evelyn pushed the shot glass aside and began drinking straight from the bottle. I could tell by her eyes and facial expression that she was seething.

"Are you okay?" I asked.

"I'm rethinking your assignment," she said.

"Are you firing me?"

Evelyn pinched my cheek and said, "Heavens, no, pretty boy. I still have plans for you."

"What, then?" I asked.

"I don't want you only to find the third copy of Mosquitoes; I want you to locate all three and get them for me."

"We haven't even found the first one yet," I said. "Locating and securing all three copies is a daunting task."

"They are a set, and I must possess them no matter the cost. Send your partner to Oxford to track down Faulkner's copy."

"And me?" I asked.

Instead of answering my question, Evelyn wrapped her arms around my neck and kissed me passionately. We were both breathing heavily when she slid her arms off my shoulders and began rubbing my private parts.

"I have a new mission in life, and you're a large part of it. A huge part of it."

After another swig from the whiskey bottle, she fished in her purse, left a wad of hundreds on the counter for Bertram, and then marched drunkenly out the door.

When Bertram returned and saw the money and the half-empty bottle of whiskey, he said, "What the hell?"

"I'd say that was the most expensive bottle of whiskey you've ever sold."

Although I live in one of the most dangerous cities, I never locked my door at night. For one thing, I didn't have much to rob. I was asleep when someone opened the door and lay beside me on the bed. It was Maya in her skimpy nightgown.

"If you knew what dreams I was having, you'd never dare lay beside me in that little bit of nothing nightgown of yours," I said.

"What dreams?" she asked.

"I can't tell you. It would make you blush."

"Make me blush," she said. "I can handle it."

"It flashed out of my brain. Now it's gone," I said.

"You are so full of shit," she said. "We missed you at Antoine's."

"I wish I had been there. I missed dinner, and I'm starving."

"What do you have in your fridge?" she said.

"Not much," I said.

"What about your pantry?"

126

"Not much there either," I said. "I'm a bachelor and don't spend much time in grocery stores."

"The French Market is just down the street."

"Like I said, I'm not much of a shopper."

Maya found a dozen eggs in the fridge and a can of Spam in the pantry. We soon feasted on Spam and scrambled eggs drizzled with lots of Louisiana hot sauce, a pot of coffee, and chicory. Though I had a hard time concentrating with a half-naked woman sitting across my little table from me, I managed to persevere.

"What did Ms. DuPont want?" Maya asked.

"To screw my brains out," I said. "So far, I've been able to resist."

"She must be pushing sixty," Maya said.

"Sometimes the cars with lots of miles are the most reliable."

Maya stopped eating and dropped her fork. "What is it with men and cars?"

She crossed her arms across her chest when I said, "There's something about a classic chassis."

"Not funny," she said. "I'm not an object. I'm a human, just like you." She couldn't keep a straight face when I grinned. "What else did your '56 Chevy tell you?" she asked.

"She confessed it was her that broke the whiskey glass and cut her hand at the Lower Pontalba Press."

"You need to tell Tommy," she said.

"No, it's you who needs to tell Tommy. Doesn't matter because he's a good cop and will find out anyway."

"You think Tommy's a good cop?"

"Tony trained him. How could he not be? You like him, don't you?"

"Tommy's a project I have no time for," she said.

"Could have fooled me," I said.

127

"You jealous?"

"You want me to be?" I asked.

"You're an asshole, Wyatt Thomas."

"And you are gorgeous, Maya Henstooth."

Neither of us spoke as we cleared the dishes and put them away.

"Feel better now?" she asked after returning to the bed.

"Not as good as I could feel," I said.

"You need to stop pressuring me."

"Me? I'm calling bullshit on that one," I said.

"My mother warned me about men like you."

"Did she also teach you how to be a tease?"

"You think I'm a teaser?"

"Gypsy Rose Lee status if you ask me," I said.

The lights went out when thunder rocked the old building. Maya and I embraced, engaging in passionate foreplay until the lights abruptly came back on. She wrestled herself from my grasp when they did and hurried to the door.

"Meet you for breakfast in the morning. You can tell me what else Ms. DuPont told you.

Chapter 14

I was still asleep the following morning when my cell phone rang and awoke me. It was Evelyn DuPont.

"Have you talked to your partner yet?" she asked.

"About what?"

"Going to Oxford, Mississippi, and finding the first copy of the Lower Pontalba Press Edition *Mosquitoes*."

"I thought you were joking," I said.

"I wasn't."

"Even if Tony finds it, what do you want him to do?"

"I have a million dollars burning a hole in my pocket. I want that book and you to find the other two for me."

"You're serious," I said.

"Dead serious. Take whatever steps are needed to secure the three copies for my collection. Possessing all three is my new mission in life."

"I'll do my best," I said.

"What are your immediate plans?"

I sensed she was smiling when I said, "Roll over and go back to sleep. I was dreaming about you."

She hung up after saying, "Sweet dreams, my amour."

Kisses was awake and insistent that I feed her even before I went to the bathroom. I fed her and made sure she had fresh water. Maya and Bertram were at the bar when I descended the stairs, the aroma of Bertram's strong Cajun coffee beckoning me even before I got a whiff of his sweet potato pecan waffles.

Maya smiled when I sat beside her, and Bertram said, "I can't believe you're just now getting out of bed."

"And I can't believe you aren't married," I said.

"Don't need a wife," he said. "Me and Lady are happy as shrimps in a bowl of spicy gumbo."

Getting the best of Bertram in the morning isn't easy, so I didn't try, turning my attention to Maya instead. She wore a white tasseled miniskirt, highlighting every inch of her gorgeous legs. Her grin told me she knew I was looking.

When Bertram entered the back, she said, "I have you figured out."

"I have no idea what you're talking about."

"Yes, you do," she said.

"Really? Tell me."

"You're an alley cat and owe allegiance to no one," she said.

"Alley cats survive by their visceral senses. Even so, there's no such thing as an old alley cat."

"You're right about that, and I worry about you."

"Don't," I said. "I'm a big boy and can take care of myself."

Tony entered the front door, saw us at the bar, and sat beside Maya before she could continue her thought. Bertram had already poured him a scotch and smiled as he handed it to him.

"Thanks," Tony said.

"No problem. Always happy to see my favorite customer," Bertram said.

Tony sipped his scotch and turned his attention to Maya. "How did you like your trip to the police district?

"If you mean Carlucci's, I loved it," she said.

"And everyone there loved you," Tony said. "Especially Tommy and Marlon."

"They are sweethearts," Maya said.

"They are seasoned cops, and you have them eating out of your hand," Tony said.

"Like I said, they're sweethearts."

Tony glanced at me for the first time. "What's up with you, Cowboy?"

"Slight change of plans concerning our case. Want to go to Mississippi?"

"Not particularly. What changes?"

"Of the three copies of *Mosquitoes* published by Lower Pontalba Press, Faulker supposedly took the original copy to Oxford, Mississippi."

"Supposedly?"

"Maya and I had drinks with Samuel Penrose yesterday. He told us Faulkner donated all his papers to the University of Virginia. Everything except the original copy of *Mosquitoes* from the Lower Pontalba Press printing."

"Who gives a shit?" Tony asked. "That's not part of our assignment."

"It is now," I said. "Ms. DuPont wants us to find all three copies published by the Lower Pontalba Press."

"For what reason?"

"She's a collector and doesn't need a reason. Collecting is an obsession, and she's suddenly positive she can't live another day without all three books. Can you find the Oxford copy for her?"

"Maybe. Even if I do, what then?"

"Purchase it for her," I said. "She told me she has a million dollars burning a hole in her pocket."

"Jesus!" Tony said. "If I had a spare million bucks, I wouldn't spend it on a musty old book."

"Collectors are worse than addicts; they're insane," I said.

"I'll have to clear my schedule," he said.

"When can you leave?"

"After I return home and pack a bag," he said.

"Lil won't be angry?"

"You haven't been married in a while, Cowboy. As long as she knows I'm not Tom catting around, she's happy to get me out of her hair for a while."

"Guess that's why I'm not married," I said.

"I have a cousin in Mississippi," Bertram said as he poured Tony's scotch."

"Mississippi is a big state. Where does your cousin live?" Tony asked.

"Biloxi," he said.

"Don't know much about Mississippi except that Biloxi's on the redneck Riviera. Oxford is about as far away as you can get from the Gulf Coast," Tony said.

"Ever been to Biloxi?" Bertram asked.

Tony grinned and said, "I spent the night in jail there once while playing minor league baseball."

"For what?" Bertram asked.

"Public urination," Tony said. "We won the game, and me and my team spent the night in the slammer."

"I ain't commenting on that," Bertram said.

Bertram had also mixed Maya a Ramos fizz and Tony noticed.

"You drinking now?" he asked.

"I'm addicted to Bertram's Ramos fizzes," she said.

"Watch yourself," Tony said. "This is the Big Easy. It's easy to get caught up in crazy behavior."

"I'm okay," she said. "I'm helping Leo and Pepper again today. Tommy and Marlon are dropping by."

"Those two boys have the hots for you," Tony said. "I have a hunch neither has a long-term chance of scoring."

"You could be wrong about that," she said.

"I doubt it," he said.

Maya finished her Ramos fizz and headed for the door. "Be careful in Mississippi," she said.

Mama and Jake entered Bertram's establishment and joined us at the bar as Maya was leaving.

"Who's going to Mississippi?" Mama asked.

"Me," Tony said. "Ms. DuPont wants someone to find Faulkner's copy of his Lower Pontalba Press version of *Mosquitoes*."

"You won't find it in Oxford. Faulkner gave all his papers to the University of Virginia," she said.

"Not everything," I said. "Maya and I had drinks yesterday with Samuel Penrose, a rare book dealer. He told us the book never reached the University of Virginia."

"Then where is it?" she asked.

"I'm going to find out," Tony said.

"I've wanted to visit Oxford since I wrote my dissertation," Mama said.

Mama shook her head when Tony said, "Never been there?"

"I've read so much about it that I feel I have. When are you leaving?"

"Soon as I pack a suitcase."

"Take me with you," Mama said. "I know all about Faulkner's life in Oxford. If the copy of *Mosquitoes* is there, I'll help you find it."

"We could be gone a week or more," Tony said. "Who's going to take care of your cats?"

Mama asked Jake, "Will you care for my babies while I'm gone?"

"You know I will," Jake said.

Mama kissed him and said, "You're a sweetheart. I'll leave the front door key in the mailbox and instructions on the kitchen table."

"You'll need some cash. Bertram, can you give Tony five grand from my account?"

"Yes, sir," Bertram said with a salute.

Bertram returned from his safe in the back with a handful of hundreds. He counted five thousand dollars on the counter and pushed them toward Tony.

"This should be enough to get you through a week or ten days on the road," I said. "If not, I'll send more."

"I feel sorry for Tommy and Marlon," Tony said. "Neither has a snowball's chance in hell with Maya. What are your plans?"

"Question Evelyn's butler, maid, daughter, and social secretary," I said.

"You think one of them stole her book?" he asked.

"I'm pretty sure Ronnie LaSalle took it."

"Knowing who took it is one thing. Recovering it is something else altogether," Tony said.

"Right about that," I said.

Jake looked bewildered as Mama and Tony exited the bar. His smile returned when Bertram handed him a Bombay gin.

"Thanks, Bertram," he said.

"You're just going to let her take off for a week with another man?" Bertram asked.

"I'm not worried," Jake said. "Mama doesn't have a deceitful bone in her body. What's the deal with Oxford?"

"Evelyn Penrose is a rare book collector. She just realized what a prize the three Lower Pontalba

Press editions of *Mosquitoes* are worth and is determined to possess all three," I said.

"Collecting becomes an obsession for some," he said. "If you need help, I'm here for you."

"Thanks, Jake. "If I get in a bind, I'll call."

The cloudy sky hung low, casting a muted gray light over New Orleans as I left Bertram's bar on Chartres and headed toward the streetcar line. The familiar sound of the old rumble-bucket grew louder as I neared Canal Street, blending with the distant hum of the city. St. Charles Avenue loomed ahead, its wide boulevard flanked by ancient oaks and stately mansions, a testament to a bygone era of Southern opulence.

The streetcar, painted in its iconic olive green, creaked to a halt with a screech of metal on metal. Its wooden doors clattered open to welcome me aboard. I climbed on and took a seat by the window.

The wooden benches, polished smooth by years of use, felt hard beneath me. I leaned back, watching the world slide by as the streetcar lurched forward with a jolt and soon began gliding down St. Charles Avenue.

Massive live oaks lined the avenue, their gnarled branches forming a canopy overhead, filtering the weak sunlight into dappled shadows that danced across the windows. On either side, grand old mansions stood like silent sentinels, their columns and wrought-iron balconies bearing witness to generations of Southern aristocracy. Tourists snapped pictures from beneath their wide-brimmed hats, oblivious to the subtle tension simmering beneath the city's surface.

As the streetcar clattered, my thoughts drifted to the task ahead. Evelyn DuPont's mansion awaited me in the Garden District, where the past seemed to cling to every brick and stone. I had many questions and intended to get answers, whether from her butler, maid, or social secretary.

When the streetcar slowed, I felt its rhythmic sway, steadying my mind for what lay ahead. I stepped into the humid air and entered the Garden District's heart.

Evelyn DuPont's mansion was a towering edifice of wealth and history, rising from behind a wrought-iron fence that gleamed black in the dim light. The house was a classic antebellum masterpiece, with white columns that soared two stories high and flanked a wide veranda around the front and sides.

The veranda, shaded by the sweeping limbs of ancient oak trees, was adorned with hanging ferns and wicker furniture. It offered a glimpse of leisurely afternoons spent sipping mint juleps and exchanging gossip beneath the oppressive weight of Southern etiquette.

The house's facade was painted a soft cream, its windows trimmed in dark green shutters that contrasted sharply with the pale plaster walls. Massive double doors framed by etched glass panels guarded the entrance like a pair of sentinels, hinting at the opulence that lay within.

Gas lamps flickered on either side of the doors, their flames steady despite the occasional gust of wind. Inside, I knew there would be a world of polished mahogany, crystal chandeliers, and plush Persian rugs. It was the kind of place where every detail was meticulously curated to project an image of old money and impeccable taste. But beneath the surface, I suspected, lurked secrets as dark and twisted as the roots of the ancient oaks surrounding the mansion.

I walked up the steps, my footfalls echoing on the veranda's wooden boards, and reached for the brass doorknocker, ready to unravel the mysteries within. After a short time, the doors opened with a creak, and a man appeared.

"Are you Mr. Thomas?" he asked.

"I am."

"I'm Jonathan, the butler, and I've been expecting you. Please come inside."

Chapter 15

Jonathan Stallings was tall, a thin man probably in his late fifties. His gaunt appearance complemented his quiet and reserved demeanor. His pale skin contrasted 666sharply with his deep-set eyes, which seemed to observe everything. His hair was silver-gray, meticulously combed back, giving him a slightly old-fashioned appearance.

"Where do you wish to begin?" he asked.

"Ms. DuPont informed me that you tend to her son Rodney's exotic snake collection when he is away. Can you show it to me?"

"Of course, sir," he said.

Stallings was dressed in traditional butler attire: a black tailcoat with silver buttons, a crisp white shirt with a stiff collar, and black trousers with a sharp crease. His polished black shoes shined immaculately, reflecting his attention to detail.

I sensed a slight smile when I asked, "It's barely eight in the morning. Do you always dress so formally?"

"On less formal occasions, I wear a black waistcoat and a simple tie. My preference for formality is evident, and I prefer to project it to all aspects of my wardrobe."

I followed Stallings through elegant hallways with polished wood floors covered by Persian rugs, antique mirrors rimmed with solid gold, and walls bearing original art. The signs of immense wealth were everywhere, and Stallings's mannerisms were precise and deliberate, never hurried or flustered. He walked up an elegant flight of stairs to the mansion's second story.

"How long have you worked for Ms. DuPont?" I asked.

Stallings answered in low and measured words, with an unplaceable accent that hinted at a well-traveled past.

"Many years," he said. He stopped at the door down a long hall toward the back of the house and touched the doorknob with reverence before opening it. "This is Rodney's bedroom."

Stallings opened the door, clasping his hands behind his back as he waited for me to follow him inside. He seemed to observe the room with a reptilian stillness, his movements smooth, almost serpentine, reflecting his affinity for snakes.

Rodney DuPont's room seemed to mirror a young man's complex and troubled mind. Located on the second floor, it was spacious yet dark, with heavy velvet drapes. The drapes were drawn, allowing only slivers of light to filter through. The walls were a muted green, reminiscent of a forest canopy, and adorned with old maps, anatomical sketches, and framed photos of exotic reptiles. Stallings opened the drapes, allowing natural light to flood the room.

The furniture was elegant but worn, with an intricately carved mahogany bed dominating the room. The bedding was dark and luxurious, with layers of heavy blankets and pillows that gave the impression of a nest more than a sleeping area. A massive oak desk sat in one corner, cluttered with journals, books on herpetology, and sketches of snakes, some of which were disturbingly detailed. The faint smell of leather and ink and the distinct odor of the snakes lingered in the air.

"How old is Rodney?" I asked.

"Forty-two," Stallings said. "The last time I saw him was in January when we celebrated his and Alicin's birthdays."

"Are Rodney and Alicin twins?" I asked.

"Yes. They were born about a year after Ms. DuPont's father died."

"Ms. DuPont still goes by her maiden name. What about Rodney and Alicin?"

"Their last name is DuPont," Stallings said.

"What was their father's last name?" I asked.

"That is a question for Ms. DuPont," he said.

Seeing he wasn't going to answer me, I moved on.

"Please show me Rodney's collection of snakes."

The room's centerpiece was the snake collection, a series of glass enclosures meticulously arranged along one wall, each housing a different species of exotic snake. The tanks were filled with carefully arranged environments—rocks, branches, and foliage— replicating the snakes' natural habitats. The soft hum of heat lamps and the occasional rustle of a snake moving through its enclosure added an almost hypnotic quality to the room.

"This reminds me of the herpetology section at Audubon Zoo," I said.

"Each species is matched with its preferred environment," Stallings said. "The temperature, humidity, and ambiance precisely monitored."

"I'm impressed."

The snakes were as varied as they were beautiful. A striking green tree python coiled gracefully around a branch, its emerald scales gleaming in the dim light. A black mamba lay coiled in another enclosure, its sleek form barely moving as it watched the room with unblinking eyes.

A giant albino Burmese python rested in a custom-built tank, its pale yellow and white skin glowing under the heat lamp. Each snake seemed to embody a different aspect of Rodney's psyche— beautiful, dangerous, and misunderstood. As Stallings guided me through the room, his demeanor softened.

He smiled when I said, "All these snakes have one thing in common. They're as dangerous as hell."

"On the contrary, Mr. Thomas," he said. I watched as Stallings put his arm in the black mamba's enclosure and lifted it out. "Kobe loves human attention."

"Kobe? Does Rodney like basketball?"

Stallings returned the snake to its enclosure and said, "I named him."

He exhibited no change in demeanor when I said, "Clever. You must like snakes as much as Rodney."

"They are intriguing creatures, Mr. Thomas," he said.

Stallings's back stiffened noticeably when I asked, "Does Rodney own a king cobra?"

"No, never," he said.

"Can you tell me about Rodney?"

Stallings touched one of the enclosures with reverence and spoke about Evelyn's only son with fondness and sadness.

"Mr. Rodney was always drawn to these creatures, even as a boy. They understood him, I think, in ways that people never could."

"He sounds like a complex individual," I said.

Jonathan's voice was almost a whisper as he gazed at the green tree python.

"Very much so. He called the snakes his 'silent friends' and said they didn't judge him, only watched and waited. I suppose that's why he loved them so."

"Is that also how you feel about them?" I asked.

Jonathan paused by the black mamba's tank, his hand resting lightly on the glass.

"Rodney was... misunderstood, just like them. People see a snake and think of danger and evil, but Rodney sees their grace and beauty. He always said that fear comes from not understanding. I think he felt that way about himself."

"Do you have any idea where Rodney is?"

Jonathan didn't answer my question. Instead, he turned to me, his expression growing more earnest.

"I've cared for these snakes since he left, but... it's not the same without him here. They miss him, I can tell. And so do I. He wasn't like other young men—there was a rare depth to him. I only hope... wherever he is, he's found some peace."

Stallings gave me a dark glance when I asked, "Did Rodney have access to his mother's rare book collection?"

"Mr. Rodney wasn't even in the house when Ms. DuPont's book went missing," he said.

"What about you? Do you have access to the collection?"

"I believe you already know the answer," he said.

142

"You've worked here for years. You live here, and Ms. DuPont trusts you."

"Ms. DuPont's rare book collection is in a room I have never entered."

He nodded when I said, "Never?"

I could tell my questioning was causing Stallings to become ever-distant.

"Three other people other than you, Rodney, and Ms. DuPont live in this house: Libby Tanner, Ms. DuPont's social secretary; Sara Sloan, her chief maid; and Alicin, her daughter. Does Sara, Libby, or Alicin have access to Ms. DuPont's rare book collection?"

"Only Ms. Tanner," he said.

"Can you describe Libby Tanner and tell me a little about her?"

Stallings's calm demeanor tightened slightly, though he remained composed. I listened as he carefully chose his words, his tone measured and restrained.

"Miss Tanner... is a young woman of many talents. She handles Ms. DuPont's social calendar with efficiency and... enthusiasm. Ms. DuPont values her for that."

"Veronica LaSalle told me they are related," I said.

"Distant relatives, I believe—family ties run deep in this household. As for her role here, beyond the social matters... She is trusted with access to the rare book collection, which is no small responsibility. Mrs. DuPont doesn't give that kind of trust lightly."

Stallings's voice remained guarded, though I detected a subtle edge beneath the surface.

"Please continue," I said.

"Miss Tanner is... close to Mrs. DuPont in ways that are not for me to judge. I serve as I'm required, Mr. Thomas. But I will say this—she is ambitious.

143

One might even say she is determined to secure her position. Whether that's for Mrs. DuPont's benefit or her own, I can't truly say."

"And?"

Stallings straightened to his full height, his hands clasped behind his back as he finished.

"If you're asking if I trust her, Mr. Thomas, let's just say trust is earned. And I've yet to see the proof of it."

"Then it's possible she could be responsible for the disappearance of Ms. DuPont's book?"

"I didn't say that," Stallings said. "Nor did I mean to imply such a thing."

Seeing Stallings becoming defensive and in danger of freezing, I said, "I can see you have no ill intent for Ms. Tanner. It doesn't matter because our conversation goes no further than you and me."

"Thank you," he said. "I'm not a gossip."

"I can tell you aren't," I said. "Please describe and tell me a few things about Ms. DuPont's chief maid, Sara Sloan?"

Stallings's expression softened slightly, and a hint of a smile appeared as he spoke.

"Sara Sloan... well, she's the backbone of this house, no doubt about it. Been here longer than most of the furniture, and she knows this place better than anyone. Frumpy, some might say, but I'd call her... practical. She's got no time for frills, not with all she manages. And manage, she does. The house runs like clockwork under her watch."

"Sounds as if you like her," I said.

Stallings paused, his tone taking on a more thoughtful quality. "She's a bit of a gossip, yes. Can't help herself sometimes, but she's careful about it. Knows what to say and what to keep under wraps. We share many secrets, Sara and I.

Comes with the territory, I suppose. You can't work in a place like this and not know things."

"I can imagine," I said.

Stallings chuckled softly, almost to himself. "Sara likes to keep up appearances—acts like she's all business, but she's got a soft spot. Looks out for the younger maids and makes sure they're not overworked. And she's got a sharp tongue, but there's kindness behind it. We've had our disagreements, of course, but... I trust her. She's one of the few here I can say that about without hesitation."

"Does she have access to Ms. DuPont's rare book collection?"

"She is the only person allowed to clean the room," Stallings said.

"Then it's possible she could have taken the book."

"Not possible," Stallings said.

"Why not?" I asked.

"Ms. DuPont never leaves the room when Sara is cleaning."

Stallings became defensive again when I said, "I thought you told me Ms. DuPont trusts Sara."

"Sara has seen a lot in this house, more than most. And she's loyal—to the family and those who've earned her respect. Don't let that fool you; she's nobody's fool. Sara's eyes and ears are everywhere. If you're looking for the truth, Mr. Thomas, you could do worse than have a word with her."

"You think Sara knows who stole Ms. DuPont's book?"

"I didn't say that," he said.

"You haven't told me about Alicin. What do you think of her?"

"Miss Alicin is Ms. DuPont's daughter. I don't feel I should talk about her behind Ms. DuPont's back."

"You told me about Rodney. Rodney is Alicin's brother. What's the difference?"

Stallings stiffened and glanced around the room as if being watched.

"I could lose my job," he said.

"Nothing you tell me will ever get back to Ms. DuPont. I promise."

Chapter 16

Jonathan's distaste for Evelyn's daughter Alicin was barely concealed. His usually calm demeanor was tinged with thinly veiled disdain. His tone was clipped, and he avoided looking directly at me.

"Alicin... Miss DuPont. She's... well, she certainly inherited her mother's looks, but little else, I'm afraid. Some might say, more attractive than Mrs. DuPont, though I'd argue beauty only runs skin-deep."

"Whatever you tell me is strictly confidential," I said.

Stallings hesitated, then continued, his voice tightening.

"She's... troubled, perhaps, though that doesn't excuse how she lives. The whiskey bottle is her constant companion—morning, noon, and night."

He nodded when I said, "Wild Turkey?"

"She has never worked a day and doesn't see the need for it. Her days are spent either in her room or by the pool, drinking herself into oblivion. And as for her... relationships, well, let's say she doesn't discriminate. Pool boys, gardeners, even some maids—none are safe from her attentions."

"She's bisexual?" I asked.

Stallings nodded and sighed, his disapproval evident.

"She's a DuPont, that's true enough, though little of the dignity or grace comes with the name. I do my duty, Mr. Thomas, but... Alicin makes it difficult. She's reckless, selfish, and utterly lost. And if you ask me, she's a danger to herself and this household."

"Please explain what you mean by that," I said.

He paused, his expression hardening. "I keep my distance as best I can. But it's hard to ignore the mess she leaves in her wake. I've seen many things in this house, Mr. Thomas, but Alicin... she's a storm that refuses to pass."

"You didn't answer my question. How is she a danger to the household."

"I fear I've said too much," he said.

"Does she have access to her mother's rare book collection?"

"Miss Alicin goes where she pleases when she pleases. She and her mother have a special bond."

"Such as?" I said.

"They drink together, swim nude together." He grew silent. "I've said too much."

"Your words are safe with me," I said. "Is Libby Tanner here?"

Stallings shook his head. "Shopping with Ms. DuPont."

"What about Sara?" I asked.

"Sara doesn't like being disturbed when she's working."

"You might remind her for me that I have Ms. DuPont's permission to question her." Stallings seemed cowed by my statement. "I didn't mean it that way. Please introduce me, and I will explain directly to her what I require."

When we returned to the first floor, I realized it was lunchtime, and the wonderful aroma wafting through the house reminded me that I was hungry. Sara Sloan was sitting alone at a table in the kitchen and had a bite of steak in her mouth when we found her.

"Sara," Stallings said. "This is Mr. Thomas, a private detective Ms. DuPont hired to locate her missing book. He wants to ask you some questions."

"I don't want to interrupt your lunch," I said. "I'll wait on the porch outside until you finish."

Sara Sloan was a woman in her late sixties with a sturdy build and a face that showed her years of hard work. Her graying hair was pulled back into a neat bun, and she was dressed in practical clothing—a simple black dress, apron, and sensible shoes that reflected her no-nonsense approach to her duties. Despite her slightly frumpy appearance, there was a warmth about her, particularly in her sharp blue eyes, which were alert and keenly observant.

"Nonsense," she said. "You're skinny as a rail. Let me put some meat on your bones. Maisie," she called. "Bring this man some meat and potatoes."

I sat across the table from Sara, and a pretty young woman named Maisie brought me a steaming plate topped with steak, mashed potatoes, and gravy."

"Dig in," Sara said. "We can talk all you want when we finish eating."

I didn't have to be asked twice. The steak was tender, and the mashed potatoes and gravy were tasty. Maisie curtsied when she brought me a glass of iced tea.

"Thank you, Maisie." When she left the table, I said, "Is all your help as pretty as she is?"

149

"It's one of Ms. DuPont's requirements," Sara said.

I didn't comment and said, "I had a long talk with Jonathan. He seems like a wonderful person."

"The best there is," Sara said. "You don't think I stole Ms. DuPont's book, do you?"

"Absolutely not," I said. "I already think I know who took the book. I'm just going through the motions."

"Who do you think the culprit is?" she asked.

"My guess is Veronica LaSalle."

Sara shook her head. "Ronnie didn't do it?"

"If not Ronnie, then who?"

"Alicin took it," she said.

"She doesn't have a key to Ms. DuPont's rare book room."

Sara grinned and put her hand to her mouth as if conveying something to me in secret.

"Alicin has the run of the place. Ms. DuPont eats out of her hand. What Princess Alicin wants, Princess Alicin gets."

"If she took it, what did she do with it?" I asked.

Sara chewed another bite of steak before answering. "Who knows with that girl? She's nutty as a fruitcake, and nothing she does makes much sense."

"I see. What about Rodney's rare snake collection? Jonathan showed them to me. He even handled a black mamba."

"Jonathan loves snakes. It was he who got Rodney to collect them."

"How so?" I asked.

Johnnie had a pet rattlesnake, which he gave to Rodney. That started him, and he soon began collecting exotic snakes worldwide."

"Does he have a king cobra?" I asked.

"King Tut," she said.

Pardon me?"

"Rodney's king cobra is named King Tut. He's as tame as a lamb and wouldn't bite anyone."

"Really?" I said.

"He disappeared a while back, and Johnnie is heartbroken. He loved that snake."

"Rodney escaped from a facility in Alabama. Is it possible he returned to New Orleans and took King Tut?"

"Anything is possible," Sara said.

She shook her head when I said, "Have you seen him?"

"He's strange and never liked me, though he adores Johnnie."

"What about Alicin? Could she have taken the snake?"

"That girl isn't afraid of anything," Sara said. "She'd French kiss a copperhead if you dared her to."

Maisie returned to the table and whispered something in Sara's ear.

"Libby's back. Want me to take you to her?" Sara asked.

"Yes, but first tell me about her."

"She's young, probably in her twenties. Very pretty with blue eyes and blond hair. Just like Ms. DuPont likes."

"Maisie's hair is black," I said.

Sara grinned. "Ms. DuPont likes pretty girls. Her favorites are pretty girls with blond hair and blue eyes."

"Let me guess," I said. "Alicin has blond hair and blue eyes."

"Blond hair, yes. Blue eyes, no. Her eyes are brown."

"Are you saying Ms. DuPont likes Libby more than her daughter?"

"It's a point of contention with both Alicin and Libby. Those girls hate each other."

"How do you know?" I asked.

They can't even stand to be in the same room. They got into a catfight once, and the other girls and I had to pull them apart. Alicin ripped Libby's dress clean off of her. Libby has long nails and put a scratch on Alicin's face that took a while to heal."

"What did Ms. DuPont do?" I asked.

"She loved it."

"Because?"

"She knew they were fighting for her attention." Sara got out of her chair and motioned me to follow her. "I'll take you to meet Libby."

As Sara led me down one of the seemingly endless hallways, I was once again amazed at the magnitude of the house. Libby's office was in a corner, separated from the noise and clatter from the kitchen. Sara knocked on the door.

"Enter," a voice inside the office said.

A smiling young woman exited her chair and met me at the door with an extended hand.

"You must be Mr. Thomas," she said. "I'm Libby Tanner, Ms. DuPont's social secretary.

Libby Tanner was the picture of polished efficiency. Her blond hair was perfectly styled and framed a delicate face with sharp blue eyes that seemed to miss nothing.

Every aspect of her appearance was immaculate, from her tailored suit in muted tones to her understated yet elegant jewelry. She walked purposefully, her demeanor calm and composed, projecting a poised professionalism that contrasted starkly with the chaos outside her office.

"Pleased to meet you, Ms. Tanner. I promise my questions won't take much of your time."

The young woman motioned me to sit in a modern side chair in front of her desk.

"Would you like a cup of coffee or glass of tea, Mr. Thomas?"

"I'm fine," I said. "I just had lunch with Sara. Thanks, anyway."

An old-fashioned intercom sat on Libby's desk, and she pushed the buzzer.

"Maisie," she said. "Please bring me a cup of hot tea. And Maisie, bring an extra cup." She smiled and said, "In case you change your mind."

Libby's office, a serene oasis within the mansion, mirrored her orderly personality—natural light from large windows overlooking the meticulously kept gardens bathed the room. The walls were painted in neutral tones, and the furniture was sleek and modern yet comfortable.

Maisie smiled when she arrived with a steaming teapot and two antique porcelain cups on an elegant tray, winking at me as she poured Libby a cup of tea. As she did, I gazed around the neatly maintained office.

Libby's glass-topped desk sat in the center of the room, its surface free from clutter. A few carefully placed items—a polished silver pen set, a leather-bound planner, and a single orchid in full bloom—added personal touches without disturbing the room's minimalist aesthetic.

Libby shooed Maisie away without saying thank you. "Plenty of hot tea. Sure you won't have a cup?"

"Why not?" I said.

As she poured my tea, I continued gazing around the office. Bookshelves lined one wall with neat rows of books on etiquette, social customs, and high society. Framed photographs of Evelyn DuPont with various dignitaries and celebrities hung on the opposite wall, a testament to Libby's role in curating and maintaining Evelyn's public image.

A discreet filing cabinet, locked and organized with precision, held sensitive documents that Libby guarded with the same care she took in managing Evelyn's social calendar. Every office corner reflected her discipline and attention to detail.

"Now," Libby said. "What questions do you have for me?"

"Veronica Lasalle told me that you are Ms. DuPont's niece."

"Not her real niece," Libby said. "Growing up, our families were close."

"The Tanners?" I asked.

"Heavens no," she said. "I was married briefly and chose to keep my married name for business purposes."

"I see," I said.

Thinking Libby might be ashamed of her maiden name for some reason, I refrained from asking what it was. She told me anyway.

"My maiden name is Malveaux."

"I met Victor Malveaux yesterday. Are you related?"

Libby's answer caught me like a straight right to the chin.

"Victor is my older brother," she said. "I know; Victor is a little strange."

I decided to move on with my questioning.

"You are one of two people Ms. DuPont trusts with the combination to her rare book room. Do you have any ideas who could be responsible?"

"Am I a suspect?"

"No, ma'am. You aren't included on my list of possible suspects."

"It could have been almost anyone," she said.

"How is that?" I asked.

"Ms. DuPont and I are the only two people with keys to this office, though its sanctity has been violated on more than one occasion."

"How do you know?"

"Everything in my office has its place. I know when something was moved."

She nodded when I said, "I see how orderly you are. How long have you worked for Ms. DuPont?"

"Two years," she said. "Ms. DuPont hired me after I graduated from Sophie Newcomb with a degree in fine art."

Libby smiled when I said, "Ms. DuPont found a keeper. I have no more questions, and I'll let you return to your work."

I had one more person to question, so I exited Libby Tanner's office to find Jonathan Stallings. I didn't have far to look, as he was waiting outside the door.

"I need to interview Alicin, and then I'll get out of your hair," I said.

"I'm afraid that won't be possible," he said.

"Why not?"

"She'd had too much whiskey and passed out by the pool. She fell and hit her head."

"Oh, no," I said.

"Ms. DuPont took her to the emergency room."

"I hope she's okay," I said.

"It happens often. The nurses and doctors at the emergency room know Miss Alicin intimately."

"Then please, show me to the front door."

The sky was still overcast, the temperature cool, and the weather humid. I left DuPont Manor and headed back to St. Charles Avenue to catch the trolley back to Canal. Someone must have followed me because I collapsed when something heavy struck me in the back of the head. Stunned, though not entirely unconscious, I was vaguely aware of someone tying something around my neck.

When I regained my senses, I was behind a live oak tree, flat on my back. A cord was tied around my neck. The other end of the cord was tied around the neck of an angry snake writhing on my stomach, struggling to get loose.

Chapter 17

Mama Mulate owned a Creole cottage in an older New Orleans neighborhood. Unlike many of the neighbors, Mama's yard was immaculately trimmed with flowering plants and hanging ferns on the front porch. Tony had been there many times as he pulled into her tiny driveway.

"Want me to wait in the car for you?" he asked.

"Come inside. It'll take me a bit to pack, and I'll get you a refill on your scotch while you wait," Mama said.

Tony followed Mama down the manicured cobblestone pathway to her house. Her three cats were waiting at the door when they opened it and entered, one of them jumping into her arms.

"You remember Bushy, Cliffy, and Ninja."

"Great cats," Tony said.

"I know," Mama said. "You're not a cat person."

"I don't dislike cats," he said.

Mama put Bushy on the floor and headed for her kitchen, where she had several bottles of booze on a cabinet. Finding a glass, she filled it with scotch and handed it to Tony.

"It won't take me long to pack. Play with the cats and make another drink while you wait."

"Take your time," Tony said. "It's an all-day drive from here to Oxford and will be dark before we get there no matter what time we leave."

Tony opened the back door and went out to the porch. It felt like a tropical oasis, with hanging ferns, pot-flowering plants, and two comfortable rocking chairs overlooking her small backyard. The eight-foot fence gave her privacy from her neighbors and enclosed her lush sanctuary, complete with a garden, fountain, and cobblestone pathway. Tony relaxed in one of the rockers.

When Mama returned from her bedroom, Tony was still in the rocker working on his second scotch, one of the cats asleep in his lap.

"As soon as I feed and check the cat's water, I'm ready," she said.

Tony glanced at his watch and noticed it was already past noon.

"I called Lil. She has gumbo waiting on the stove for us," he said.

"Good idea," Mama said. "It'll save time if we don't have to stop on the way to Oxford and eat."

Tony grinned and said, "Neither my bladder nor my car's gas tank will last six hours, so we'll have to stop along the way no matter what."

"Let's take ice and bottles of scotch and vodka," Mama said.

"Road trip, here we come," Tony said.

Lil had gumbo waiting. After eating, they put Tony's suitcase in the trunk and headed toward Oxford. The weather was overcast and drizzly as they headed north on I-55 in Tony's red Mustang convertible. The top was up because of the weather, which was a good thing, making conversing easier.

The road stretched before them, a ribbon of highway leading north from New Orleans into the heart of Mississippi. Tony and Mama were drinking tall alcoholic beverages from plastic cups. When Tony finished one, Mama made him another.

"Nothing like tooling down the highway with a good buzz," Mama said.

"Unless the Mississippi Highway Patrol stops us."

"We're miles from nowhere, and not many cars on the road," Mama said. "We'll be okay."

"I wasn't only talking about our drinking and driving."

"Then what were you talking about?" Mama asked.

"This is Mississippi. You're a black woman; I'm a white man."

"This is the twenty-first century, Tony. People aren't as sensitive to such things as they were in the past," Mama said.

Mama laughed when Tony said, "I don't want to get lynched."

"They wouldn't lynch either of us. You're white, and I'm a woman."

"Just saying. We'll have to deal with being a mixed couple when we reach Oxford."

"Oxford is small though sophisticated. It's the home of Ole Miss and William Faulkner. Several influential authors live there, and it has become the literary hub of the south. No one will bat an eye."

"Then let's make sure we make it to Oxford," Tony said. "I can't get the last scene of *Easy Rider* out of my mind."

Mama laughed again. "Captain America and Billy were killed by a redneck in rural Louisiana, not Mississippi."

"Hope you're right," Tony said.

Their journey took them through the loess hills of western Mississippi, where the landscape undulated in gentle waves. Once deposited by ancient winds, the fertile soil gave rise to lush forests and rolling farmlands. The road curved and dipped, flanked by towering oaks draped in Spanish moss, their branches forming a leafy canopy over the highway. The occasional clapboard church or weathered barn appeared like ghosts of the past, reminders of the deep history etched into the land. A sign advertised several filling stations at the next exit.

"My red monster needs gas. Ready for a potty break?" Tony said.

"I thought you'd never ask," Mama said.

They spent the next twenty minutes in the superstation, perusing souvenir coasters and designer candy. Tony left the all-night truck stop with a full tank of gas, an empty bladder, and a hot link.

"Shame on you," Mama said. "Save your appetite for Oxford. It's the culinary capitol of northern Mississippi."

"Can't stop at a truck stop without eating some of their junk food," he said.

"I wouldn't know," Mama said.

"You seem to know lots about Oxford. Tell me about it," Tony said.

Cruising north in Tony's red convertible Mustang, the lush Southern landscape zipped by. Mama settled back in her seat, her mind already in Oxford, Mississippi.

"Oxford's a place with a lot of soul. It's a small town but steeped in history and literary significance. William Faulkner put it on the map, of course. He called it 'Jefferson' in his books, but it's Oxford through and through."

She nodded when he said, "Were most of his books set there?"

"Oxford is in Lafayette County. Faulkner lived there most of his life. Many of his books occurred in Yoknapatawpha County, Lafayette County's fictional name. Many of his characters were conceived from people he knew."

"Sorry I interrupted," Tony said.

"Oxford's town square is the heart of it all, with its courthouse in the center, surrounded by quaint shops, restaurants, and old buildings that have seen everything from Civil War skirmishes to modern-day football celebrations.

"You'll find a little bit of everything—antique stores, bookstores, cafés, and, of course, Square Books, one of the best independent bookstores in the country. That's a must-see for sure."

Tony nodded, taking it all in. "Hope they have plenty of bars."

"Lots of bars," she said. "Then there's Rowan Oak, Faulkner's home. His old Greek Revival house is nestled among trees, almost hidden from the world. Faulkner bought it in 1930 when it was falling apart. He spent years restoring it. You can walk through the rooms where he wrote and see his typewriter and books. It's like stepping into his mind for a moment. You can feel the presence of his stories in the very air."

Tony chuckled. "You really love this place, don't you, Mama?"

She grinned, nodding. "I do. It has a certain magic to it. And then there's the University of Mississippi, or Ole Miss as everyone calls it."

"The same football conference as L.S.U.," he said.

"Don't you boys ever grow up? Ole Miss is so much more than a football school. The campus is beautiful, with big oaks, magnolias, and a deep sense of tradition. Walking through it, you can almost hear the echoes of protests and civil rights

161

struggles. Faulkner once said it was the South's 'special burden,' and that history is still woven into every brick and blade of grass."

"All fine and good, but where will we stay?"

Mama paused, her eyes twinkling.

"As for hotels, you can't go wrong with The Graduate—right in the heart of town, near the square. It's got this quirky vibe that pays homage to Faulkner and Ole Miss. Or if you want something more historic, there's the Chancellor's House. It's elegant, with all the Southern charm you'd expect. You'll feel like you're stepping back in time with all the modern comforts."

"They both sound great, as long as they have a bar from where we can walk to our rooms. Whichever, it sounds like we're in for a treat."

"Oxford is special. A place where the past and present intertwine, where stories linger in the air like the scent of magnolias. I think you'll feel it also once we get there."

"Can't wait, though you need to pour me more scotch before this hot link destroys my gut."

"You're hopeless," Mama said as she poured him another scotch.

As they passed through small towns, life seemed to slow. In places like Crystal Springs and Hazlehurst, time felt suspended, Tony, imagining the quaint downtowns dotted by mom-and-pop shops and diners that looked like they'd been there for decades.

Further north, the road climbed into the higher ridges of the hills. The trees became denser, and the greenery more vibrant. Tony noticed the change in the air—cooler, crisper, with a hint of pine. Small towns like Senatobia and Sardis punctuated the drive, each with its own character, from faded murals on brick buildings to old service stations turned into antique shops.

The closer he got, the more the landscape began to flatten out, giving way to the rolling countryside surrounding the historic town. By the time they reached Oxford, the sun had started to set, casting long shadows across the university town.

The redbrick buildings of the University of Mississippi, with their columns and stately architecture, stood proudly against the evening sky. It was a town steeped in literary history. As Tony drove down Lamar Boulevard, he could almost feel the presence of William Faulkner himself, his spirit lingering in the humid Southern air.

They decided to make The Graduate Hotel their base of operations. As Mama had said, the person at the front desk didn't bat an eye when they checked in.

"Let's have a look at our rooms," Mama said. "I need a shower and a change of clothes. I'll meet you at the downstairs bar in an hour."

"You got it," Tony said.

His room was much more than he'd expected, and he had a fantastic view of the historical square. When he went downstairs, Mama was waiting on a barstool, looking fresh in a short skirt with mesh stockings and heels.

"You look great," Tony said. "I didn't know you were going to dress up."

"I bought this dress for Jake when we go to Tulsa. I decided to try it on you."

"You're a knock-out, and that dress shows off your killer legs. If you're trying to seduce me, forget it. I'm a happily married man."

"You're cute," Mama said. "Jake's my only man."

"Hey," Tony said. "When you have a set of wheels like yours, you don't want to keep them locked in the garage."

"Let's grab a bite at the restaurant and then have drinks at the Rooftop Bar. I hear it's the best view in town."

"You had me at hello," Tony said.

The cuisine at the hotel restaurant was excellent. Mama ate fresh Gulf snapper while Tony enjoyed a chicken-fried steak. Mama insisted they both try a piece of Key lime pie, and Tony didn't protest.

After dinner, they sat in the darkness of the Rooftop Bar. As Mama had said, the bar atop the old four-story building overlooked the square, the cool haze in the air making the scene feel almost psychedelic.

"This is so atmospheric; I wish Jake and Lil were here," Mama said.

"Me too," Tony said. "Lil and I recreated many old memories during our trip to Italy."

"I'll bet you did," Mama said.

"That was play; this is work," he said. "Where do we start?"

"Faulkner had a large house on thirty acres he called Rowan Oak. It isn't far from here and is now a museum. The book may be in the museum. If not, perhaps someone there can direct us. Let's hit it after breakfast tomorrow."

"I'm tired as hell," Tony said. "It's beautiful up here on the roof. Doesn't matter because I'll fall asleep if we don't leave soon."

"Me too," Mama said. "And I need to call Jake before I crash."

Mama motioned to their waiter and had him bring their tab. When they reached the elevators, she kissed Tony's forehead.

"What was that for?" he asked.

"For bringing me to Oxford. I've wanted to visit for years, and you made it possible."

Chapter 18

Tony was waiting when Mama met him downstairs at the café in the hotel. He had a frown on his face and a telephone book in his lap and was thumbing through it.

"You look frustrated," she said. "What's wrong?"

"There's not a single Faulkner in the phonebook," he said.

"Because he was born William Falkner and not Faulkner. The printer misspelled his name on the first book he wrote. He liked it, and that became his name."

"Glad you told me," Tony said. "Lots of Falkners. Thought for a minute I was losing my touch."

"Have you eaten already?" she asked.

"I waited on you," he said.

"Thank you. What are you having?"

"Continental Breakfast," Tony said.

Mama glanced at the menu and said, "That's enough food for two people."

"I'm hungry," he said.

"Go for it," Mama said. "I'm having a bowl of oatmeal."

Both Mama and Tony agreed that they liked strong black coffee. The waitress brought them an extra carafe before they finished breakfast. Tony cleared the tab, looking satisfied.

"Need to powder your nose before we go?" he asked.

"Do you?" Mama said.

"As a matter of fact."

Mama grinned. "I'll wait for you."

When Mama and Tony left the hotel, the weather was gorgeous, and Tony immediately lowered the top of his convertible. Rowan Oak wasn't far. The old modified Greek Revival house surrounded by trees was large, reminding Tony of a plantation home.

Rowan Oak stood tall and stately beneath the warm Mississippi sun, the scent of pine and oak leaves mingling in the air. As they stepped onto the porch of the two-story white house, Tony adjusted his sunglasses, the corners of his mouth lifting in appreciation.

"Feels like Faulkner's spirit might still be in the air here," he said, glancing at Mama, who nodded with a knowing smile. She adjusted the colorful shawl draped around her shoulders, eyes scanning the weathered shutters and old brick pathways.

An Ole Miss student named Amy greeted them at the door with all smiles and energy. "Welcome to Rowan Oak, y'all. I'll be your guide today. My name's Amy."

As Amy led them through the house, her voice took on a soft reverence. "This was Faulkner's home for more than thirty years. He wrote some of his greatest works here, right in this very office."

She paused by a large desk with Faulkner's old typewriter perched on top. Next to it, his pipe rested on a silver tray as though waiting for him to return.

Mama leaned over the desk. "Is it the same one he used to bang out *Sanctuary*?"

Amy smiled. "Yep. It's said he typed *Sanctuary* and *Light* in August on that one. He liked to write late into the night."

Mama, eyes gleaming with curiosity, traced a finger over the desk's wood. "And he and his wife had separate rooms?"

"That's right." Amy led them upstairs, her ponytail bouncing as she ascended. "Faulkner's study had a view of the thirty-acre forest out back. His wife Estelle had her room down the hall. Not uncommon back in the day, I guess."

Amy grinned when Mama said, "Whatever floats your boat."

They stood in Faulkner's second-story study, the light streaming in through tall windows that overlooked the lush greenery outside. Tony whistled.

"Not a bad spot for inspiration."

Mama's voice was soft, contemplative. "I imagine the trees whispered many stories to him."

Amy tilted her head, sensing their interest. "So, what brings y'all to Rowan Oak? Y'all writers, too?"

Mama smiled warmly. "In a way, yes. But we're also here on a different sort of search. We've heard of a... special copy of *Mosquitoes*. One that never made it to the publisher's final version."

Amy's brow furrowed as she shook her head. "I've heard rumors but never seen anything like that here. If it exists, it's long gone from Rowan Oak." She paused, a thoughtful expression crossing her face. "If anyone might know something, it'd be Blind Jim."

Tony raised an eyebrow. "Blind Jim?"

Amy nodded. "An old man, been around Oxford longer than anyone can remember. He used to parch peanuts and sell them on the Ole Miss campus. Some say he's as old as Faulkner's nephews, and he might've known Faulkner himself. Jim might have a clue if that book's still out there."

Mama's eyes sparked with interest. "And where might we find this Blind Jim?"

Amy smiled. "You'll likely find him on campus, near the Grove. He's usually there when the weather's nice, sitting on a bench, selling his peanuts and telling stories. If anyone knows Oxford's secrets, it's him."

Tony gave a nod of thanks. "Much obliged, Amy."

Mama Mulate looked out the study window once more, her gaze distant. "Seems we have a new trail to follow."

"Good, because the book's not here," Tony said.

Tony didn't speak as he drove away from Rowan Oak.

"You think this is a wild goose chase, right?" Mama asked.

"Don't know. Seems a longshot some old blind man knows where the book is. What do you think?" he said.

"I believe in destiny. If we're destined to find Faulkner's book, we will."

"Doesn't matter if he knows where the book is. You want to meet Blind Jim," Tony said. "I've known you long enough to see how you think."

"Get out of here," she said. "If you think this is a waste of time, we can take another path."

"No way. Homicide detectives have an extra sense. My extra sense tells me to listen carefully to everything you say."

Mama reached across the console and patted Tony's arm.

"That might be the nicest thing anyone has ever said about me," she said.

The Grove at Ole Miss was a peaceful expanse of green, dappled in soft sunlight filtering through the canopy of towering oaks. Spring had settled over the campus, bringing a cool breeze and the faint scent of blooming dogwoods. The expansive lawns stretched out in all directions, though the usual hustle and bustle of students was absent. In the quiet of April, only a few were scattered across the benches, and their faces turned to books or the distant horizon.

Tony parked the Mustang under the shade of a sprawling magnolia, its thick branches spreading low over the sidewalk.

"Nice place to be a student," he said. "If I'd had this place to study, I might not have flunked out my first semester."

"You're hopeless," Mama said with a chuckle.

She joined him, adjusting her African shawl as they entered the Grove. Not far from the iconic open green, they spotted two elderly men seated on a weathered wooden bench, sharing a small paper bag of parched peanuts. One of them was blind, and quite obviously, it was Blind Jim.

Blind Jim, dark-skinned with a toothy grin, tilted his head as they approached as if sensing their presence long before they arrived. Next to him, an old white man with a thin frame and sun-spotted hands chuckled at something only the two seemed to know.

Tony and Mama exchanged a look before approaching.

"Afternoon," Tony said, his New Orleans accent blending into the Southern warmth of the campus. "I'm Tony, and this beautiful woman with me is Mama Mulate. Are you Blind Jim?"

The old black man straightened, his smile widening. "Afternoon, folks. People call me Blind Jim, and this is my friend, Deacon Winter. What brings y'all to this neck of the woods on such a fine day?"

Mama Mulate stepped forward, her voice rich with a quiet energy. "We're here looking for some answers, and we were told you might be the ones to help."

"You're a voodoo woman," Blind Jim said. "I feel your power."

"Yes, and I'm also an English professor. Our tour guide at Rowan Wood informed us you knew William Faulkner when you were younger."

"Me and everyone else in town," he said.

Mama smiled. "I'm betting not many of those people are still alive."

"That's a fact," Blind Jim said. "Deacon was. Maybe he can answer your questions."

Deacon's brown eyes twinkled beneath the brim of his worn hat. "Answers, you say? Well, now, that depends on the question."

"What are you doing here?" Mama asked.

Deacon smiled and said, "My outgo exceeded my income, so my upkeep is my downfall."

Mama said, "You sound supernatural. Are you sure you aren't a ghost?"

"Angels are more like it," Blind Jim said. "Do you believe in angels?"

"Of course we do, and what a place to look. Oxford is absolutely hallucinatory," she said.

"Beautiful, all right," Deacon Winter said with a grin. "Soil's so poor, it takes seven acres to rust a nail."

Mama laughed. "I love your sayings," she said.

"Ol' Deacon has a saying for just about everything," Blind Jim said.

171

"Love them," Mama said. "They should be in a book."

"That's why you're here," Blind Jim said. "You're looking for something."

A book," Mama explained, her eyes sharp as she studied their faces. "A missing copy of *Mosquitoes*. Word is, y'all might know what happened to it."

Blind Jim and Deacon Winter exchanged a glance, the kind that passed whole stories without a word. Deacon gave a soft chuckle and tossed a peanut shell to the ground. "Book, huh? You ain't the first to come askin' about that."

"No one knows about it," Mama said. "Seems it was a secret."

Blind Jim nodded slowly, the smile never leaving his face. "Faulkner, he had all kinds of secrets. That book, well, it's one of them. But you see, books don't just disappear into thin air around these parts."

Tony crossed his arms, leaning against a nearby tree. "So where did it go?"

Deacon Winter emitted a soft whistle and shifted on the bench, leaning toward them.

"There's a place," he said, his voice low and slow, "on the edge of town—a cemetery where Confederate and Union soldiers are buried side by side. Folks around here know it well. Not many go after dark. Some say it's haunted. I know it ain't a place you want to visit alone."

"What's the name of the cemetery?" Mama asked.

"Used to be called Whispering Oaks," Blind Jim said. "Now, people that have gone there call it the abandoned cemetery."

"Sounds creepy," Mama said.

Blind Jim nodded. "It's eerie and quiet, with ancient oak trees swaying in the wind and their branches murmuring the stories of those long departed."

Been abandoned for decades," Deacon said. "Grown up because no one tends the graves anymore."

"What is it we're looking for there?" Mama asked.

Blind Jim's sightless eyes seemed to brighten at the mention. "A gravestone y'all need to see. Old, cracked, and nearly forgotten. But the story it holds... might lead you to that book you're after."

Mama's brow furrowed as she listened. "What does a gravestone have to do with Faulkner's missing manuscript?"

"Old William's life was filled with ghosts and insecurities of his past," Blind Jim said.

Deacon Winter popped another peanut in his mouth, chewing thoughtfully.

"Faulkner wasn't the only one with stories around here. And some stories are written in stone. Might take some looking, though when you find it, you'll have the answer to your question."

"Can't you tell us which gravestone to look for?" Mama asked.

Blind Jim shook his head. "Faulkner knew that place well. Might've even written a few lines about it. But the truth? It's buried deep, like all secrets worth keepin', and the truth is in your minds."

Tony cast a glance at Mama, his curiosity piqued. "Guess we'll have to pay this cemetery a visit."

Mama Mulate smiled softly, the mystery swirling around them like the Mississippi wind. "Seems we will. Thank you both."

Deacon Winter waved them off with a wrinkled hand. "Good luck to y'all. Just remember... You must go after midnight to see the veils of secrecy stripped off the answers you seek."

Tony had more questions. Mama grabbed his hand and tugged him toward the car.

"They aren't telling us all they know," he said.

"Turn and look," Mama said.

When Tony turned, Blind Jim and Deacon Winter were gone, a wispy cloud floating over the bench with peanut hulls on the ground beneath it.

"Where'd they go?" Tony asked.

"Nowhere," Mama said. "They were never here. What we saw were apparitions."

Tony started walking back to the bench and said, "Impossible. I saw them."

"This town is filled with spirits of the past, and we just saw two of them. They told us where to go and what to look for," Mama said.

"Then what do we do until dark?" Tony asked.

"Get some dinner, and then find a friendly bar and see how many drinks we can knock down between now and midnight," Mama said.

Chapter 19

The sun hung lazily over the horizon, casting a golden light over Oxford's rolling hills. Mama leaned back in her chair, sipping her martini with regal ease. The Graduate Hotel's rooftop bar was bustling with a low hum of laughter and conversation, but the noise faded into the background.

Below them, the town shimmered in the late spring light, its streets winding through a sea of blooming trees. Tony swirled his scotch, his eyes fixed on the distant line where the sky met the horizon.

"I'm telling you, Mama, this is nuts," he said, shaking his head. "Ghosts don't give directions. And why would they be interested in Faulkner's book even if they did? Doesn't make any sense."

Mama Mulate smiled, that knowing smile she always had when Tony got riled up.

"You should know by now that sense has nothing to do with our world. Blind Jim and Deacon Winter are as real as you and me. They live in a different plane of reality, is all."

"Their 'plane' doesn't pay the bills," Tony said.

Taking a long sip of his drink. He watched the ice cubes clink together, feeling the smooth burn of the whiskey down his throat.

"Quit grumbling and enjoy the marvelous view," Mama said.

"Whispering Oaks sounds like something out of a bad horror movie," he said.

Mama set her glass down gently, her dark eyes meeting Tony's.

"It's an old place, older than Oxford itself. Lots of pain, lots of history buried in that soil. Union, Confederate, and all the people caught in between. But the spirits? They know things, Tony. Things that are unwritten in books or told in stories. You can learn a lot if you listen."

Tony leaned back, crossing his arms. "Maybe. I'll believe it when I see it."

The breeze picked up, carrying with it the faint smell of honeysuckle. Shadows stretched longer now, creeping over the rooftops and turning the vibrant greens of the landscape into a dusky gold. The day's warmth was starting to give way to the coolness of evening. Tony eyed his watch, then glanced at the horizon again.

"Still too early," Mama said. "Let's have another drink."

Tony motioned to their waiter and said, "Good idea. Dinner's starting to wear off. I'm going to order snacks."

"Go for it," Mama said. "Matter of fact, I could eat a dozen raw oysters."

"Me too, now that you mention it. You really think we're going to find anything out there?"

Mama chuckled, lifting her glass in a slow toast. "If Blind Jim says the answer is on a headstone, it is. Trust the spirits, Tony. They never lie."

"Lord help us!" he said.

Tony rubbed his temple, feeling the familiar ache of skepticism battling against the strange world he'd been pulled into ever since meeting Wyatt Thomas and Mama Mulate. He drained the last of his scotch and set the glass down with a dull thud.

"I can go alone," Mama said.

"Ain't happening, Mama. I'll trust them—for now. But if I see one zombie, I'm out."

Mama laughed, her melodic voice rising above the gentle clatter of the bar. "It's not the zombies you have to worry about. It's yourself."

Darkness cloaked the mysterious old town of Oxford, and midnight finally arrived. As Mama and Tony left the hotel and headed toward the edge of town, few businesses remained open. The farther from town they went, the darker it got.

"We're in the middle of nowhere as it is. How are we supposed to find this place?" Tony asked.

"Quit carping. You're going in the right direction," Mama said.

"How can you tell?"

"I feel the haunted spirits who live there," she said. "They're calling to me."

Tony shook his head, not knowing if she was serious or pulling his leg. Either way, he continued driving until she told him to stop.

Off the main blacktop, an old wagon path twisted through dense trees, their gnarled branches reaching overhead like skeletal fingers. The night sky stretched wide and deep above them, stars twinkling in a sea of darkness. A full moon bathed the land in an ethereal silver light, casting ghostly shadows as Tony guided the car over the bumpy road. Finally, the cemetery emerged from the woods—abandoned, overgrown, forgotten.

"Park the car," Mama said. "This is it."

"You sure?" Tony asked. "Looks like more of the same to me."

"We're here," she said. "I can see reflections off of the headstones."

Tony followed Mama out of the car and through a wrought iron arch almost rusted away. Whispering Oaks spread before them like a dark dream, the gravestones tilting, half-sunk into the earth, tangled in weeds and overgrown grass that reached Tony's knees.

The ancient oaks surrounding the cemetery swayed gently in the night breeze, their moss-laden branches whispering secrets into the darkness. No light from Oxford could be seen; they were alone now, bathed only in moonlight as the soft sound of a mournful dirge floated through the air. His heart quickened, and he froze.

"You hear that, Mama?" he whispered, straining to see through the shadows.

Mama Mulate stepped beside him, her flowing skirt brushing against the grass. Her eyes gleamed in the moonlight, excited, alive.

"I hear it. The spirits are with us tonight and are singing for those long lost."

Tony swallowed, his gaze shifting nervously to the high grass.

"Screw the spirits. I'm more worried about stepping on a rattlesnake. This place looks like it ain't seen a lawnmower in decades."

Mama chuckled softly. "You worry too much, Tony. The snakes nor the ghosts will bother you. It's the living you should fear, not wildlife or the dead."

Tony wasn't listening, his eyes locked on something moving in the distance. As they ventured deeper into the cemetery, the source of the dirge became clear. There, under the heavy branches of an ancient oak, sat a group of ghostly figures—men, both Confederate and Union soldiers, spectral and pale, their uniforms tattered and stained with the dirt of battle.

They sat on fallen logs gathered around a flickering fire that cast no light, only shadows. The fire burned with a strange glow—blue, like the cold flame of a distant star.

The soldiers' faces were worn with the weight of centuries, their eyes hollow, fixed on some distant memory. Their voices were low and mournful as they sang, the sound of men who had seen too much and had been left behind by time. The dirge rose and fell in the night air:

Through fields of gray, we marched away,
Our souls adrift, our bones to clay.
No victory won, no glory found,
We sleep beneath this hallowed ground.
The drums are still, the battle's done,
But still, we wait, where light's undone.
In whispered winds, our names are lost,
We paid the price, but what the cost?

Tony's heart pounded. "What the hell is that?" he whispered, stepping back. "Mama, those... those are ghosts."

Mama's eyes gleamed with a reverent joy. "Yes, and they've been waiting long to tell their story."

"Waiting for what? For us to join them?"

Tony shifted his gaze between the soldiers and the gravestones. The air felt heavy with unseen eyes.

"No," Mama said, her voice steady, calm. "They're waiting for us to find the truth. We're close now, Tony."

Tony shook his head, the hairs on the back of his neck standing on end.

"You can't be serious. You want me to start reading gravestones while a bunch of dead soldiers sing backup? We didn't even bring a flashlight."

Mama smiled, unfazed by the ghostly figures. "The dead have much to say if you're willing to listen."

Tony took a cautious step forward, the weight of the situation sinking in.

"I'm not in the mood for a conversation. Let's find this headstone and get the hell out of here."

As they waded through the grass, the ghostly soldiers continued their lament, their words a haunting echo in the night. The moonlight revealed the gravestones in patches, their names and dates barely visible beneath layers of dirt and time. Mama moved purposefully, her hands brushing the stones as if sensing something beyond the physical world.

Finally, they reached a weathered headstone, its surface cracked, nearly illegible. Mama knelt before it, her fingers tracing the faded inscription.

"Here," she whispered. "This is the one."

Tony's breath caught in his throat as he glanced over his shoulder. The soldiers by the fire seemed to watch them now, their dirge fading to a low hum like the distant roll of thunder. He wanted to run, to get as far away from this haunted place as possible. Mama's steady hand on the gravestone held him there.

"How do you know?" he asked, his voice barely above a whisper.

Mama looked up, her eyes bright in the moonlight.

"It's so obvious. I can't believe I hadn't thought of it already."

"Mind explaining it to me?"

"One of Faulkner's benefactors offered him a beachfront cottage in Pascagoula, Mississippi, as a writer's getaway. He spent the summer there writing *Mosquitoes* and started on *The Wild Palms*."

"And?"

"While living in Pascagoula, he fell in love with a woman named Helen Baird and dedicated both *Mosquitoes* and *Wild Palms* to her. Literary scholars think *Wild Palms* was modeled after her."

"Faulkner never married her, did he?" Tony asked.

"Their lives were too different. She was a southern aristocrat. He was little more than a mostly unknown Bohemian," Mama said. "When she married someone else, Faulkner gave her a handwritten book of love poems. They would be worth a fortune now."

"So, you think he gave her his copy of *Mosquitoes*?" Tony asked.

"Faulkner supposedly ran into her in 1955 while strolling on the beach. No one knows what they chatted about. I think I know,"

"What?"

"He sought her out, intending to give her one of the books he'd dedicated to her. The same one we're looking for."

"A woman named Helen Baird has the book?"

Mama shook her head. "Helen is long dead. One of her heirs has the book. We need to drive to Pascagoula and see if we can locate it."

"Tomorrow?"

"It's already after midnight, and Pascagoula is more than five hours away. Let's check out of the hotel and head that way. We'll be there when the sun comes up."

"It's been a while since I drove all night," he said.

"I'll help you drive if you get tired."

When they left Whispering Oaks, the fire was still burning, and the ghost soldiers still singing.

As they exited the wagon path, Tony glanced in his rearview mirror. The cemetery was gone.

"You sure we saw what we saw?" he asked.

"Never doubt it," Mama said.

They reached the Graduate, packed their clothes, returned to the empty lobby, and checked out. It was almost two before they got on the road. Mama was already mixing them drinks.

"One thing bothers me," Tony said.

"Only one?" Mama asked.

"One of many. If Helen Baird lived in Pascagoula, why is she buried in Oxford?"

"She isn't," Mama said. "Her headstone said she was born and died in Pascagoula."

"Then how. . .?"

"The grave was and still is in Pascagoula. What we saw was a spectral mirage."

"Mirages are real," he said. "Their appearance is random. What we saw was meant for us to see."

"You're right about that. The universe runs like a well-oiled machine, and everything happens for a purpose. Accept it, and don't stress your pretty little head trying to explain things."

"Thanks," he said.

"They'd driven for two hours, seeing only big trucks and no cars on the road.

"What now?" Tony asked.

More humidity and puffy clouds covered the moon as they approached the Gulf of Mexico. Lost in thought, Mama took a moment to answer.

"Pull into the next truck stop. Your car probably needs gas, and I need a potty break. You must be tired, and I'll drive the rest of the way."

Chapter 20

There can't be anything much more traumatic than opening your eyes and seeing a squirming reptile attached to your neck by a 1piece of twine. I did my best not to panic.

I was eyeball to eyeball with the snake. Luckily, my training as a boy scout kicked in, and I recognized the squirming reptile as a non-poisonous king snake. The snake wriggled like a worm on a hook when I reached for his head, hoping I didn't grab his tail.

I somehow managed to extricate the struggling snake from the noose and released it on the grass beside me. I lay in the damp grass for a long minute as it slithered away, and my racing heart began returning to normal. When it did, I headed toward St. Charles Avenue with caution.

My head ached as I rode the rumbling streetcar toward Canal. I was still wincing when I entered Bertram's and strode to the bar.

When Bertram saw me, he said, "What happened to you."

"Someone nailed me," I said.

"I can see the knot from here," he said. Bertram quickly prepared a bag of ice and handed it to me. "Put this on it. It'll bring down the swelling pdq,"

The throbbing lessened the moment I applied the ice bag to it. Bertram handed me a glass of lemonade and two aspirins.

"Take these," he said. "They'll help."

Darkness had fallen on the French Quarter, tourists and locals pouring into Bertram's following the shutdown for the night of the French Quarter Fest. Tommy and Marlon were two new customers. They saw me sitting at the bar and pulled up stools beside me.

"What the hell happened to you?" Tommy asked.

"Something that might have relevance to your murder investigation," I said.

"Tell us," he said.

"I was at Evelyn DuPont's house in the Garden District. When I finished and was walking back to St. Charles, someone hit me in the head, knocking me unconscious."

"Good thing he has a hard head," Bertram said. "What are you boys drinking?"

"Abita for me," Tommy said. "Marlon's like Wyatt and he don't drink."

"Cowboy likes lemonade. I got a fresh pitcher made," Bertram said.

"Love lemonade," Marlon said.

Still stinging from Bertram's comment, I said, "When I came to, behind an oak tree, I was flat on my back, with a noose around my neck and the other end of the cord around a snake's head."

"You're kidding me," Tommy said. "Wasn't a king cobra, was it?"

"King snake," I said. "Good thing, or I'd be pushing up daisies now like Toby Coleman-Labissiere."

"Who'd you talk to?"

"Four people: Jonathan Stallings, the butler; Sara Sloan, the Chief Maid; a server named Maisie; and Libby Tanner, Ms. DuPont's social secretary."

"Tell us about Jonathan Stallings," Marlon said.

"Big man, maybe in his sixties. He takes care of Ms. DuPont's son's snake collection. He showed it to me and physically handled a black mamba named Kobe."

"Call downtown and have someone pick him up and bring him to the station for questioning," Tommy said.

"Wait," I said. "Stallings isn't the only suspect."

"One of the women?" Tommy said.

"Libby Tanner is Ms. DuPont's social secretary. Her brother is a man named Victor Malveaux. It's possible she called him after I interviewed her."

"Why would she do that?" Tommy asked.

"Ms. Tanner is one of only two people with the combination to Ms. DuPont's rare book room. She could have let her brother into the room to steal the book."

Marlon asked, "How does he tie in with the murder and rare books?"

Maya and I met him and his boyfriend, Samuel Penrose, yesterday at The Office. Penrose is a rare book collector and dealer, and he and Malveaux knew Coleman-Labissiere. They also knew the victim was killed by a snake even though the police haven't released the cause of death yet."

I nodded when Tommy said, "Ms. Tanner could have gotten spooked when you quizzed her about the missing book."

"How does Stallings fit into the scenario?" Marlon asked.

"When I interviewed him today, he told me Rodney DuPont has never owned a king cobra. Sara Sloan informed me that Rodney owned a king cobra named King Tut. It's missing, and Stallings is heartbroken because he loved the snake."

"Who killed Coleman-Labissiere, Malveaux or Stallings?" Tommy asked.

"This morning, I thought I had the answers. Now, I'm not so sure," I said.

"We should pick up both of them for questioning," Tommy said. "One of them tried to kill you."

"If they'd wanted to kill me, they would have tied a poisonous snake to my neck. They didn't because they were only trying to scare me. There's more to Coleman-Labissiere's murder than meets the eye."

"We're homicide detectives," Tommy said. "Our job is to find the murderer and put them behind bars."

"The person who stole Evelyn DuPont's book is also responsible for the murder of Toby Coleman-Labissiere. Give me two more days before you question anyone, and I'll deliver your murderer to you on a silver platter."

"Not going to happen," Tommy said.

Maya entered the bar and overheard the conversation. She stood on her tiptoes and kissed Tommy.

"Give Wyatt and me two more days," she said. "It's important to me, and we won't disappoint you."

"Well. . ."

"Please," Maya said.

"Where's Tony?" Tommy asked.

"Mississippi," I said.

"What the hell's he doing in Mississippi?" Tommy asked.

"Tying up loose ends," I said.

"Okay, Cowboy. Two days. Hope the hell you know what you're doing. We're going to Carlucci's, Miss Maya. Want to come along?"

"You bet I do if you'll give me a ride back to Bertram's," she said.

"You got it, pretty lady," Tommy said.

When Tommy reached for his wallet, Bertram said, "As always, drinks are on the house for you boys."

Tommy killed his Abita, smiled, and said, "Thanks, Bertram."

"Great lemonade," Marlon said. "Thanks."

"You boys come back anytime when you're out slumming," Bertram said as they headed for the door.

"Thank you, Maya," I said.

When they were gone, Bertram said, "If you know who the killer is, why didn't you just let them arrest him?"

"They're homicide detectives working for the city of New Orleans. I'm a private investigator working for Evelyn DuPont. We have similar goals, though they aren't the same."

Bertram left to wait on a customer when my cell phone rang. It was Evelyn DuPont. It was well after dark, and she was slurring her words.

"Wyatt, where are you?"

"Bertram's," I said.

"I thought you were here. I've been looking for you."

"I questioned Jonathan, Libby, and Sara. You weren't around, so I left and returned to Bertram's."

"I have something important to tell you," she said.

"Tell me."

"In person so that we can talk face-to-face," she said.

"It's pouring down rain outside. Can't it wait until tomorrow?"

"I'm not taking no for an answer. My chauffeur is on his way there. He'll honk when he pulls up outside."

Evelyn hung up the phone before I could answer her.

Bertram had returned to the bar and asked, "Who was that?"

"Evelyn DuPont. She wants me to see me."

"You ain't going, are you?"

"She's sending her chauffeur," I said. "Will you feed my cat?"

"You planning to stay awhile?"

"I probably won't leave until the rain stops, and it sounds like an all-nighter."

"I'll feed her, though it don't sound like a good idea for you to go out in the middle of a storm."

"You my mother now?"

"Just saying," he said.

"I'm a big boy," I said. "I can take care of myself."

"Tell that to the knot on your head," he said.

"Your icebag and aspirins are working," I said. "Thanks. I'll be back when I get back."

I hurried outside when Evelyn's chauffeur honked the horn outside on the street. The spring storm had stalled over the French Quarter, water pooling in the streets and blowing in sheets as I climbed into the backseat.

Evelyn's chauffeur was the antithesis of Bradley, small and feral. He drove away without asking me where I wanted to go. It was raining even harder when he pulled the sleek limousine into the Garden District drive. He held an umbrella for me as we hurried to the porch and into the house.

"Ms. DuPont's bedroom is at the top of the stairs."

188

The little chauffeur disappeared into the darkness. I assumed he knew where Evelyn's bedroom was because he'd performed the same function many times. Before I could start up the stairs, someone spoke behind me. I must have jumped because they laughed.

"Scare you?" a woman asked.

I turned to see a voluptuous young woman dressed in little more than a revealing slip. She was grinning like a Cheshire cat.

I didn't have to ask if she was Alicin because I could see the family resemblance. Like Ronnie Lasalle had said, she was a knockout, even more attractive than her supermodel mom.

I smiled and said, "I'm not easily frightened."

"Who are you?" she asked.

She grinned when I said, "Wyatt Thomas. I work for your mom."

"Mom and Ronnie are passed out drunk upstairs." She took my hand and said, "I'm Alicin. Come with me. I'll take care of you."

Alicin led me down the hall to her room. She was a striking woman, even in her state of disarray. Her long, blond hair, unkempt and falling in loose waves, contrasted with her bronzed skin— a testament to countless hours spent lounging by the pool.

She had the kind of beauty that drew attention, with a curvy figure and expressive brown eyes that would be captivating if they weren't glazed over from alcohol.

According to Jonathan, when she bothered with it, her wardrobe consisted of designer bikinis, sheer robes, and occasionally a slip or dress that clung to her figure. More often than not, he said, she didn't care much about modesty, letting the world see her as she was—drunk and indifferent.

The door to her bedroom was ajar, and I followed her inside.

The room was dim, lit by only a single candle and the lightning flashing through the undraped French door. She didn't bother turning on the lights as she kicked a loose shoe under the bed.

Alicin's room was a chaotic reflection of her lifestyle, with expensive clothes strewn carelessly, half-empty whiskey bottles on every surface, and the lingering scent of perfume and alcohol mixing in the air. Outside, the patio and pool area were her domain—where she reigned with reckless abandon, indulging in sunbathing, drinking, and fleeting encounters with those she found amusing.

"What happened to your head?" she asked.

"Long story," I said.

She opened a small bottle and said, "I have something to help. Put two of these under your tongue."

"What are they?" I asked.

"Arnica. It reduces swelling and bruising. You'll be a new man shortly."

I'd heard of arnica and put the two tablets under my tongue. She was right, as my head felt instantly better.

A beautiful pool was right out the French doors from Alicin's room. As I watched, she let her garment slip to the floor. She was naked, and even in the dim light of a single candle and the lightning show outside, I found it hard to take my eyes off of her.

She didn't seem to mind and said, "See something you like?"

"I think you already know the answer to that question."

"Let's go swimming," she said.

"You crazy? There's a lightning storm outside. We'd be electrocuted."

"No, we won't," she said. "Come on."

Alicin's naked body, backdropped by the lightning storm, electrified my soul. She grinned and began stripping off my clothes. I just kept seeing her mother's full-frontal poster in my brain, and I was powerless to resist. After clasping my hand, she pulled me toward the door.

Against my better judgment, I followed her into the pool, heavy rain pounding our heads as we embraced in shallow water. Lightning struck nearby. It didn't matter because another part of my body other than my brain was calling the shots.

Chapter 21

I fell asleep sometime during the night and awoke alone, the wet bed a testament to my skinny dipping during a lightning storm. To make matters worse, my head was pounding like a church bell.

The pain didn't mask the smell of Alicin's warm body or perfume lingering on the damp sheets, nor did it make me forget the carnal pleasures we had shared. The bed was comfortable, and the sheets were soft as I blinked against the morning light streaming through the tall windows.

The scent of rain lingered though the storm had passed. The sound of a door creaking open drew my attention. Alicin entered, her blond hair neatly tied back, and she wore a modest sundress that clashed with the memory of the reckless woman from the night before. A little dog pranced at her heels, his fluffy white fur spotless despite their walk.

"You have a dog," I said. "What's his name?"

"Bijou. It's French for Jewel. He's my heart and soul."

"Where have you two been?" I asked.

Alicin glanced at me, the past night's haze of drunkenness and mania replaced by an eerie clarity.

"Bijou loves our walks. The group, you know, they meet every morning and afternoon. It's a routine."

"Group?" I said.

She bent down to unclip the dog's leash, her fingers tender as they brushed the fur on his tiny head.

"He loves it," she said softly. "We walk, we talk about our dogs. It's... normal."

I sat up, watching her. "The group?"

"Mmm-hmm," Alicin said. "Just some Garden District neighbors. People like me, with nothing else to do but fawn over our dogs. Funny. How something so small can make people feel grounded."

Bijou hopped onto the bed, nestling into my lap. Alicin smiled a genuine smile that nearly threw me off balance.

"You're different this morning," I said.

She shrugged, her eyes trailing to the window. "Sometimes the world feels less crazy. Like today. I can focus when it's just me and Bijou. He keeps me sane, even when I'm not."

For a brief moment, I saw the woman Alicin might have been before the booze, the pills, the madness. Then, just as quickly, her expression shifted back into something more familiar— distant, unfocused.

I got out of bed, found my clothes, and put them on. I was pulling on my shoes when Alicin began her rant.

She began pacing the room, her bare feet padding across the hardwood floor, agitation bubbling beneath the surface. She lit a cigarette, took a deep drag, and exhaled with a shake of her head as if trying to dispel an invisible cloud of frustration.

"They're poisoning us, Wyatt," she said, her voice trembling with conviction. "All those vaccines, all that crap they push on us—they're not for our health. They're for control."

I watched silently, fully aware that this conversation was teetering on the edge of something darker. Bijou sat perched on the bed beside me, blissfully unaware of his owner's brewing storm.

Alicin's eyes glinted, wild and feverish. "Do you know what's in those shots? Mercury, formaldehyde, God knows what else. They pump that filth into babies, Wyatt! Babies! And people just let them. They don't ask questions. They roll up their sleeves like sheep. Did you take the COVID-19 shot?"

"I meant to but never got around to it," I said.

"Good for you. We have to protest against the group trying to enslave us. Do you watch the videos on YouTube?"

"I never have," I said.

"I'll send some to your phone. You won't believe what they're doing to us," she said.

"Okay," I said.

She tossed the cigarette into an ashtray, pacing more vigorously now. "It's a conspiracy. They want to keep us sick and make us dependent on their drugs and their hospitals. The pharmaceutical companies are in bed with the government, with the media, all of them playing us like fools."

"Alicin, you really believe that?"

She spun around to face me, her expression a mixture of defiance and anger.

"Of course, I believe it! Why do you think I've never let a needle touch me? Why do you think I stick to natural remedies—plants, oils, things from the earth? Everything we need is already here, Wyatt, but they don't want us to know that. They want us hooked on their pills, sick and dependent, living in fear of the next manufactured pandemic."

She sat on the edge of the bed, her manic energy simmering into something more focused. "You think I'm crazy, don't you?" Her brown eyes bore into me, unblinking.

I realized I needed to choose my words carefully and said, "I think you're passionate, Alicin."

She snorted, shaking her head. "You'll see. One day, the truth will come out, and everyone will realize they've been living a lie. But not me. I've seen through their games for years, and I'll never let them put one of those damn needles in me or Bijou. They're not touching us."

I glanced at the little dog, who yawned, oblivious to the weight of his owner's convictions. Alicin lit another cigarette, marched into the bathroom, and slammed the door behind her. I wanted to leave. Walk back to St. Charles and take the streetcar to Canal. I waited because I had questions to ask.

I was shocked when Alicin emerged from the bathroom in panties, black lace stockings, and nothing else. She was unpredictable and provocative, and the stockings evoked her sensuality and mystery and emphasized her boldness and disregard for convention.

It deepened my unease as her erratic behavior contrasted sharply with moments of vulnerability or coherence. I honestly was unsure of what to expect next.

"Tell me about your brother," I said.

"What about him?" she asked.

"I visited his room with Jonathan, and I sense that I know him, though I'd like to hear your take."

Alicin stared at the ceiling fan, her fingers absently tracing patterns on the sheets. The air felt thick, charged with something unspoken. I sat up, watching her, sensing the shift in her mood. She suddenly laughed—a hollow, sharp sound that made me uneasy.

"You want to know about Rodney, don't you? Everyone does," she said, her voice lilting and unsteady. "He's always been... different."

I attempted to keep my voice calm and gentle. "Tell me about him. I need to understand."

Alicin turned her head, her brown eyes wide and shimmering like a dam ready to break. "Understand? You can't. No one can. Not about Rodney. Not about us." She smiled, but it didn't reach her eyes. "He was always mine, you know? Since we were little. Mom tried to keep us apart, but we were twins, Wyatt. Twins share everything... even the things they shouldn't."

Though my breath caught in my chest, I remained silent, letting her speak.

"You think it's sick, don't you?" Her voice was harsher now, more frantic. "But Rodney and I, we knew. We knew what we were—what we came from. Mom tried to keep it buried, but we felt it in our bones. We were never normal. We weren't supposed to be." She laughed again, that unsettling sound. "Mom and Grandfather... they did this to us. We were their dirty little secret. Just like everything in this house."

I was having a hard time keeping my voice steady. "Alicin, what do you mean? What did they do to you?"

Her laughter stopped abruptly, her gaze locking onto mine with an eerie intensity.

"You really don't get it, do you? They were lovers, Wyatt. Our mother and our grandfather. That's why Rodney and I... that's why we..."

Her voice broke, and for a moment, she seemed fragile, teetering on the edge of madness. My stomach twisted as the gravity of her words sank in, and I felt the weight of her twisted legacy pressing down on me.

"Rodney... Rodney couldn't handle it," Alicin whispered, her voice barely audible now. "He was always the weaker one. He tried to escape it, though he never could. That's when he found them."

"Who, Alicin? Who did he find?"

Her eyes glinted with a wild light. "The Order, Wyatt. The Ordre du Sang. Penrose and his friends. They promised Rodney salvation, promised they could free him from all this... from us. But they didn't save him. They broke him. They made him do things... awful things." She shuddered, wrapping her arms around herself as if to ward off a chill. "I saw it. I saw what they did to him, and I couldn't stop it. I... I couldn't save him."

Wyatt leaned closer, his heart racing. "Alicin, what did they do to him?"

"They took him," she whispered, her voice trembling with fear and anger. "They took him and made him one of them. He's not my brother anymore. He's... something else now. And Penrose... Penrose is using him, Wyatt. He's controlling Rodney, just like they tried to control me."

Her face twisted in pain, her expression caught between fury and despair. "You have no idea how deep this goes. If you don't stop them, they'll take everything. And you'll lose yourself, just like Rodney did."

"What do you mean?" I asked.

"I mean, they're coming for you. Beware, Wyatt! Beware!"

Alicin grabbed a pillow, hugging it. Bijou licked her face, and I touched her shoulder.

"It's okay," I said.

"No, it isn't," she said. "I begged Mom to have me lobotomized like she had Rodney lobotomized. She laughed at me, Wyatt. I need to escape this madhouse. Will you help me?"

When Alicin clutched my hand, I felt her naked pain jabbing a red-hot poker through my heart.

"No one's going to lobotomize you. I promise I won't let them."

Alicin's sobs were palpable. She pulled herself to me, her soul as naked and bare as she was. She pressed her breasts into my clutched hand, and I could feel her heartbeat. It was racing almost as fast as my own.

"You're looking for Mom's book, aren't you?"

"It doesn't matter," I said.

"I have it," she said, letting go of my hand. I watched as she reached under her pillow and pulled it out. The same pillow I was sleeping on the previous night. "Take it."

Alicin thrust the book into my hand. "I can't," I said.

"I was going to burn it. I couldn't. Take it," Alicin said. "Don't let Ordre du Sang have it."

"Why would they want it?" I asked.

"The volume Uncle Toby had is their bible. It's sacred to them. They study it and believe every word has a deeper meaning."

She nodded when I said, "Ordre du Sang has the Lower Pontalba Press's original copy of *Mosquitoes*? Did Rodney kill your Uncle Toby to help Ordre du Sang?"

"Rodney would never kill anybody," she said.

"His snake might have," I said. "What's your blood type?"

"B," she said.

"The same as your mother's."

Alicin shook her head. "Rodney and I have Type B. Mom's type is AB+," she said.

"She told me her blood type is B, same as yours," I said.

"It's AB+, like I told you."

"Was it you and not your mother who found your uncle after the snake killed him."

Alicin shook her head. "It wasn't me."

"Your Mom said it was her that found him, and that's how she cut her hand," I said.

"She slashed her wrist with a butcher's knife because she didn't want to incriminate Rodney."

"If Rodney is lobotomized, how could he have done it?"

"I don't know. I do know Ordre du Sang has powers beyond comprehension. They have ways."

Alicin began sobbing again and shook her head when I said, "Is Jonathan part of the cult?"

"Libby Tanner is. She's a slut and a whore and consorts with Satan himself."

"Is that why you fought with her?"

"Libby Tanner has called for my sacrifice," Alicin said. "The cult wants to cut out my heart and eat it. I'm ready to let them. Only my mom is protecting me."

Alicin's words shocked me, though I didn't know if she was speaking the truth or talking insane nonsense. Realizing she was capable of both, I had no clue.

"I'm never going to let that happen," I said.

"Let it. I'm ready to die."

"What about your mom?" I asked.

"Grandfather was part of the order. Mom isn't."

"Then why did she allow her son to be lobotomized?"

Alicin's face was red from the tears. "I'm crazy, but Mom is genuinely insane. Not only does she not understand the concept of right and wrong, she suffers from congenital dementia."

"What about Ronnie? Is she a cult member?"

"She knows all about the cult, though she isn't a member. She covets the cult's Bible and would do anything to possess it, though she's deathly afraid of Penrose and Malveaux."

I touched her hand and said, "I have to go now."

Alicin wrapped her willowy arms around my neck and said, "I'll probably never see you again. Make love to me one last time before you go."

Chapter 22

I returned to St. Charles Avenue, feeling the world's weight on my soul. The rain had begun again, and I huddled beneath a streetcar stop, awaiting the next rumbling vehicle to arrive.

My conversation with Alicin DuPont raised many questions, all unanswered. I knew one person in the Quarter who might have answers to my questions. Realizing it was a long shot, I headed for the Wild Magnolias bookstore. My phone rang before I got there.

"Armand, what's up?"

"Something I can't talk about over the phone," he said. "Can you drop by Allemand's?"

"Sure," I said. "I'm just around the corner."

"See you when you get here," he said.

It was still early when I arrived at Allemand's, though it didn't matter. Regulars lined the bar, some on the same stool as the last time I was there. The bartender recognized me and waved.

"I'll bring your lemonade to the booth," he said.

"Thanks," I said.

The old jukebox was blasting out hits from the sixties and seventies, and the clack of pool balls sounded in a room at the back of the bar.

Madam Toulouse and Armand were at their usual booth, and the Madam scooted over so I could join them.

"That was fast," Armand said. "You must have been right around the corner."

"Anytime you and Madam Toulouse call, I'm Johnny on the spot," I said.

He and Madam Toulouse both shook their heads. "You don't have to hype us, Cowboy. We're not one of your clients."

"I just stepped off the streetcar at Canal. I wasn't far away," I said.

"You weren't at Evelyn DuPont's house," he asked.

He grinned when I said, "Guilty as charged, Your Honor."

"Any luck finding her book?" Madam Toulouse asked.

I pulled Evelyn's copy of Mosquitoes out of my coat pocket and showed them.

"Found it," I said.

Armand examined the book as if I might somehow have the wrong one. He handed it to Madam Toulouse, and she quickly thumbed through it before handing it back to me.

"Where did you find it?" Armand asked.

"Alicin DuPont had it under her pillow," I said.

"Interesting," Armand said.

"Not as interesting as some of the things she told me."

"Such as?" Madam Toulouse said.

"That Evelyn and their grandfather were her biological parents."

"Whoa!" Armand said. "That's one I never heard, though it might explain why Alicin and Rodney are a couple of bricks short of a load."

"Congenital mental illness," I said. "She also told me Evelyn had Rodney lobotomized." Armand glanced at Madam Toulouse with a knowing smile. "What?"

"That's false," Armand said.

"He's not lobotomized?"

"No way. Even Evelyn DuPont isn't wealthy enough to have that procedure done," he said.

"Then why did Alicin tell me?"

"Alicin's grasp of sanity is a little loose," Madam Toulouse said.

"Then Rodney could have been the person who put the king cobra in Coleman-Labissiere's lap," I said.

"Coleman-Labissiere was murdered for a reason," Madam Toulouse said. "He had something the murderer wanted, and the only way to get it was to kill Coleman-Labissiere."

"The first copy of Mosquitoes printed by the Lower Pontalba Press?"

"Yes," Armand said. "Samuel Penrose has the book."

"How do you know?" I asked.

The tattooed bartender brought my lemonade and fresh drinks for Armand and Madam Toulouse before Armand could tell me. I handed him a twenty, and he seemed happy.

"Never knew you to be a big tipper, Cowboy," Armand said.

"Things change when you're on Evelyn DuPont's payroll."

"What we're about to tell you may be too rich for even her," Madam Toulouse said. "There's a book auction tonight, and the final book for sale is so valuable that every collector desires it."

"Let me guess," I said. "Samuel Penrose is auctioning the Lower Pontalba Press 1st edition *Mosquitos*."

"Bingo," Armand said. "In the ballroom of his plantation on River Road."

"How do I gain admission to this event?" I asked.

"Can't help you on that one. Invitations to the world's wealthiest book collectors have already gone out, and they've been arriving in droves. Ronnie LaSalle can probably get you in," he said.

"Might not make any difference since I can't stop the sale," I said.

"There's a way," he said.

"Please tell me."

"The book will be on display, with armed guards looking on, of course, and Penrose is allowing potential purchasers to examine it."

"What'll I do? Grab it and run?"

"If you want to get shot in the back," Madam Toulouse said. "We have a better idea."

Armand produced a book from his black blazer.

"A first edition *Mosquitos*, signed by William Faulkner. It's yours for five hundred dollars."

"What will I do with it?" I asked.

"Switch it for the more valuable book," Madam Toulouse said.

"I'm good, though I doubt I'm magician enough to pull the switch," I said.

"Billionaires are foaming at the mouth over this auction and flying in from all over the world. Penrose's ballroom will be standing room only. Switching the books is your only way to save it."

"Sounds daunting to me," I said. "Penrose knows my face because I interviewed him."

"That's your problem, Cowboy. Here's the exchange copy of *Mosquitoes* if you want it."

I quickly forked over five hundred dollars and stowed Armand's copy of *Mosquitoes* in the inside pocket of my sportscoat.

"Though you may have to wear a disguise, Ronnie LaSalle can get you in," Madam Toulouse said.

"But will she?" I asked.

"If anyone can sweet talk her, Cowboy, that person is you," Armand said.

"One thing bothers me," I said.

Armand snickered and said, "Only one?"

"How did Penrose get Rodney to use his cobra to kill Coleman-Labissiere?"

"We're clueless," Madam Toulouse said.

"Not your problem anyway, so don't worry about it," Armand said.

I finished my lemonade and said, "Thanks for the information and the book. I'm sorry to drink and run."

"You're family, Cowboy. We're always happy to see your smiling face."

I slid out of the booth and said, "Thanks. I owe you one."

"What else is new?" Armand said as I headed for the door.

The French Quarter is small, and Wild Magnolias wasn't far from Allemand's. With Armand and Madam Toulouse's copy of Mosquitoes in the pocket of my sportscoat, I headed in that direction. Ronnie LaSalle smiled when I entered the bookstore.

"Evelyn and I waited for you last night. You never showed."

"Alicin said the two of you were passed out drunk."

Ronnie shook her head. "Alicin lied because she wanted you for herself. Did she get her wish?"

I didn't answer her question, saying, "Alicin told me some disturbing things about her mother."

"Alicin's a liar if you haven't figured that out already," Ronnie said.

"What she told me didn't sound like a lie."

"What did she tell you?"

"That her father is David DuPont, her maternal grandfather."

"That rumor is false and was debunked years ago," Ronnie said.

"Laceigh Rutherford's poem in Evelyn's missing book accuses her grandparents of incest. Alicin and Rodney would mark the fourth generation of incest within the DuPont family."

"What else did Alicin tell you."

"She told me Evelyn arranged to have Rodney lobotomized when she realized Alicin and Rodney were sexually active with each other."

"Another lie," Ronnie said. "Rodney isn't lobotomized."

"How do you know?" I asked.

"I know," she said.

"Alicin said Rodney is living with Samuel Penrose. Is it true?"

"Yes," Ronnie said.

"For what reason?" I asked.

"Samuel is Rodney and Alicin's father. Their real father."

"Penrose is gay," I said.

"Gay men can procreate, and he didn't always know he was gay."

"Samuel and Evelyn are cousins and grew up together. Samuel impregnated Evelyn, and the result was Rodney and Alicin?"

Ronnie nodded. "Distant cousins. Evelyn has no siblings. Your premise is correct."

"Alicin told me she was thirty-two," I said.

"More like forty-two," Ronnie said.

"If that's true, how old was Evelyn when she conceived Alicin and Rodney?" I asked.

"Thirteen," Ronnie said. "Evelyn's mother raised the twins."

"And her father?"

"David DuPont couldn't have conceived them because he was already dead," Ronnie said.

"So, Samuel Penrose is the father of Alicin and Rodney."

"Samuel got Rodney out of the mental facility in Alabama. He's living with him and Victor in his house on River Road."

"Evelyn told me Rodney escaped from the facility," I said.

"She knows where he is."

"Did Penrose take Rodney because he wanted a relationship with his son, or did he have an ulterior motive?"

"What motive?"

"Alicin said Penrose is the head man of a cult called Ordre du Sang, and they worship Faulkner's copy of *Mosquitoes* as their Bible."

Ronnie laughed and said, "That's absurd."

"He wanted something Coleman-Labissiere possessed, and cousin Toby had other ideas."

"What other ideas?" Ronnie asked.

"Don't play coy, Ronnie," I said. "You know Penrose has the book and is auctioning it to the highest bidder tonight."

"I have no idea how he got the book," she said. "I know Sam isn't a member of any cult, much less its head man."

"Maybe he was manipulating his son Rodney, a person he has no real love for, to murder Coleman-Labissiere so he could steal the most valuable book on the planet."

"What you say is nothing but conjecture. How do you know Toby didn't sell the book to Samuel? No matter how he obtained it, I had nothing to do with it," she said.

"His possession of the book is his motive for having Coleman-Labissiere murdered. The police will soon put two and two together."

"Tonight's auction is private," Ronnie said. "Who told you about it?"

"You said yourself there are many rare book collectors in New Orleans. You can't keep that a secret for long."

Ronnie's head sagged. "I'm not part of any of this and don't want to be implicated."

"Then get me into the auction."

"What purpose would that serve?" she asked.

"I'll think of something," I said.

"The police can't stop it because no judge will issue a search warrant. How do you intend to prevent the sale?"

"I don't have a clue."

Ronnie threw up her hands. "Don't tell me. I don't want to know."

"One other thing. I've recovered Evelyn's book," I said. "At least I've completed that part of my assignment."

"Where did you find it?" she asked.

"Alicin had it."

"Have you told Evelyn?"

"Not yet," I said. "It isn't the only book Evelyn is looking for. My partner Tony is in Mississippi looking for Faulkner's copy."

"I suppose she also wants the signed Lower Pontalba Press's edition of *Mosquitoes*. So do lots of collectors," Ronnie said.

"Penrose told me it's possibly the most valuable book in the world."

"He isn't exaggerating," she said.

"Evelyn and Penrose are distant cousins, and Toby Coleman-Labissiere is also a cousin. Am I wrong to assume Penrose and Coleman-Labissiere are also related?"

Ronnie sniffed. "There are blood connections between every influential family in the Big Easy. You know that."

"I know all too well about power and influence in this town," I said. "What's the connection between Rodney and Jonathan Stallings?"

"Rodney was strong, had an explosive temper, and often got crazy. Jonathan was the only person who could control him."

"Did Rodney ever hurt anyone?" I asked.

"In a fit of anger, he ripped Evelyn's blouse off and strangled her. If Jonathan hadn't interceded, he would have killed her."

"Jonathan could control him?"

"Jonathan was a father figure to Rodney," she said.

"I'd say the feeling was mutual from his reverence when he showed me Rodney's room and snake collection. "That brings me to another question. What motive would Jonathan have to kill Toby Coleman-Labissiere?"

"I don't know," Ronnie said. "Why do you think he had anything to do with Toby's murder?"

Jonathan told me that Rodney never owned a king cobra. Rodney's cobra, King Tut, killed Toby Coleman-Labissiere. Jonathan lied because Evelyn's maid Sara told me Tut was his favorite snake. Is Jonathan complicit in the murder?"

"I have no clue who killed Toby or what motive they may have had. Now, no more questions."

"Fine," I said. "Provide me an invitation to tonight's sale.

"And the police?" she asked.

"Half the blue-blood elites in New Orleans know about the auction tonight. I don't think you have much to worry about."

"This isn't going to be a typical book auction," Ronnie said. "It's formal only with the ladies in designer gowns and the gentlemen in tux and ties. There's be a regal buffet, a string quartet, and enough armed guards to overthrow a small Central American country. It's set to be the event of the season."

"Thanks, Ronnie," I said.

With the gold-engraved invitation in hand, I headed for the door when Ronnie stopped me.

"Watch yourself, Wyatt. Victor Malveaux is a dangerous man, and I have no doubt he wouldn't hesitate to kill you if he thought you might interfere with the sale of Sam's prized book."

Chapter 23

Tony guided his red convertible Mustang along the narrow road that wound through the coastal pines, the salty tang of the Gulf thick in the humid air. Pascagoula stretched before them like a town suspended in time, the low-slung skyline defined by shrimp boats bobbing lazily in the harbor and the remnants of the old shipyards, weathered by decades of storms and salt.

The once-vibrant pastel colors of the main street's wooden buildings had faded to muted shades, their shutters hanging askew as if the town were caught between a memory and a dream. In the distance, seagulls circled over the shimmering blue water, their cries mingling with the distant hum of an old shrimp trawler returning from the Gulf.

Mama sat in the passenger seat, her large hoop earrings swinging gently with the breeze as she took in the surroundings with eyes that saw more than the physical world. Spanish moss hung like spectral veils from the ancient live oaks lining the quiet streets, and the wide porches of the antebellum homes hinted at stories buried deep in the town's past.

They passed St. Peter's Catholic Church off the main drag, its weatherworn spires rising like sentinels over the bayou. Every corner of Pascagoula seemed to pulse with forgotten energy. It was a place where history and myth merged, leaving a feeling that anything—good or evil—could happen here.

The Gulf's murmur was constant, like a whispered warning, and as the wind picked up, it carried the scent of brine and something else, faint but unmistakable—an undercurrent of decay beneath the veneer of coastal charm.

"We're here," Mama said. "What now?"

"Locate the person who inherited Helen Baird's books," Tony said.

"How do we do that?" Mama asked.

"Find a place to eat breakfast and quiz the locals. If everything fails, we borrow a phonebook and start cold calling."

"Sounds boring," Mama said.

"All P.I. work isn't glitz and glamour," Tony said.

"No kidding," Mama said. "Where do we find this café?"

"Downtown Pascagoula, where all the oldest locals have eaten for years. I'll know it when I see it. Someone will point us in the right direction."

"I'm game," Mama said. "Let's do it."

It wasn't far to the center of the old town, and Tony quickly spotted Harley Jane's Café.

"That's it," he said.

Tony pulled into a parking space in front of the café between an old Ford pickup and a vintage green Cadillac from the 1990s. There were no parking meters.

Tony and Mama stepped out of the humid Mississippi air into a cozy little café on Pascagoula's Main Street. The screen door creaked behind them as they entered, the sound of sizzling bacon and the low hum of quiet chatter filling the air.

The café, like much of downtown Pascagoula, seemed frozen in time. The old brick buildings lining the street had faded, sun-bleached signs of a more prosperous past. The sidewalk was cracked but clean, and the occasional car rumbled by on the narrow road.

Inside the café, fresh coffee and homemade biscuits mixed with the faint aroma of grits and frying sausage. The décor was simple— mismatched tables and chairs, floral vinyl tablecloths, and a row of framed black-and-white photos on the wall showing the town's history in faded snapshots.

A few regulars, mostly older folks, were scattered around the café, seated at the tables, engrossed in their morning routines of quiet conversation, folded newspapers, and refilled coffee cups. An older man behind the counter wearing a red checkered shirt was making change from an antique cash register.

"Sit wherever you want," he said, barely averting his gaze from the cash register.

A plump, middle-aged waitress in a pale blue uniform with a frilly white apron approached their table with a notepad. Her name tag read Darlene, and her warm smile spoke of years spent serving regulars and out-of-towners alike.

"Well, good morning, y'all! I'm Darlene. What can I get you this fine day?"

"Morning, Darlene," Tony said. "We're hoping for something hearty for breakfast. Eggs, bacon, grits, maybe?"

"With a side of biscuits. I could use a little sweetness in my life, so maybe with some honey," Mama said.

Darlene nodded and said, "You got it. Bacon's crispy, and the biscuits are fresh from the oven. Coffee for both of you?"

"Black for me," Tony said.

"Me too," Mama said.

Mama took a sip from her cup when Darlene returned with their coffee.

"Wonderful," she said.

"It's strong but always fresh," Darlene said. "I see to it. What are you folks doing in Pascagoula?"

"Looking for someone," Tony said.

"Me and Al know about everybody in town," Darlene said. "Who you looking for?"

Darlene nodded when Tony said, "Is Al your hubby?"

"Both of us have lived here our whole lives," she said. "Who you looking for?"

"A woman named Helen Baird had an insurance policy. She lived and died here in Pascagoula."

Tony nodded when Darlene said, "You two insurance people?"

"Midcon Life," Tony said. "We have a thousand dollars for her nearest heir."

"I know all the Bairds but not Helen Baird," Darlene said.

"That's because she died back in the sixties. We have a hundred-dollar reward if you can help us find an heir."

Darlene paused, tapping her notepad with her pen.

"Baird, huh? Now that's a name I know. Billy Baird comes to mind. Old bachelor who fixes up televisions. Went to high school with him. Nice fellow, a bit of a recluse, but sharp as a tack with electronics."

Tony glanced at Mama and smiled. You think we could borrow a phonebook if you got one lying around?"

"You're in luck. We're a little old-fashioned here and keep one under the counter, though It's been a while since anyone asked for it. I'll bring it over when I get your breakfast. Have it out in a jiffy."

"You're good," Mama said when Darlene disappeared through the kitchen door.

Darlene soon returned with their breakfast, though not the phonebook.

"You don't need to make any calls. Give me your cell phone number, and Al and I will spread the word about what you're looking for."

"You're an angel, Darlene," Tony said.

Darlene smiled as she jotted their numbers on her order pad. "Enjoy breakfast," she said

Tony's phone rang before he had a bite of eggs. He grabbed a pen and pad from his coat and began taking notes. Mama's phone soon rang, so Tony gave her a blank page from his pad and the extra pen he always carried.

Mama and Tony barely had time to eat between conversing with potential heirs. They looked dejected when Darlene returned with more coffee.

"No luck?" she asked.

Tony shook his head. "I think we've talked with every Baird heir around. No one's panned out so far."

"Dammit!" Darlene said with a smile. "Al and I already had that Benjamin spent."

"The first person you told us about. Can you give me his name again?"

"Billy Baird," she said. "Come to find out, he died last night."

"Does he have heirs?"

"Afraid not. Like I said, he was an old bachelor."

Tony pulled a hundred-dollar bill from his wallet and handed it to Darlene.

"Here's the reward. You earned it. However you spend it, you and Al have fun," he said.

"You're a sweetheart," she said, kissing his forehead.

When she headed for the cash register to share her good fortune with her husband, Tony said, "Wait. How do we find Billy Baird's house."

"He lived in a little place near Bayou Casotte."

She scribbled the address on a blank sheet from her order pad and then hurried to the cash register. Tony followed her, clearing their tab and returning to the table to leave a twenty-dollar tip.

"You're the angel, Tony. I've never seen someone's eyes light up like Darlene's when you handed her the hundred. What do you hope to find at Billy Baird's house?"

"We spoke with every Baird in town. Either Billy is our man, or we aren't going to find him."

They drove out of town, soon reaching a narrow two-lane road that cut through green Mississippi woods and the humid air still clinging to the heat of the late morning sun.

Spanish moss hung from the towering oaks lining the road, their crooked limbs forming a natural canopy overhead. The pavement was cracked in places, a testament to years of neglect, and gravel patches crunched under the tires as they headed deeper into Bayou Casotte.

The farther they went, the more remote it felt. The sound of civilization faded, replaced by the constant hum of insects and the occasional bird call. The air smelled of damp earth and fresh-cut grass mixed with the salty tang of nearby marshes. Every so often, they passed an old shotgun house or a rusted mailbox, but for the most part, the road was empty, framed by the endless sprawl of cypress and palmetto.

As they approached Bayou Casotte, the landscape revealed a vast expanse of wetlands. Patches of tall reeds and cattails swayed gently in the breeze, and the murky water of the bayou glistened in the sunlight, reflecting the blue sky above.

The road turned to dirt, and Tony slowed as the car kicked up small dust clouds. They found Billy's house on the bayou's edge, a weathered structure raised on stilts to guard against flooding. Once painted white, the wooden exterior was faded and chipped, its boards warped from years of humidity and neglect.

The tin roof, streaked with rust, creaked in the breeze. A crooked porch ran the front length of the house, shaded by a massive oak tree whose roots stretched into the water below.

The yard was wild, though not wholly untamed. Sunflowers grew tall near the house, their bright heads bobbing in the wind, and a few neglected vegetable plants—okra, tomatoes, and peppers—clung to life in a garden near the porch. A rusted pickup truck sat beneath a lean-to off to the side, its tires half-sunken into the marshy ground.

Beyond the house, the bayou spread out in lazy loops, dotted with lily pads and herons stalking fish in the shallows. As Tony and Mama parked the car, they saw a group leaving the house, murmuring to each other as they climbed into their vehicles.

When Tony knocked on a car window, a smiling woman opened it.

"Pardon me, ma'am. Are you relatives of Billy Baird?"

"Sadly, Billy had no family and died alone. We're members of his church, helping clean out his house."

"Thank you," he said.

The older woman nodded to Tony as she shut the door of her car. Dust kicked up as the small convoy of vehicles drove away, leaving the house quiet again. Mama and Tony stepped onto the porch, the boards creaking beneath their feet.

Inside, the house was dimly lit, with sunlight filtering through thin curtains that hung limply in front of the windows. The main room was simple— a mix of faded wallpaper peeling at the edges and bare wood floors that creaked with every step. A single ceiling fan spun lazily overhead, barely stirring the heavy air.

The furnishings were sparse but comfortable in an old-fashioned sort of way. A worn-out armchair sat near the front window, its upholstery threadbare from years of use. Next to it, a small wooden table held a half-read paperback novel and an old rotary phone.

Against one wall was a TV, the kind with a wooden console. Its screen was dark and dust-covered, a testament to Billy's lifelong work as a television repairman. Tools, spare parts, and old manuals were scattered on the floor next to it as if he had been in the middle of a project before he passed.

A narrow hallway led to the back of the house, where the kitchen and bedroom were. The kitchen was modest—yellowed linoleum floors, faded cabinets, and an old stove that hadn't been used in days. A small table in the corner still had a coffee cup and plate, as if Billy had left it there just yesterday. A Catholic father sat at the table, praying."

"Who are you?" he asked.

"Tony Nicosia and Mama Mulate," Tony said.

"I'm Father Bandini," the man said. "My parishioners and I cleaned Billy's house and are taking care of his burial. Are you the people with the insurance company?"

Tony didn't like lying to a priest, though he saw he had no choice.

"Yes," he said."

Tony and Mama nodded when Father Bandini asked, "Want a look through the house?"

In the bedroom, a simple iron bed with a patchwork quilt dominated the space. A wooden dresser held a few framed photos of family members long gone, along with a wind-up alarm clock that ticked softly in the background.

Neatly folded clothes sat on a chair in the corner, and a pair of well-worn boots rested at the foot of the bed. The house smelled faintly of old wood and the marsh outside, with a hint of the lavender-scented cleaner the church members must have used before they left.

"Billy lived a solitary life, and there's a sense of peace in the simplicity of his home, as though the bayou itself was his closest companion," Father Bandini said.

Model planes, many working models, lined the walls and corners.

"Did Billy make these model planes," Tony asked.

"He was a talented man. He often flew his model planes," Father Bandini said. "They were his passion."

"They are beautiful," Tony said.

"Take one," Father Bandini said. "Otherwise, they are going in the trash."

"Don't do that," Tony said. "I'll give you a hundred dollars for them. I don't have enough room in the trunk of my car."

"We'll save them for you," Father Bandini said.

Tony opened his wallet and counted a hundred dollars for the model planes and a thousand in hundred-dollar bills.

"This is for your church," he said. "Sounds as if Billy had no heirs."

"Billy was a good man, though not perfect," Father Bandini said. "He was an artist and drew pornographic pictures." The priest held a handful of three-by-five cards and flashed one so Tony and Mama could see. "I'll burn these so none of the parishioners learn of his predilections."

"Let me see," Mama said.

The priest reluctantly handed the cards to Mama. On each were pin-up pictures of voluptuous women. None were nude, and there was nothing pornographic about the drawings that Mama could see.

"This is art," Mama said. "You can't destroy them."

"I'm afraid I must," Father Bandini said.

"Nonsense," Mama said, reaching for her wallet.

She only had thirty-nine dollars and handed all of it to the priest.

"I can't take your money," Father Bandini said.

"Then I better have my thousand dollars back," Tony said.

Father Bandini thought about Tony's words and said, "Okay, keep the pictures."

"Thanks," Mama said. "Did Billy have any books?"

"Lots of them," Father Bandini said.

"Where are they?" Tony asked.

"St. Peter's had a book sale today. The proceeds will help us build a new chapel. Please excuse me because I must go now."

"Where will I pick up the model planes?" Tony asked.

"I live in the rectory on the church grounds. If I'm not at St. Peter's, I'll probably be in the rectory or not far away."

"Thanks, Padre," Tony said. "I'll find you."

Chapter 24

Mama and Tony watched the priest drive away in an old Chevy station wagon. Standing in the house's stillness, they felt the weight of Billy's life—quiet, unassuming, and forever lonely. The peacefulness of the bayou and the faded beauty of the old house seemed to speak of a man who found comfort in the simple things, even as the world outside passed him by.

"What now?" Mama asked.

"St. Peter's Catholic Church," Tony said. "Maybe we can get there before the books are sold."

Mama was reveling in purchasing Billy Baird's pen and ink drawings of World War II pinups.

"What will you do with five hundred three by five cards?" Tony asked.

"You kidding? Each card is a snapshot of an unknown artist's soul, the culmination of their life. I'll treasure them until I die."

"Whatever," Tony said.

"You're one to talk," Mama said. "You paid a hundred bucks for Billy's model planes."

"So sue me. It's getting late. Let's get the hell out of here."

Tony and Mama returned to Pascagoula in the late afternoon as shadows began creeping across the greenery. St. Peter's Catholic Church loomed in the fading light, its tall steeple casting long shadows across the gravel lot. Tony parked in front.

"No one's here," Tony said, cutting the engine and glancing at Mama.

"Maybe someone's inside," Mama said. "Let's check."

They found the wooden doors shut tight, a 'SALE ENDED' sign taped to the heavy oak, the stained-glass windows glowing as if guarding past secrets, and the faint scent of incense lingering in the cool air as they returned to the car. St. Peter's Catholic Church stood quiet, its tall spire reaching toward a cloudless sky. The doors were closed,

"We're screwed," he said.

"Maybe not," Mama said. "Drive to the alleyway in the back, and let's check the dumpster."

"You have to be kidding," Tony said.

"I'm not," Mama said.

A weathered fence separated the alleyway from the parking lot of an apartment complex. Tony parked the car beside it and gazed around to see if anyone was observing them. Mama got out of the car and opened the dumpster's lid.

"Oh, my God!" she said. "Someone threw the books they didn't sell into the dumpster. Help me."

"Do what?"

"I'm going dumpster diving. Help me."

"You have to be kidding," he said.

"Not kidding. Help me."

Mama stepped into Tony's hands, her colorful skirt sweeping across the ground as she disappeared into the dumpster. Tony peered inside at the mess of paperbacks, hardcovers, torn pages, and dog-eared novels. To him, it was just trash. To Mama, it was something else entirely.

"We're taking all of them," she said.

223

Tony blinked. "All of them? You sure? It's just a bunch of old books—"

"Somewhere in this mess, there could be *Mosquitoes* or another treasure. If it's in here, I'll find it. Even if it's not, we're taking the rest."

Mama tossed out an empty box and said, "Start packing them."

"This is bullshit!" Tony said. "We aren't going to have enough room in the trunk."

"Then stack them in the backseat."

"This is crazy," he said. "The boxes will be hanging out the windows."

She said, "We'll take them to the bus station, pack them up, and have them sent to New Orleans."

Tony shook his head, half-amused, but began collecting the books she handed him. Mama worked with fierce precision, sifting through volumes, her fingers dancing over the spines as if each held a secret waiting to be told.

"Anything?" Tony asked.

Mama paused, holding up a worn book. Her breath hitched. "Not yet... but I feel it. We're close. I won't stop until I've rescued every book."

"Some of these paperbacks don't even have covers," Tony said.

"Doesn't matter. Books are the writer's souls," Mama said. "We can't just let them rot in a garbage pile."

As Tony stuffed another box full of books, he couldn't help but feel it. The thrill of discovery. The chase for something more than just paper and ink. Maybe Mama was right. Maybe there was something worth saving in this forgotten pile of stories—maybe even Faulkner's lost words. He stopped what he was doing when she stuck her head out of the dumpster.

"I've found something."

"Faulkner's *Mosquitoes*?"

"Maybe something even more valuable."

"What?" he asked.

"The handwritten volume of love poems Faulkner wrote for Helen Baird."

"Let me see," he said.

Mama handed him an old leather-bound book filled with loose poems.

"Faulkner's unpublished poems," Mama said. "You realize how much something like this is worth?"

"Ms. DuPont didn't hire us to find it," Tony said.

"It's not ours. We can't keep it."

"We found it in a dumpster," Tony said. "It's our book. I say we give it to Father Bandini and his new chapel. It's what Billy Baird would have wanted."

"I can live with that," Mama said. "Only a few more books are in the dumpster, and it's almost too dark to see."

"I have a flashlight in the car," Tony said. "I'll get it."

Daylight was fading as Tony handed Mama the flashlight. Suddenly, she began screaming.

"I found it. It's Faulkner's *Mosquitoes*. Help me out of this hell hole."

Tony reached over the dumpster and grabbed Mama beneath her arms, lifting her high enough to climb out alone.

"My skirt is ruined," she said.

"We'll get you a new skirt," Tony said. "I can't believe you found the book."

Mama smiled when she showed it to him.

"It was the last book in the dumpster. Now, can you believe it?" she asked.

Boxes of books filled the trunk, backseat, and console area of Tony's Mustang. He barely had room to turn the steering wheel.

"This is bullshit!" he said. "We'll never make it home with this load."

"You're right," Mama said, reaching for her cell phone.

"Who are you calling?" Tony asked.

"Jake," she said. "I'm going to have Colley pick up the books and your planes in Jake's helicopter."

"Sounds like a plan," Tony said.

"I saw Father Bandini's rectory on the other side of the church. Let's wake him and give him the book of love poems," Mama said.

Father Bandini's rectory was a modest brick structure tucked behind St. Peter's Catholic Church. Its simple charm was enhanced by weathered shutters and ivy creeping up the walls. Tony pulled in front and stopped the car, barely having enough room to open the door.

"There are no lights in the house," Mama said. "You think he's here?"

"Probably asleep is my guess," Tony said. "The padre didn't seem the type to party until all hours."

There was no doorbell, and Tony pounded on the door. They were about to give up and return to the car when they heard someone padding toward them.

"Who in heaven's name knocks at this hour?" the priest asked.

"Tony Nicosia and Mama Mulate, the insurance people you met at Billy Baird's house."

"What is it you need?" he asked.

"We found something of value and are here to give it to you," Mama said.

"Can't it wait until tomorrow?"

"Tony and I won't be here tomorrow. I think you'll want to see what we have."

They heard the clunk of deadbolts being unlocked and more grumbling as the priest opened the door and peered out.

"All right," he said. "Come in."

"Thanks, Padre," Tony said. "You won't be disappointed."

Like the outside of the rectory, the inside décor was minimal, dominated by wooden furniture and religious icons. A small crucifix hung on the wall above a well-worn couch, and the faint scent of incense lingered in the air. Father Bandini's nightshirt dragged to the floor as he led them through the little house.

"Let's go to the kitchen. I'll put on a pot of coffee."

"Right behind you, Padre," Tony said.

The kitchen was humble—linoleum floors, a round table with four mismatched chairs, and a single light bulb hanging from a string. It was quiet and unadorned, much like Father Bandini himself, and he motioned them to have a seat.

No one spoke while Father Bandini brewed a pot of coffee, and its wonderful aroma soon filled the kitchen.

"Now, what do you have for me that couldn't wait until tomorrow?"

Mama showed him the leather-bound volume of poems.

"William Faulkner met Helen Baird in Pascagoula years ago," she said. "So taken by her was Faulkner that he wrote love poems in her honor. He had them bound and presented them to her."

Father Bandini glanced unimpressed at the book of poems.

"What is something like this worth?" he asked.

"Possibly millions," Mama said.

"More than enough to complete your chapel edition," Tony said.

"Are you sure?" Father Bandini asked.

"The volume is one-of-a-kind, handwritten by Faulkner himself," Mama said. "Trust me when I tell you it's invaluable."

Father Bandini rubbed his eyes, barely believing what he was hearing.

"William Faulkner wrote this?"

"It'll fetch more than enough to build that chapel—and maybe throw in a new roof for your rectory while you're at it," Tony said.

"This isn't stolen property, is it?" he asked.

"Billy Baird was the last heir of Helen Baird. We found the book in the church's dumpster. We're donating it to St. Peter's. Please accept our donation."

It was raining when Tony and Mama hurried to the Mustang.

"Return to Billy Baird's house," Mama said. "Colley can land the helicopter in the field in the back."

"How will he know how to find it?" Tony asked.

"He has the coordinates of my cell phone," Mama said.

Tony followed the rural road back to Billy Baird's house on the banks of Bayou Casotte. Rain peppered the surface of the scenic bayou as they reached the house.

"Wait in the car, or inside the house?" Tony asked.

"The house," Mama said. "Maybe we can converse with Billy's ghost while waiting for Jake and Colley."

"Hope not," Tony said. "This place is creepy enough with the rain and all."

Though the lights were dim, the electricity was still on in the little house. Mama began looking through the cabinets.

"I need a drink, and I don't mean coffee."

Tony pulled a silver flask from his coat pocket.

"I have scotch," he said.

"I'm not picky," Mama said, taking the flask from him.

"Save me some," Tony said.

"Jake has plenty of booze in the helicopter. We can mix a real drink when he gets here."

The already dim lights flickered when thunder shook the house.

"Hope they hurry. This place is getting spookier by the minute."

"We didn't get any sleep last night, and I'm not looking forward to driving all night in the rain back to New Orleans," Mama said.

"Go back with Jake and Colley," Tony said. "It's only about a hundred miles, and I can stop if I get too tired."

"No way!" Mama said. "I won't let you drive alone."

They soon heard the thump-thump-thump of Jake's chopper landing in the field behind Billy Baird's. It was raining, so Mama and Tony waited in the house. Colley and Jake soon joined them. They weren't alone. Bradley, the chauffeur, was with them.

After a long embrace with Mama, Jake said, "We brought Bradley. He's going to drive the car back to New Orleans. You two are coming with me in the chopper."

They waited for a break in the rain to begin loading the boxes of books and the model airplanes. Bradley waved and watched them rise into the air when they were done.

The helicopter lifted off as the rain began to fall steadily, streaking across the windows like slashes of silver under the dim moonlight. The rhythmic hum of the rotors filled the cabin as Jake, seated beside Colley, his trusted pilot, glanced back at Mama and Tony in the rear. Mama, relaxed and lost in thought, looked out into the misty night while Tony adjusted his seatbelt, never quite comfortable with flying in small aircraft, especially in the rain.

Mama poured him a glass of scotch and said, "Relax and be glad we're not down there on the road."

Below them, the coastline stretched like a dark ribbon, faint lights dotting the horizon where the Gulf of Mexico kissed the shore. The rain gave the world a dreamlike quality, blurring the boundary between land and sea as if the two were slowly merging. Now and then, a flash of lightning illuminated the dark waters, revealing the whitecaps rolling beneath them, restless from the storm.

The helicopter cut through the night, hovering just above the coastal towns dotting the Mississippi Gulf. As they passed, the lights of Biloxi shimmered faintly through the rain, a mix of casino neon signs and sleepy neighborhoods, their lights dulled by the heavy clouds. The view from above was a patchwork of pine forests, marshlands, and winding rivers, all fading into the misty expanse of the Gulf.

Tony leaned closer to the window, his breath fogging up the glass as he peered at the churning waves. He could make out the stretch of Highway 90, hugging the coastline like a fragile thread dotted with the occasional car's headlights cutting through the storm.

Mama, always more at ease with the unseen, rested her hand on Tony's arm, sensing his unease.

"We're in good hands. Jake's flown through worse than this," she said with a reassuring smile.

As they flew further west, the rain began to lighten, but the distant rumbles of thunder still echoed over the water. Colley adjusted their course slightly, angling them toward New Orleans. The silhouette of oil rigs and shrimp boats blinked faintly on the horizon, tiny beacons of light in an otherwise vast sea of darkness.

"Look at that," Jake said, nodding toward the faint glow of the Crescent City just beginning to appear ahead. "A storm's not enough to dim those lights."

The helicopter banked left, preparing to descend into New Orleans, the familiar sight of the city's skyline emerging through the mist. Mama sat back, closing her eyes for a moment, the sound of the rain against the helicopter blending with the steady thrum of the rotors. Feeling the slight shift in altitude, Tony looked ahead at the city and felt the tension in his chest begin to ease.

Chapter 25

On the last day of the French Quarter Fest, Bertram's was empty when I returned from my visit with Ronnie LaSalle. The Cajun bartender was alone, polishing a glass for his next customer.

"Where you been?" he asked.

"You know where I was. Evelyn DuPont sent her chauffeur for me last night. Said she had to see me."

"How come?" Bertram asked.

"Who knows? She was drunk and passed out when I got there."

"Well, you stayed with somebody because you didn't come back here," he said.

"Alicin DuPont, Evelyn's daughter, gave me a place to sleep."

"Did she now?" he said. "Want to tell me about it?"

"I'd rather not. She told me some interesting things."

"Word on the street is she's crazy as a coot," he said. "Probably can't believe a thing she says."

"She has reason to be crazy, though I already know some of the things she told me aren't true," I said.

"Such as?" he asked.

"She accused her mom of having her twin brother Rodney lobotomized. Armand, Madam Toulouse, and Ronnie LaSalle said she was lying."

Before he could respond, Maya came out of the back, saw me sitting at the bar, and joined us. It was misting outside as a customer came in off the sidewalk.

"Got to take care of business. You two have fun," Bertram said.

Maya sat beside me and said, "I went to your room last night and waited on you. You never came home."

"It was raining. I didn't have a ride."

"Bradley would have picked you up. Why didn't you call him?"

"I did," I said. "He's out of town."

"You're a liar, Wyatt Thomas," she said.

I reached into the inner pocket of my damp sports coat and produced Evelyn's missing copy of *Mosquitoes.*

"I found Ms. DuPont's lost book," I said, showing it to her.

"Where was it?" Maya asked.

"Evelyn's daughter, Alicin, had it," I said.

"Is that where you were last night?"

Maya turned away when I said, "You're jealous, aren't you?"

After crossing her arms tightly around her chest, Maya said, "French Quarter Fest is almost over. I'm helping Leo and Pepper again today. What are your plans?"

"Of the three special copies of *Mosquitoes* printed by the Lower Pontalba Press, I now have one. Tony and Mama are in Mississippi looking for Faulkner's copy."

Maya's arms unfolded, and she asked, "Are they having any luck?"

"Don't know," I said. "I think Toby Coleman-Labissiere had one of the copies. When he refused to make a deal, Penrose had him murdered and took it."

"Who killed Coleman-Labissiere?" Maya asked.

"Could have been Rodney, Ms. DuPont's son, or Jonathan Stallings, her butler."

"Because of Rodney's snake collection?" Maya asked.

"And, as it turns out, Samuel Penrose is Rodney's father."

"Who told you that?" Maya asked.

"Ronnie LaSalle."

"Interesting," Maya said. "Have you informed Tommy and Marlon?"

"Not yet," I said. "It isn't my job to find the murderer. Ronnie LaSalle told me something else that affects the case."

"What?"

"Penrose has the book. He's hosting a book sale tonight at his plantation home on River Road. The original copy of Lower Pontalba Press's *Mosquitoes* is the star attraction. I have an invitation."

"Tell me again about Ordre du Sang," she said.

"A cult disguised as a secret society. They are Satanists and practice all manner of evil."

Lydia and Adano arrived before I could answer.

"You're talking about Ordre du Sang, aren't you?" Lydia asked.

"What's Ordre du Sang?" Adano asked.

"A cult of Satanists," Lydia said. "It's how I met Wyatt."

"Please explain," he said.

"When I was working for the Greater Archdiocese of New Orleans, we became aware of a Satanic shrine in the Old Ursuline Convent. Not wanting to get the police involved because of the adverse publicity it would generate, we hired Wyatt to investigate," Lydia said.

"The shrine was only the tip of the iceberg," I said. "City politicians, police commissioners, and many influential people were members of the cult."

"What happened to it?" Adano asked.

"An explosion destroyed their meeting place and killed many of the members," I said.

"What caused the explosion?" Adano asked.

"Long story," I said. "The bottom line is the cult was destroyed. At least, we thought it was. Alicin, Ms. DuPont's daughter, informed me that Samuel Penrose revived the cult and is now its head man."

"Is it true?" Lydia said.

"Maybe not," I said. "Veronica LaSalle was quick to inform me that Alicin was lying."

Ordre du Sang was forgotten when Mama and Jake arrived and joined us.

"What's up?" Jake asked.

Maya showed them Evelyn's lost copy of *Mosquitoes*.

"Wyatt found Ms. DuPont's missing book."

Then your job is completed and successful," Adano said.

"Not quite," I said. "Ms. DuPont decided she needs all three copies printed by Lower Pontalba Press for her collection. Mama and Tony were in Mississippi looking for Faulkner's copy."

"We got back early this morning," Mama said. "Jake picked us up in his chopper."

"Any luck?" I asked.

"We found it," she said. "Tony's on his way and will tell you the story."

"Where is the third book?" Lydia asked.

"Toby Coleman-Labissiere's grandfather kept it to sell at auction in London. The sale never occurred."

"What happened to it?" Adano asked.

"My best guess is it remained in the possession of the Coleman-Labissiere family," I said. "They'd either forgotten about it or didn't realize its value. Someone else did."

"The person who murdered Coleman-Labissiere?" Adano said.

"At least the person responsible," I said.

"And that person is?" Lydia said.

"Rodney DuPont and Jonathan Stallings are the only two snake handlers I know, except for Adano. They have to be the prime suspects."

"Unless. . ." Maya said.

"Unless what?"

"Unless something else killed Coleman-Labissiere and not the snake."

"The autopsy would have told the police if something other than the snakebite had killed him," I said.

"There were no other marks on the body, and the toxicology report showed he died from the venom of a king cobra," Maya said.

"So?"

"Maybe someone injected Coleman-Labissiere with the venom, and the coroner overlooked the injection site."

"Surely not," I said.

"A needle puncture beneath the hairline would be easy to overlook," she said.

"Coroners scrutinize the skulls of victims. They wouldn't have missed a puncture, even a small one. Besides, how did they emulate the bite of a snake?" I asked.

We looked at Adano when he said, "They used the skull of a cobra with the fangs intact. I knew a witch who used a snake skull to inject venom."

Adano smiled when Lydia said, "You knew a witch? Maybe I should reconsider our relationship."

Mama nodded. "Vodoun practitioners often use venomous snake skulls when practicing dark magic."

"Why would Coleman-Labissiere let them do that to him without a struggle?" I asked.

"His blood alcohol content was off the chart," Maya said. "Maybe he was passed out. Besides, Rodney had no motive."

"Who did?" Lydia asked.

"Victor Malveaux and his lover Samuel Penrose. Penrose is a rare book dealer and is hosting an auction tonight. *Mosquitoes* is the biggest and final book on the agenda."

"Is it that valuable?" Lydia asked.

"When Maya and I interviewed Penrose, he told us it is the most valuable book in the world," I said.

"What do you intend to do?" Lydia asked.

"It'll be the auction prize, the final book of the night, and the crowd will be at a fever pitch. I obtained tickets to the event from Veronica LaSalle. My friends Armand and Madam Toulouse sold me a 1st edition version of *Mosquitoes* from the New York publisher."

"For what purpose?" Lydia asked.

"To switch it with the Lower Pontalba Press version and then get the hell out of Dodge. There's a problem."

"What problem?" Lydia asked.

"Penrose and Victor Malveaux know me and Maya. I'll have to wear a convincing disguise."

Lydia turned her attention to Adano when he said, "I'll do it for you."

"Thanks, Adano. This switch requires certain skills. There will be armed guards and book collectors watching. I'm unsure if I have the sleight of hand to pull it off."

"I can do it, and no one will ever know," he said.

"You're a priest," Lydia said. "You have no such skill."

"Oh, but I do," Adano said. "My family moved to Rome when I was eight. I supplemented my parents' income by picking the pockets of tourists."

"You didn't," Lydia said.

"I still have the touch," he said. "I could remove your bra; you would never know it."

Lydia grinned and said, "Get out of here."

"Let me take your ticket," he said. "I'll get the book for you."

"You're going no place without me," Lydia said.

"Sounds like a plan to me," Maya said. "I'll borrow Leo and Pepper's truck, park outside, and wait for you to complete the switch."

"Your plan has a moral problem," Lydia said.

"What problem?" I asked.

"Faulkner commissioned the book. His heirs are the owners."

"He donated his notes and manuscripts to the University of Virginia," I said.

"Then that's where this book must go," Lydia said.

"Ms. DuPont may have something to say about that," I said. "That isn't the only problem," I said. "The auction is a black-tie affair with a string quartet and Vegas-style buffet. How will you get fitted for a tux and gown by then?"

"What fun," Mama said. "I want to go."

"I can help," Jake said. "I have a wardrobe department at my studio if you let Mama and me tag along. We can all go in the limo."

"I don't have extra tickets," I said.

"No problem," he said. "Angie can get us as many as we need."

"What time does the sale begin?" Lydia asked.

"The banquet begins earlier, though the auction starts at ten," I said.

Jake was on the phone calling Angie. When he hung up, he said, "We don't have much time. Let's go."

Lydia, Adano, Jake, and Mama were barely out the door when Tony entered with a smile and something in his hand. Bertram saw him walking toward the bar and had a scotch waiting when he sat beside me. He placed a book on the bar and pushed it toward me.

"Is that what I think it is?" I asked.

"Better," he said. "It's the first copy of the Lower Pontalba Press's version of *Mosquitoes*. Faulkner had it, after all."

"Mama and Jake beat you here and told me. They just left," I said.

"Mama called Jake after we'd found it. He and Colley picked us up in his chopper."

"What about your car?" I asked.

"Bradley drove it home, and I gave him a ride back to his limo when he reached my house," Tony said.

He nodded when I asked, "First time in a helicopter?"

"I had the jitters. Jake's full-service bar relaxed me, and I enjoyed the awesome ride back to New Orleans."

I glanced inside the front cover and saw the numeral one, signifying it was the first copy printed.

"Awesome job! How much did you have to pay for it?" I asked.

"Nothing. We found it in the bottom of a dumpster."

"How?"

"Long story," he said. "What about you? Any luck?"

Maya showed him Ms. DuPont's missing book.

"Ms. DuPont's daughter had it," she said.

I could see by Tony's expression that he wanted to ask why she gave it to me. After correctly reading the jealousy in Maya's expression, he asked another question instead.

"What about the third book?" he asked.

"Samuel Penrose has it. He's auctioning it tonight at his plantation home on River Road."

"Sounds like a motive for murder to me," he said. "Did he kill Coleman-Labissiere?"

"Either him or Victor Malveaux is my guess. They're setting it up as death by snakebite so they can pin the murder on Rodney DuPont."

"You're saying that a snake didn't kill him?" he said.

"Maya's the one who needs to tell you," I said. "She has a theory that makes lots of sense."

"Let me call Tommy," he said. "She can tell all of us at the same time."

Tommy and Marlon weren't far away and soon sitting at the bar with us. Bertram brought Tommy an Abita and a lemonade for Marlon.

"This better be good," Tommy said. "We were planning to arrest Rodney and Jonathan Stallings today. What's this cockamamie theory you have?"

"It's Maya's idea and not cockamamie," I said.

"Let's hear it," Tommy said.

"Coleman-Labissiere was killed by cobra venom but not by a live cobra," she said.

"Impossible," Tommy said. "The snakebite on the victim's neck was the only wound."

"What if an accomplice got the victim drunk and then used something to make it appear a snake had bitten him?"

"Like what?" Marlon said.

"The skull of a cobra with its hollow fangs intact," she said. "They used the fangs to make the snakebite wound on Coleman-Labissiere's neck and then injected cobra venom through the fang hole."

"Where did they get the venom?" Tommy asked.

"I'm sure it's rare," Maya said. "If Penrose bought it somewhere, the purchase should be easy to trace."

"What about the cobra we found on location?" Marlon asked.

"Rodney DuPont's snake," I said. "They released it there because they were setting him up to take the fall."

"How do we prove Rodney's snake didn't kill Coleman-Labissiere?" Tommy asked.

"Measure the distance between puncture marks and compare it with Rodney's snake." Maya said. "It seems highly unlikely that they would be the same."

Tommy glanced at Tony and said, "What do you think?"

"I like it," Tony said. "Rodney has no motive. Penrose and Malveaux do."

"Say, Tommy, Maya said the blood you found at the crime scene was type B. Did you find a match for the lone fingerprint you found on the broken glass?" I asked.

"It doesn't match anything in our system," he said. "Maybe we'll find out when I put a warrant out for the arrest of Penrose and Malveaux," Tommy said.

"They're at Penrose's plantation on River Road. You have no jurisdiction in St. Charles Parish. Besides, you need to get the fang measurements first, or some savvy defense attorney could deep-six your case."

"Tony?" Tommy said.

"Cowboy was a defense attorney. You should probably heed his advice," Tony said.

"I like it," Tommy said. "Maya, you're a genius. Let's go, Marlon. We have calls to make." Tommy killed his beer and started for the door. "Thanks for the drinks, Bertram."

"Wait for me," Maya said. "I'll walk out with you." She turned and said, "See you later tonight, Wyatt."

Chapter 26

When Bertram's front door opened, we could hear the noise of the French Quarter Fest. The rain had ceased, and it appeared that the tourists and locals would have the remainder of the day of jazz and gluttony. I had other things to worry about.

"What now?" Tony asked.

"Evelyn DuPont. I need to take these two books to her. Before I go, I have a few questions to ask you."

"Shoot," he said.

"Ms. DuPont told me her blood type was B, the same type as the blood found at the scene. She also had a bandage on her hand."

"You think she was at the murder scene?" Tony asked.

"When I quizzed her, she told me she was. She was lying."

"How do you know?" Tony asked.

"Alicin told me her blood type is B and that so is her twin brother Rodney's. She said her mom's blood type was AB+. She also told me she used a butcher knife to cut her hand with."

"Moms know their kid's blood type. Why would a daughter know or even care about their mother's?"

"Maybe because it's AB+ is unusual and memorable. Is it possible for children to have a different blood type than their mother?"

"Yes," Tony said. "If a mother has AB+ and the father O+, the kids could have A or B, unlike either of the parents. There are all sorts of possibilities."

"How do you know so much about blood types?" I asked.

"There was no DNA testing when I broke in as a detective. Fingerprints and blood type were our primary forensic tools. Though both have limitations, they were all we had to work with."

"Alicin said it was her at the crime scene," I said. "Ms. DuPont was protecting her son. Maybe Alicin was trying to do the same. Whatever, it implies Rodney was at the scene."

"Why would he release his favorite snake in the office of the Lower Pontalba Press?" I asked.

"Maybe he didn't," Tony said. "Lots of people have type B blood. The match on the fingerprint will tell the story."

"Hope so," I said.

"Let's go see Ms. DuPont. I'll give you a ride," Tony said.

"Good. We can double-team her."

The weather was sunny with a spring nip as we tooled down St. Charles Avenue, the top of Tony's red convertible Mustang down and a cool breeze blowing over us. He parked in front of Evelyn DuPont's sprawling Garden District mansion.

I glanced at the house, its columns stark against the backdrop of moss-draped oaks, as the humid air clung to everything like a thick film. The mansion's windows reflected another approaching storm system, casting the place in an almost oppressive stillness.

As we approached the grand entrance, one of the maids, her eyes wide with worry, opened the door before we could knock. Inside, the mansion's usually composed elegance seemed frayed at the edges. The staff was a flurry of movement—maids darting from room to room, keeping their heads low and their steps quick. One of the housekeepers nearly bumped into us, muttering a hurried apology before rushing off.

"Something's brewing," I said.

Tony chuckled. "And it ain't the weather."

Sharp and edged with frustration, Evelyn's voice cut through the air. She appeared at the top of the grand staircase, clutching the railing as if it were the only thing keeping her from tearing into one of the terrified servants. Her usually pristine appearance was slightly disheveled; the hem of her silk robe trailed loosely behind her, and her hair, though still elegantly styled, had a wildness to it. She barked at one of the maids who had been too slow with a tray of drinks.

"You! If you spill another drop, you're out of here!"

The maid nodded, her hands trembling as she retreated toward the kitchen. Evelyn finally noticed Tony and me at the base of the stairs, her expression shifting from anger to irritation.

"I hope you've got better news than the incompetents that I'm paying a fortune to clean this place."

"We have something you might like—two of your special editions of Mosquitoes."

Evelyn's eyes flicked toward the package Tony held, her interest momentarily breaking through her foul mood. She descended the staircase slowly, her irritation ebbing, but only slightly.

"Two, you say? I assume that includes the copy from Mississippi?"

Tony nodded. "Faulkner's copy. Mama Mulate and I found it in Oxford."

"Mama Mulate?" Evelyn said.

"A professor of English literature at Tulane, and she's a Faulkner scholar," Tony said. "If it weren't for her, we'd never have found the book."

Evelyn's lips twitched into something resembling a smile, though it was laced with impatience. As she drew closer, the pungent smell of whiskey told us she had started tipping the bottle early.

"Let's see what you've brought me."

She turned sharply, motioning for us to follow her down the hallway. I exchanged a glance with Tony, the tension still palpable, the air thicker than just the humidity.

"She's in a mood all right," I said, muttering.

Evelyn led us into her private study, where the mood was no less stormy. The study was a sanctuary of old-world elegance, starkly contrasting with the chaos outside its doors.

Enveloped in rich mahogany paneling, Evelyn's study exuded a timeless charm. Intricate crown molding adorned its high ceilings. Large, arched windows framed by velvet drapes let streams of muted sunlight filter in, casting a warm glow over the space.

The scent of aged leather and polished wood, mixed with the faintest hint of lavender from a vase of freshly cut flowers, filled the room. An antique desk dominated, its surface covered with an organized chaos of papers, letters, and elegant stationery. Evelyn sat at the desk, pushing the button on an intercom.

When the box squawked, she said, "Maisie, we need drinks."

Two well-stuffed chairs were in front of the desk, and Evelyn motioned us to sit. We did, and I continued gazing around the room. A glass display case along one wall housed some of her prized rare books, their worn spines gleaming under soft lighting. The bookshelves that flanked the desk were filled with volumes bound in leather and cloth, each spine telling its story of literary and historical significance.

Above the fireplace, an ornately framed portrait of Evelyn's twins, Alicin and Rodney, loomed. Rodney looked regal, like a young prince, and nothing like I had imagined. Maisie appeared with a silver tray before I could ask Evelyn about the picture.

"Your drink, Ms. DuPont," the pretty maid said.

Evelyn nodded and said, "I know Wyatt is drinking lemonade. What about you."

"Scotch," Tony said.

"I'll be right back with your drinks," Maisie said.

The dark marble fireplace remained cold, its mantel cluttered with precious trinkets—family heirlooms, a delicate crystal clock, and framed photos of a much younger Evelyn with her children.

Two high-backed armchairs upholstered in deep burgundy velvet faced the desk. They were inviting yet somehow intimidating, as if the weight of the room's history made it impossible to relax.

The only light emanated from a brass floor lamp beside one of the chairs, its warm glow casting long shadows across the walls. An underlying tension pervaded everything as if the past was never far from Evelyn's thoughts.

Tony put the two books on the desk and slid them toward her. Her smile grew as she thumbed through Faulkner's volume.

"How much did you have to pay for this?" she asked.

"Nothing," Tony said. "Mama Mulate and I found it in a church dumpster."

Evelyn's demeanor had changed, and she said, "Thank you. I'm Evelyn DuPont. I don't believe we've met."

"Tony Nicosia. I'm one of Wyatt's partners on this case."

"Tony was a homicide detective with the N.O.P.D. He was, and still is, one of the best detectives anywhere."

"I'm impressed," Evelyn said. "Who took my book?"

"Your daughter, Alicin," I said. "She had it under her pillow, and it never left your house."

"Figures," she said.

Maisie returned with our drinks. Evelyn's anger had disappeared, as had her short-lived smile. She laid her head on the desk and began to sob. Tony gave me a perplexed look. Maisie looked disturbed as I walked around the desk and rested my hand on Evelyn's shoulder.

"What's wrong?" I asked.

"I'm afraid."

"Of what?"

"Rodney killed Toby, and now he's going to prison for the rest of his life."

"Rodney killed no one," I said.

"His snake did," she said.

"No, it didn't. Rodney's cobra is so tame he wouldn't harm anyone."

"Was it Alicin?" she said.

"None of your kids killed Toby," I said.

"Then who did?" she asked.

"Alicin and Rodney's father," I said.

Evelyn's head sprang up from the desk, and she said, "Jonathan killed Toby?"

"Samuel Penrose," I said. "The father cf Alicin and Rodney."

"Sam isn't their father. Who told you that?" Before I could answer, Evelyn noticed Maisie still in the room, taking in our conversation.

"Maisie, bring me another drink." Maisie hurried out the door. Evelyn asked me, "Who told you Sam is Alicin and Rodney's father?"

"Ronnie," I said.

Evelyn shook her head. "That's the story I told her, though it isn't true."

"Jonathan, your butler is the father of Rodney and Alicin?" I asked. "Does he know?"

"He knows," Evelyn said. "We had a single unprotected night of bliss, and I got pregnant. I was only thirteen."

"How old was Jonathan?" I asked.

"Not much older. It was years before he became my permanent butler."

A slight smile returned to Evelyn's face when Tony said, "Then the butler did it."

"That's funny, though I shouldn't laugh," Evelyn said. "How did you learn that Rodney isn't the killer?"

"Maya Henstooth," I said. "Our fourth partner. She's a homicide detective with the Rapides Parish Police and is singing here during French Quarter Fest."

"What reason does Samuel have for killing Rodney?" Tony asked.

"He's a ruthless man," she said.

"Ruthless and murder are two different things. It's no motive for murder," I said.

"Sam was extorting me," Evelyn said.

"For what?" I asked.

249

"He's obsessed with owning the first copy of *Mosquitoes* published by the Lower Pontalba Press. He thought I had it and kidnapped Rodney, threatening to kill him and throw his body to the alligators unless I sold it to him."

"But you don't own the first copy," I said.

"I told him that. He didn't believe me. He must have used Alicin to get the book for him."

"Why would she have done it?" I asked.

"She loves Rodney as much as I do. When he saw it was the volume with the extra chapter, he gave it back to her."

"Then what?"

"I told him the truth. Faulkner had mistakenly taken the second copy, and the Coleman-Labissiere family had the original version."

"You were wrong," Tony said. "Faulkner did have the original version."

"And Toby's family had the second copy printed," Evelyn said. "I knew where it was. No one else, not even Toby, did."

"Then how did Penrose know where to look?" Tony asked.

"Because I told someone where to find it," she said.

"Alicin?" I asked.

Evelyn shook her head. "Libby Tanner."

"Who is Libby Tanner?" Tony asked.

I answered for her. "Evelyn's social secretary. It all makes sense now," I said.

"Not to me, it doesn't," Tony said. "What does Ms. DuPont's social secretary have to do with Samuel Penrose?"

"She's the sister of Victor Malveaux," I said.

"I had all but forgotten," Evelyn said. "Still, I never imagined that she would betray me."

"My guess is the fingerprint on the broken glass is hers," I said.

Evelyn began crying again. "What can we do to help, Ms. DuPont?" Tony asked.

"Rescue Rodney," she said.

"Where do you think he is?" Tony asked.

"Sam's plantation on River Road," she said.

Tony came around the desk and rested his hand on Evelyn's other shoulder.

"Ma'am," he said. "I'm making a solemn promise right now. We'll have your son here tomorrow, and he'll be unhurt."

Evelyn reached up and grabbed Tony's hand. "We just met, but I trust you."

When Tony and I exited her study, Evelyn's head was still on her desk. Maisie was outside the door.

"I need to speak to you," she said.

"Of course," I said.

"Not here," she said.

Maisie led us down a long hallway to a quiet nook before stopping.

"Rodney is in danger, though Ms. DuPont didn't tell you all you need to know."

Maisie was upset, so I took her hand and gently squeezed it.

"It's okay," I said.

"It's not okay. Rodney is in danger. He may even be dead."

"How do you know?" Tony asked.

Maisie glanced at the ceiling before answering. "Rodney and I are lovers. Samuel Penrose didn't kidnap him. He went willingly."

"Because?"

"Mr. Penrose is the head man for a group called Ordre du Sang. He and Mr. Malveaux recruited him into the order."

She nodded when I said, "Is Libby Tanner a member?"

251

"Rodney called me when Toby Coleman-Labissiere was murdered. He had his snake with him at Mr. Penrose's house. It was taken during the night and used in the murder."

"If he's a member of the cult, why did they have to take the snake from Rodney?" I asked.

"Rodney was disillusioned and planned to leave the order."

"How do you know?" I asked.

"He told me so. The order imprisoned him. He said they were going to sacrifice him."

"What the hell do you mean by that?" Tony asked.

"Kill him and offer his body to Satan in an Ordre du Sang ceremony," she said.

"We're going to a book sale at the plantation tonight," Tony said. "Do you know what part of the house they keep him in?"

"The house has three stories. He's kept in a room on the top story," Maisie said.

She nodded when Tony asked, "Is he guarded?"

"The order has many young followers ready to kill if necessary. That's why I didn't call the police," she said.

Maisie had begun to cry, and I squeezed her hand again. "Does the room where they keep Rodney have a window?"

She nodded again and said, "Yes, but the roof is too steep for him to escape."

"Stay strong," I said. "We'll get him out of there."

When Tony and I left the DuPont mansion, the sky had darkened, and it was sprinkling when we reached St. Charles Avenue. Tony pulled up the top before we drowned, then reached into his jacket and produced his silver flask. Opening it, he took a swig straight from it.

"Sorry, Cowboy. After all that drama, I needed a drink. What now?"

"Tonight's book sale will be a gala affair with a buffet, string quartet, and all the out-of-town guests crowding into Penrose's banquet hall. Let's take advantage of the event's clamor and rescue Rodney."

"We don't have a tux," Tony said. "How will we get in?"

"The place will be swarming with caterers, security, waitstaff, and workmen. If we dress in the right outfit, we'll be as good as invisible."

"What about Maya?" Tony asked.

"She'll be pissed if we don't include her. I'll call her."

"And then call Jake," Tony said. "Maybe we can find something appropriate in his wardrobe department."

Chapter 27

When I phoned Jake, he gave me the address of his production studio in the Central Business District. Tony called Maya, and she and Jake's assistant, Angie, who was back from vacation, were waiting for us when we reached the studio along with Mama, Jake, and Colley, dressed to the nines, Mama in a lime green designer gown and Jake and Colley in tuxedoes.

"Jake said you have information about Rodney," Mama said.

"The playing field just got bigger," I said. "Alicin, Ms. DuPont's daughter, wasn't lying when she told me about the Ordre du Sang."

Mama's hand went to her mouth. "I thought we were rid of them," she said.

"They're back, and Samuel Penrose is the head of the snake," I said. "His plantation home is swarming with cult members."

"You mentioned on the phone that someone had told you where they're keeping Rodney," Jake said.

"Maisie, one of Ms. DuPont's maids, is Rodney's lover. Rodney was a cult member until he became disillusioned. Penrose has him imprisoned in a room on the third floor of the mansion on River Road," I said.

"Is he in imminent danger?" Jake asked.

"In addition to pinning Coleman-Labissiere's murder on him, the cult plans to kill him," I said. "Tony, Maya, and I will try to free him tonight."

"We're here for you," Jake said. "We have something that might help."

Jake and Colley led us to a room in the large warehouse studio and gave us each a tiny hand-held transmitter-receiver.

"State of the art walkie-talkie," Colley said. "Ultra secure and with a range of two thousand meters. We'll use them to keep in touch."

"When you key the device, everyone with a receiver can hear," Jake said. "If you can get Rodney out the window, Colley and I can hoist him into the helicopter."

"Maisie said all the stairways are guarded. It'll be a daunting task to reach him. We'll figure something out. Where is Lydia and Adano?"

"Waiting in the limo," Angie said.

Angie was a gorgeous young black woman with the intelligence and ability to solve almost every problem that came up with the Cryptid Hunter. She was also Bradley's girlfriend. She had already discussed our situation with Maya and had a solution.

"The catering service booked for tonight's auction is the same one that Cryptid Hunter Productions uses," she said. "I have exact uniforms and nametags. If you are questioned, the catering office will cover for you."

"You're the best, Angie," I said.

"I'm also going," she said. "I get few chances to wear a ballgown and attend a fete like the one tonight. Bradley's jealous because he'll have to wait for us in the limo."

"Bradley's a good man," I said.

She smiled. "He's a big jealous baby."

Jake looked at Mama and said, "Sorry about the party. I'm going with Colley in the chopper."

"Me too," she said. "I'm not missing all the fun."

Jake smiled and said, "I'll make it up to you."

"Don't worry about it," Mama said.

"We're leaving," Jake said. "The helicopter is on the roof and ready to fly."

Mama, Jake, and Colley left the warehouse still dressed like they were attending a formal fete.

"Leo and Pepper are waiting in the parking lot," Maya said. "Let's change clothes and head upriver."

Leo's brand-new double-cab rattled down River Road, hugging the curves of the Mississippi as twilight settled over the water, the horizon melting into streaks of orange and indigo. The utilitarian vehicle was a stark contrast to the luxury awaiting us.

I adjusted my caterer's cap and focused on the road as Leo drove with a steady hand, his gaze darting to the rearview mirror to check for any signs of trouble. Tony sat beside me in the back, his fingers brushing over his blackjack, a leather-wrapped club weighted with lead.

"This reminds me of a swat team mission I once volunteered for," he said. "Except we didn't have a string quartet."

"At least no one will recognize us in these outfits," I said. "We'll be invisible for all practical purposes."

The river beside us swelled, the moonlight now glimmering on its surface as the last rays of the sun disappeared. The air was thick with the scent of swamp and magnolia, mingling with the sharp odor of gasoline.

Tree branches hung over the road, casting skeletal shadows stretching toward the truck as if they knew something we didn't. As we rounded a bend, the Penrose plantation came into view, nestled behind wrought-iron gates and flanked by ancient live oaks whose branches twisted like the fingers of skeletal giants.

A gravel driveway lined with flickering lanterns stretched toward the house, a colossal structure that loomed ahead, its white columns illuminated under the soft glow of spotlights. The home was a grand ode to Old Southern wealth—a two-story Greek Revival mansion with a wraparound porch, the railings draped in ivy that hung down like tendrils, and the walls pristine white, reflecting the lights that bathed them.

The effect was haunting, a façade beautiful and chilling, exuding an aura of forgotten times steeped in secrets. We could see the caterers and staff bustling around in the courtyard and several expensive cars parked along the driveway—guests already arriving, champagne flutes glinting in the hands of well-dressed men and women.

Leo pulled in, keeping to the side, his eyes scanning for the delivery entrance. The plantation seemed to pulse with life and luxury, an unpredictable blend of the living and the past. The air felt charged as if the ground beneath us knew what the house concealed.

"We're temps," Maya said. "Charlotte is in charge and will assign each of us a job. Angie says we'll find her by the catering truck."

Charlotte was an older woman with brown hair that was turning gray. When she gave us our assignments, she neither smiled nor frowned.

The ballroom was a lavish expanse of polished marble, towering columns, and glittering chandeliers that cast golden light across the well-dressed crowd. Crystal sconces adorned the walls, their warm glow reflecting off the expansive mirrors, making the room seem even more extensive.

A string quartet played near the far end of the ballroom, their music elegant and restrained— Mozart, perhaps, or something similarly timeless. Their notes drifted above the hum of conversation, the chime of laughter mingling with the clink of champagne flutes.

The guests moved with practiced grace, their designer gowns and perfectly tailored tuxedos shimmering under the chandelier's light, each fabric a testament to affluence.

Dressed as a caterer, I lowered my gaze and maneuvered through the guests with a tray of hors d'oeuvres. Maya's expression was neutral as her eyes darted to each doorway and every hallway leading out of the ballroom. Tony moved between us, his arms laden with fresh trays of food. A flicker of unease danced in his eyes every time a guest bumped into him.

"Keep it moving," a stern voice called behind me.

Maya caught my eye across the room, her fingers brushing a stack of plates as she gave a slight nod, her silent confirmation that she had found nothing out of the ordinary. Tony approached the buffet table, setting down a fresh platter of poached shrimp and leaning in toward Maya, his voice barely a whisper.

"Too many eyes in here," he said, "We need a distraction."

"Give it time," Maya said. "Once the drinks start flowing, people will get sloppy. We only need one moment."

Tony nodded toward the room's many security guards stationed strategically along the walls, their earpieces conspicuous against the backdrop of luxury.

"Might do us no good. This place is swarming with security."

"At least they aren't Ordre du Sang," I said.

"How do you know?" Tony asked.

"Their uniforms and nametags," I said.

I moved back toward the kitchen, my heart pounding as I caught sight of Samuel Penrose dressed immaculately. A dark tuxedo framed his tall, almost statuesque figure, his expression one of cold civility as he spoke with a group of wealthy guests. His eyes, however, seemed distant, as if he were only half-listening, his thoughts elsewhere— perhaps even on the captive hidden within the house.

I returned to the catering truck, exchanging a knowing glance with Tony as he passed. We were all thinking the same thing: how would we get upstairs?

It was all about patience. We needed one slip in the perfect facade, one small moment to vanish from the ballroom's blinding extravagance and slip into the shadows beyond.

By ten, most guests had arrived and partaken of the regal buffet and copious alcoholic drinks. An auctioneer appeared and began auctioning books without much ado. I glanced across the room, looking for Lydia, Adano, and Angie. I jumped when my walkie-talkie squawked. It was Maya.

"I took the chance to venture into the central part of the house. Four guards are at the foot of the grand staircase. They're not part of the security company."

"How do you know?" I asked.

"They're all wearing black sportscoats, and I'm guessing they're packing," she said.

One of the catering supervisors, a middle-aged man with a pencil-thin mustache and a sharp eye, urged me back toward the kitchen. I nodded in return, forcing a smile that never reached his eyes.

A darkened hallway led from the ballroom to the kitchen, and another hall intersected it. I was alone and took the opportunity to peek around the corner. One man in a black sportscoat was seated at the end of the stairs. The dim lighting prevented me from seeing much detail, though I assumed he was packing. I keyed the walkie-talkie.

"I located the servant's stairway. One guard, and he's armed," I said.

"Roger that," Maya said.

Tony keyed the walkie-talkie. "I found a dumbwaiter. No guards and it's accessible, though too small for me to get inside."

After Tony had given us directions, Maya said, "I'm on my way."

I keyed my walkie-talkie and said, "Me too."

When we reached Tony's location, the hallway was dark. It was on the far side of the large house, and the auction sounds were muted.

"I think I can fit," Maya said.

"You're the only one who can," Tony said. "Are you up to this?"

"I'm a cop," she said. "It won't be the first dangerous situation I've faced."

"Except you don't have your service revolver," Tony said.

"Here's hoping I won't need it," she said.

We helped Maya squeeze into the service dumbwaiter. When the door closed and we pushed the up button, the whir of electricity began, and thirty seconds passed until she keyed her walkie-talkie.

"I'm in an alcove on the second floor. There's a stairway leading to the third floor with no guards," she said. "I'm going up."

Five minutes passed with no word from Maya, and we began to worry. I keyed my receiver.

"Maya, are you okay?" I asked.

"There's a single door at the top of the stairs. It's locked. It must be where they're keeping Rodney. I'm looking for something heavy to knock the handle off the door."

"There are guards at the base of the stairs," I said. "Don't make too much noise."

Maya's walkie-talkie went quiet, and Tony and I waited in the darkness, wondering what was happening.

Maya could hear someone moving behind the door. Hoping it was Rodney, she knocked.

"Rodney DuPont," she said. "Is it you?"

"It's me," a voice said. "Who are you?"

"Maya Henstooth. I'm here to rescue you, but the door's locked."

"There's a key under the doorstop," he said.

A chunk of limestone sat near the base of the door. When Maya nudged it with her foot, she saw the glint of metal. It was the key to the door.

Rodney's room was small and dark and had an odor Maya instinctively knew was the smell of snakes. Rodney had blond hair and brown eyes. He wasn't smiling.

"There's no way out of here," he said. "Believe me, I've tried."

Maya shut the door and opened the room's lone window. The roof was too steep to stand on, and a fall to the ground would almost certainly result in broken bones. She keyed her receiver.

"Jake, I'm in Rodney's room.

"We're on the ground," Jake said. "About ten miles away. Open the window. We'll drop a line and hoist you and Rodney into the helicopter."

"I'm going no place without my snakes," Rodney said.

Rodney nodded when she asked, "Are they poisonous? We can't take them."

"Then I'm not going," he said.

A large terrarium, lit by a heat lamp, occupied a wall of the room. In the distance, they could hear the whump whump whump of an approaching helicopter. Maya pulled a pillowcase from a pillow on the bed.

"Put them in here," she said.

"No," he said.

Maya keyed her receiver. "Jake, Rodney won't leave without his snakes."

"Bring them," Jake said.

"There are ten of them. Too many to get to the helicopter."

"Hand Rodney the walkie-talkie." Mama complied, and Jake said, "Rodney, Maisie's in the chopper with us."

Maisie's voice trembled when she said, "Rodney, please."

Rodney took the pillowcase and reached the terrarium to remove the snakes. The chopper was outside the window as someone banged on the door.

Maya pushed Rodney and the snakes out the open window and said, "Now or never."

Rodney reached back and grabbed Maya's hand as Jake began hoisting them toward the chopper. Maya wrapped her arms around his waist and held on. When members of Ordre du Sang fired out the window at the helicopter, Jake grabbed an AR-15 and returned fire.

Someone keyed the walkie-talkie. It was Jake.

"Maya, Rodney, and Rodney's snakes are in the helicopter, and we're on our way to the Big Easy. Get the hell out of there, and don't get yourselves killed.

When Tony smiled, I gave him a high five.

"This place is going to explode any minute now. You go first," he said. "I'll drop back and bring up the rear."

I hurried down the darkened hallway toward the noise and music coming from the grand ballroom when someone poked the barrel of a handgun into the small of my back.

"What are you doing here," the person behind me asked.

"Delivering some shrimp from the buffet," I said.

"No, you weren't. Hands over your head and turn around slowly."

When I raised my arms and turned, I saw the shadowy figure of someone behind the man in a black sportscoat. It was Tony, and the eyes of the man with the pistol closed when Tony smacked him on the back of the head with his blackjack. Upstairs, we heard the commotion of people swarming the room where they'd held Rodney.

"Let's get out of here before all hell breaks loose," Tony said.

As we entered the grand ballroom, we heard muffled gunshots, which were dissonant. The music had stopped, and the auctioneer had everyone's attention.

"It's time for the book you've waited for: the first edition of the Lower Pontalba Press's *Mosquitoes*, signed by William Faulkner. The bidding starts at a hundred thousand dollars. Good luck and good bidding."

With the crowd at a fever pitch, no one noticed as Tony and I slipped out of the grand ballroom and hurried to the parking lot where Leo and Pepper awaited us.

"Where's my sister?" Leo asked.

"Safe," I said. "In Jake's chopper, heading back to New Orleans."

"Did you get the book?" Pepper asked.

"Don't know," I said. "We got Rodney and his snakes, and they're in the helicopter with Maya."

"What now?" Leo asked.

"Get the hell out of here and put the pedal to the metal," Tony said.

Chapter 28

It was late when Leo, Pepper, Tony, and I entered Bertram's. French Quarter Fest was finally over, and most of the tourists were on their way back home. It didn't seem to matter. Bertram's was rocking, and almost everyone at the bar wore gowns and tuxes. Tony grinned as we approached the bar.

"Looks like the aftermath of a Mardi Gras ball," he said.

When we joined the crowd, Pepper and Leo embraced Maya. Bertram smiled as he filled drink orders. Jake, Mama, and Colley were among the group.

"Your little sis is a hero," Jake said.

Evelyn, Maisie, and Rodney were also at the bar, Evelyn smiling as she sipped on one of Bertram's New Orleans milk punches.

"She's number one in my book," Evelyn said.

Maisie, still dressed in her maid's uniform, had her arms around Rodney's waist and was also smiling.

"Mine too," she said.

They weren't the only ones enjoying Bertram's cocktails. Lil was there and wasn't smiling when she and Tony embraced. Tommy and Marlon stood beside her. When Lil and Tony's embrace ended, they pumped Tony's hand.

"Good work, Lieutenant," Tommy said.

"I still got it," Tony said with a grin.

"You're going to get it if you don't stop risking your life," Lil said.

"Maya did most of the dirty work," Tony said. "Cowboy and I played backup."

Still dressed in her caterer's uniform, Maya joined them and was soon the meat in a Tommy and Marlon sandwich. Her smile showed she was enjoying every minute.

Lydia and Adano were present, happy as they savored Bertram's martinis.

"Did you get the book?" I asked.

Adano nodded and said, "I still got it, too."

Evelyn showed me the world's most valuable book and then tapped her glass with a spoon to get everyone's attention.

"He certainly did," she said. "I'd like to make an announcement. After speaking with Sister Lydia, I'm donating all three Lower Pontalba Press's versions of Mosquitoes to the University of Virginia museum."

"Here, here," Lydia said.

"Two more things," Evelyn said. "Maisie and my son, Rodney, are getting married, and I intend to host the biggest and most lavish wedding ever held in the Garden District of New Orleans."

Bertram said, "Here, here," as everyone drank to the upcoming wedding.

"Everyone here is invited," Evelyn said. "Also, everyone involved in Rodney's rescue will receive a check from me for fifty thousand dollars as a reward."

"Here, here," everyone said as one.

"My chauffeur is waiting, and we're going now," she said. Evelyn pinched my cheek before exiting with Rodney and Maisie. "I have other plans for you. Can you come by my house tomorrow?"

She laughed when I said, "I'll be there, though it might be later in the day."

Bradley and Angie joined us as Evelyn and her crew walked out the door. Bertram handed Bradley an Abita.

"What are you having, pretty lady?" he asked.

Evelyn had left most of her drink untouched.

"What was she drinking? It looks good."

"New Orleans milk punch," Bertram said. "Coming right up."

Leo and Pepper had finished their beers, and Leo yawned.

"The Fest wore us out. I enjoyed the hell out of it, but I'm glad it's over," Leo said.

"Doing it again next year?" Bertram asked."

"It's addictive," Pepper said.

"We wouldn't miss it for the world," Leo said. "We're returning to Rapides Parish early tomorrow and leaving now."

"We'll miss your famous ribs," Colley said.

Leo laughed. "You got that fancy chopper. Fire it up and come see us anytime."

Leo and Pepper waved goodbye and then left Bertram's arm-in-arm.

"You and Maya were right," Cowboy," Tommy said. "Malveaux killed Coleman-Labissiere, and Libby Tanner was his accomplice."

"We got a match between Ms. Tanner's fingerprints and the one we found on the broken glass," Marlon said.

"When we hauled her in, she squealed like a baby," Tommy said.

"She copped a plea and gave up her brother and Penrose in exchange for a lesser charge," Marlon said.

"Hallelujah!" Adano said.

"State police and St. Charles Parish police have Penrose and Malveaux in custody as we speak," Tommy said.

"Good job," I said.

"What about the Ordre du Sang?" Lydia asked.

"In disarray," Tommy said. "They won't be bothering anybody for a while."

"Wonderful," Lydia said.

Tommy and Marlon had finished their beer and lemonade.

"We're on our way to Carlucci's to celebrate. Want to come along?" Tommy asked.

"Wouldn't miss it for the world," Maya said.

"Lil, you've never been to Carlucci's," Tommy said.

Tony winced, and Lil grinned when she said, "Why not? Maybe I'll uncover some of my husband's secrets."

Bertram's group was thinning as Maya and the troupe exited to head for Carlucci's.

I glanced at Mama and said, "What now?"

"Jake, Colley, and I are flying to Tulsa tomorrow. We're staying at least a month and taking the cats with us," she said.

"How did you like your tour of Mississippi?" I asked.

"A dream come true," she said. "Oxford is intoxicating. I'm taking Jake next fall."

"I can't wait," Jake said. "It's near Kilgore Hills, Mississippi."

"Never heard of it," I said.

"Kilgore Hills is the most supernatural place in the Magnolia State and home of the legend of the Moon Man."

"Moon man?" I asked.

"Aliens supposedly visited in 1883, and the Cryptid Hunter intends to get to the bottom of the legend."

"Lord help us!" Mama said.

"What about you, Colley?" I asked.

"I'm an aviation nut, in case you haven't already figured that out. Tony sold me all the model planes he and Mama saved in Pascagoula. Believe me when I tell you I'm in heaven."

"You finished with your beer, Bradley?" Jake said. "Mama and I need some sleep."

"You got it, Bossman," Bradley said.

Soon, no one remained at the bar except Lydia and Adano.

"What about you two?" I asked. "Is there another wedding in the future?"

"Heavens, no," Lydia said. "Adano and I have taken vows of celibacy."

She smiled when I asked, "Does that also mean you're abstaining from sex?"

"We're visiting Italy, the land of romance, next month if that tells you anything," Adano said.

"We're human," she said. "Let's leave it at that."

"Everything I need to know," I said.

Bertram and I watched as they exited the bar hand-in-hand, looking like lovestruck teenagers.

"Those two are about as celibate as you and Eddie Toledo."

"Did someone call my name?"

We glanced toward the door to see Eddie Toledo, one of my closest friends I hadn't seen in over a year. Bertram's smile had returned, and he had a tall scotch ready when Eddie sat beside me at the bar.

"Speak of the devil," he said.

"What are you doing in the city?" I asked.

"I have a problem I'm hoping the best ex-attorney in the Big Easy can help me with."

Bertram was laughing and said, "Here we go."

Chapter 29

It was very late before Bertram, Eddie Toledo, and I shut down the bar and even later when I finally reached my bed and fell asleep. Sometime during the early morning hours, someone slipped under the covers beside me. It was Maya, dressed in her blue nightgown.

"How did you get Tommy and Marlon to bring you home," I asked.

"They know I'm returning to Rapides Parish later today and need some sleep."

"You came to the wrong place for that," I said.

"I don't need much sleep," she said.

The first light of day was dawning over the French Quarter, a breeze whipping my open balcony door curtain.

When I wrapped my arms around her, she didn't pull away, and I said, "I was hoping you'd say that."

End

Book Notes

Wild *Magnolias* is loosely based on William Faulkner's short time living in the French Quarter. *Mosquitoes* is a novel about artists and their benefactors during a summer in New Orleans. While it's true that the publisher of *Mosquitoes* edited three chapters from the original manuscript, the Lower Pontalba Press and Faulkner's three extra copies are purely fictional.

I hope you enjoyed reading *Wild Magnolias* as much as I enjoyed writing it and that you liked all the eccentric characters. I hope you'll read all my *French Quarter Mystery Series* books featuring moody private detective Wyatt Thomas and be around for Book 14 for the return of Eddie Toledo to the Big Easy.

You might also like my *Paranormal Cowboy Series, which* features Buck McDivit, my modern-day cowboy detective who likes horses, cowgirls, and Australian sheepdogs. My *Oyster Bay Mystery*, set on a Louisiana island near New Orleans, shares many *French Quarter Mystery* characters.

Thanks for being a fan. My stories would be little more than morning fog wafting across a forgotten lawn without beautiful readers like you. Thank you.

About the Author

Eric Wilder is an American author known for his gripping mystery novels set in New Orleans. He was born and raised in Louisiana, where he discovered his love for storytelling at a young age. After completing his education, Wilder spent several years in the oil and gas industry before pursuing a career as a writer.

Wilder's breakthrough came with the publication of Big Easy, which introduced readers to his signature blend of suspense, action, and local color. The book instantly succeeded, drawing critical acclaim and a devoted following. Wilder followed up with a collection of thrillers set in the heart of New Orleans.

Wilder's writing is characterized by his deep knowledge of the city and its unique culture and his skillful use of suspense and plot twists to keep readers on the edge of their seats. His books have been praised for their authenticity, vivid descriptions, and compelling characters.

Today, Eric Wilder is a respected author with a loyal fan base and a reputation for delivering top-notch thrillers that transport readers to the heart of New Orleans.

Eric Wilder

Wilder is the author of twenty novels, several cookbooks, many short stories, and Murder Etouffee, a book that defies classification. His series features characters who often find themselves involved in the paranormal.

Eric Wilder lives in Oklahoma near historic Route 66 with his wife, Marilyn, two gorgeous pit bulls named Moebius and Sage (and her seven puppies born seven days before publication), two small-breed strays named Buddy and Shorty, three remarkable cats, Buttercup, Blanco, and Mama, and a beautiful parrot named Paco.

www.ingramcontent.com/pod-product-compliance
Lightning Source LLC
Chambersburg PA
CBHW011516240626
47154CB00010B/3047